David Rice was born in Ireland, and has worked as a journalist on three continents. He has also been a Dominican friar and a Catholic priest. During the 1970s he was an editor and award-winning columnist in the United States, and in 1980 he returned to Ireland to head the prestigious Rathmines School of Journalism; his guidelines for writing are published in *The Rathmines Stylebook* (Folens, 1993). In 1989 he moved to Beijing to train journalists on behalf of the New China News Agency, and to work as an editor with China Features. His photographic work is carried by agencies in New York and London. His No. 1 best-seller *Shattered Vows: Exodus from the Priesthood* was followed by his acclaimed television documentary *Priests of Passion*, broadcast on Channel 4 in 1992.

ALSO BY DAVID RICE

BLOOD GUILT

DAVID RICE

THE
BLACKSTAFF
PRESS
—————
BELFAST

First published in 1994 by
The Blackstaff Press Limited
3 Galway Park, Dundonald, Belfast BT16 0AN, Northern Ireland

© David Rice, 1994
All rights reserved

Typeset by Paragon Typesetters, Queensferry, Clwyd

Printed in England by Cox and Wyman Limited

A CIP catalogue record for this book
is available from the British Library

ISBN 0-85640-531-0

for
Luci
who knows why

PROLOGUE

The spike of a crescent moon came up out of the line of scudding cloud above Newry. Low in the sky, it cut through the cloud like the dorsal fin of a great white shark.

It gave little light that spring night in 1957, as two vehicles glided through the sleeping streets of the Northern Ireland town. They pulled to the kerb near Corry Square, a little way up from the police barracks.

The windows in the bleak, red-brick façade of the barracks were sightless eyes staring down on the street.

From a Morris van two figures alighted, and three climbed out of an Austin Cambridge saloon car. All had Sten sub-machine-guns slung from their shoulders. Two of them opened the back of the van, and took out a coil of cable and a square packet. They moved silently up the street to the heavy oaken door of the barracks, while the others waited by the car.

Equally noiselessly two windows in the second floor of the barracks slid up, arc lights came on, and automatic fire shattered the silence.

Over by the Austin two figures fell; the men at the barracks door rushed back to the van, and one collapsed as he reached it. The other grabbed him, hurled him through the rear doors of the van and jumped in after him. With tyres squealing the van took off down the street.

The Austin was screeching away ahead of it.

Sirens wailed as the van raced along by the canal, swung right into Bridge Street, and roared up the long hill out of town towards the three-mile-distant border. Where the road levels off and curves right under the railway bridge, the van screeched left off the road onto a half-hidden rocky track, and the sound of police sirens faded along the main road towards the border.

The van bumped and thumped its way along the track that clings to the mountainside. The thin moon had sailed clear of the cloud and was reddening as it neared the horizon.

Some miles along the track the van bumped to a stop, at a silent spot overlooking Carlingford Lough, where fir and pine trees slope steeply down to Narrow Water. Whimpering and shivering, a young man climbed out, went to the back of the van, shone a flashlamp on the remains of a human being lying there, and vomited.

Across from the trees was a low wall of loose stones, and the young man moved hesitantly across to sit on it. He threw the flashlamp on the grass beside his feet and, shivering as if with ague, buried his face in his hands.

He sat there for a long time, the only sound the wind sobbing in the pine trees below the road.

From far ahead, where the road curves and descends towards the border, came the sound of a car climbing in low gear. The sound came closer, and the man on the wall raised his head from his hands to listen.

Just before the headlamps swung around the last bend, the young man grabbed his gun from the van, swung his legs across the wall and crouched behind it. The headlamps were now boring straight up the road.

Closer and closer the car came – an elderly Hillman Minx. It drew level, passed. Then it stopped.

Two men climbed out, wearing armbands of the B Specials,

the part-time auxiliary police force. They shone a flashlamp into the cab of the van, then moved around to the open rear doors.

One gave a low whistle. 'Jesus, would ya take a look. Thon's a right mess, an' no mistake.'

'Who d'ya think done it?'

'Probably our fellas. He's one a them Fenians, was down at the Newry barracks th'night. Sure look at the kyarr number: thon's the one we got on the wireless.'

They stood in silence in the moonlight.

'Malcolm. Give us a lend a your penknife, willya?'

'Whaddiya want a penknife for?'

A snigger. 'I'm goin'ta cut it off an' stick it in his fuckin' mouth. Like Churchill's fuckin' cigar. Hold the torch, willya?'

He bent down, intent on his grisly task.

A figure rose from behind the wall, a Sten gun spoke, and the lamp went out as the men crumpled. Forcing the muzzle down, the figure pumped round after round into the still heap. With a click the gun emptied. The figure withdrew the magazine, turned it around to reload and clicked it back in place. He climbed across the wall and, breathing deeply, gazed down at what he had done.

The stench of burst bowels assailed his nostrils, mingling with gunsmoke and the sweetish, butcher's-shop odour of flesh. A spreading pool of blood was black in the faint moonlight.

A movement inside the Hillman caught the man's eye: the Sten gun roared at the car, shattering the rear side window, and there was a shriek from inside. Silence. The young man waited. He walked to the car and peered in.

Dying eyes met his. A girl of about fifteen was trying to raise herself from the rear seat, and blood was pumping in rhythmic spurts from what remained of her neck. The blood seemed black.

'Oh God, oh no, oh no, oh no, oh no,' screamed the

young man, as he hurled the gun by its hot muzzle out over the tops of the pine trees, a black Excalibur that arced under the red moon.

He turned away from the dying thing, and stumbled whimpering down the road towards the border.

1

Clongowes Wood College, celebrated Irish boarding school where James Joyce set the opening of his *Portrait of the Artist as Young Man*, has a 150-year-old tradition – that the student who wins the annual debate medal invariably becomes eminent later in his chosen walk of life.

It is a remarkable boast, but one borne out by the list of winners down the years. It includes famous lawyers and judges, men of letters, churchmen, physicians, academics, statesmen – statesmen like John Redmond who, after Parnell, led the Irish Party at Westminster in the early twentieth century.

When young Conor Emmet left Clongowes for the last time, in the mid-1950s, he carried in his school trunk not only the massive silver debate medal with its purple and white ribbon, but also the senior medal for best essay and a colours blazer for cricket.

'There's a young fellow to watch. Hmmm? Hmmm?' said Father James Gracey, SJ , Prefect of Studies, standing with the Clongowes rector at the great castle window, watching the Emmet car scrunch across the gravel and down the avenue. 'A young fellow to watch. Hmmm? You mark my words, Father Rector. You mark my words.'

And within a couple of years people were indeed watching. Con's father, widowed old Doc Emmet, well-liked physician in the Northern Irish town of Newry, had sent his only son across the border to Galway's small but famous university because he believed there would be more personal supervision there.

'And a fella can make his name quicker at a small place like that,' he told Con. 'Big fish, small pond – know what I mean, young fella me lad? Y'know, your mother'd a been proud of ya so far. Och, sure you never remember her. I forget that.'

You lay low for the first year, of course. Everybody did: it took a while to find your feet in the strange, exhilarating world of university. And Con needed that year just to savour the sheer freedom, after the grim and punitive regimen of a Jesuit boarding school.

There were the pubs to enjoy, with their camaraderie and marvellous conversations that never quite got anywhere. And each pub was so different: the Skeff at Eyre Square where the med students met; the Kelpie, favoured by the republicans; the Cottage Bar at Salthill, favoured by the mountaineering club; the Galway Arms where they all talked sport; the pubs near the Claddagh where the real Connemara men came – big slow-moving men with faces like the Cliffs of Moher and cloth caps forever affixed to their heads, some of them talking real Irish instead of the ersatz Irish of the students.

And you learned early to relish the tart black brew that poured creamily from the Guinness tap, and you watched in thirsty wonder as the fawn foam separated itself from the dark stout, while the glass waited for the barman to top it up. And you learned to draw a shamrock on the foam with a matchstick, so thick the foam was.

'A pint, please, Mick,' was all you had to say, and Mick would draw you a Guinness. Sure what else would you be wanting? If you wanted anything else, you uttered its name.

'A glass, Mick' meant a half-pint. But if it was hard liquor you were drinking, then 'a glass' meant a double. It took a bit of learning, but you learned fast.

'Aw, come on now, ladies and gents. Drink up please!' the barman would be saying, a half-hour after legal closing time. 'Come on now, can't ye see the time that's in it? Ladies and gents, have ye no homes to go to, at all?'

You pretended not to notice, until the barman got to your table and started wiping it and lifting the empty glasses and saying 'aw come on now'. And then you mooched in the general direction of the door, if you felt you had to.

'How about Nora Croobs', lads?' someone might say, and Nora Croobs' it would be. You tapped at the door of a high, ancient house in a gloomy back street and, if your tap sounded right, old Nora or her gentle sister would shuffle out and bring you into the kitchen.

You might just manage to discern fifteen or twenty students crammed onto the tiled floor as well as on all available chairs and benches, as you blinked in the cigarette smoke and the steam from the pot that simmered forever upon the black, shiny stove. It was from there that Nora ladled you her famed stew and croobeens, the pig's feet from which came her nickname.

Nora's rules were of the strictest. You had to be introduced and vouched for the first time. And the first word of bad language brought instant banishment. If you happened to be drunk you stayed very quiet, for Nora would not approve. She would, however, be more forgiving than for the bad language.

Not indeed that you had to drink wildly to enjoy life. To be sure there were fellows who felt they had to prove something by getting 'mouldy', as they called it, and sometimes a fellow would tank up before a hop or a dance out of sheer terror of the opposite sex, or to get the courage to cross the dance floor to the line of girls along the wall and ask one to dance.

And sometimes, just sometimes, some girl might take a drink or two too many and forget the absolute necessity of keeping her knees together, and the ensuing disaster would encourage all the other young women to count their drinks very carefully indeed.

But for Con and most of the youngsters, a couple of pints sufficed, thick and black and rich, topped with that dreamy creamy foam.

'Good luck!' you said solemnly, as you raised the virgin pint to your lips. A couple more of those, along with an ocean of splendid conversation, and any man would be content.

And there were the girls to get used to. After six years at an all-male boarding school where you talked girls from morning to night but rarely saw any, it was a strange and delightful experience to find them right beside you as fellow students.

In the great Gothic Latin Hall, with its rising tiers of benches, during one of those first lectures, Con had dropped a pencil. When he bent down to get it he encountered, not the mousey flannel knee of a boarding school mate, but a silken female knee descending to a shapely ankle. Con had groped for that pencil longer than had been strictly necessary.

'You're welcome back!' the ankle's owner had whispered, with a cheeky grin, when Con came up for air. Con had blushed.

He hadn't slept overly well that night.

But in those days you didn't try to go very far. Con's female companions were mostly convent-trained youngsters who just occasionally might let you have a kiss and a canoodle in the dark street outside their digs, after you walked them home.

'Look, I have to go,' the girl would say then. 'Stop it, now. Arragh will ya behave yourself! Look, the landlady's watching. Conor Emmet, you just put that hand right back where it came from!' And she'd break away with a giggle and scurry into the house.

And often the landlady had indeed been watching. Most of them had the mind of a mother superior and eyes in the back of their heads.

But sure who minded, with so much to do? There was a bit of rowing on the river, there was the mountaineering club and

Connemara to be explored and the Twelve Bens to be climbed, and the incomparable Lough Corrib to be fished and the occasional horse-riding along the edge of Galway Bay.

Above all, there was the debating at the Lit and Deb – the university's famous Literary and Debating Society – the weekly meetings of which drew Con as a candle draws a moth.

For a long time Con just listened. And even after they asked him to speak for the first time, he continued unwittingly to follow the advice that had once been given to the young Disraeli: 'Speak briefly, but speak often. And soon the House will sigh for the wit and eloquence they know is in you.'

By the beginning of Con's third year at university, it had all come together.

The Greek Hall would be crowded to the windowledges on a Wednesday night when Conor Emmet was to speak in a debate. Lesser speakers would be merely suffered, and would have to stammer along under a barrage of catcalls and heckles and paper darts.

The nonsense might stop, of course, for Maeve Halloran, the lovely young medical student, if only because she looked so gorgeous down there at the rostrum with the red-gold hair to her waist, and the proud, graceful figure. The strength of her political beliefs gave the youngster a power beyond eloquence.

Still, they would really be waiting for Con.

Finally the long thin figure would uncoil from a seat at the front of the tiered hall, and Con would be standing, slightly stooped beside the auditor's rostrum. He would pull a few notes from an inside pocket and place them at the edge of the rostrum. And the long, angular, unlovely face would look up at the sea of faces that rose in tiers to the back of the hall.

Silence would fall.

The craggy face would break into a grin and Con would tell a joke so ridiculous nobody else could have got away with it.

'The speakers we have had to listen to remind me of the Red

Indian that didn't know heads from tails,' Con might say. 'And of course we all know what happened to him, don't we?'

'No! Tell us, Con!' the hall would roar.

'Well, I don't know either,' Con would answer. 'But you should've seen the scalps he brought home!'

And they'd howl and groan and stamp their feet with delight at the sheer nonsense of it. And when they ran out of breath and were ready to listen again, there'd be a different Con down there, unsmiling, with contemptuous eyes.

'These buffoons here,' Con might say, 'who also cannot tell heads from tails, are in the finest tradition of those who run our country, who, in half a century of dithering about Northern Ireland, are content with war dances that frighten nobody but themselves, with wearing green war paint as a substitute for action, and with pathetic rituals that conjure up no spirits but the spirit of Irish national apathy.'

It was the most marvellous of all drugs, to stand in front of a mass of people and make them into a single, panting thing that groaned and laughed and wept and cheered and roared. Savonarola must have known that ecstasy. And Hitler, when he stood in the searchlights at Nuremberg and promised 'one Reich for the next thousand years', and brought those uniformed masses to the thumping, hypnotic chant of *Ein Volk, ein Reich, ein Führer*. And Cicero too, denouncing Catiline to the Romans; or Churchill, promising his people only blood, sweat and tears. Or Furtwängler, bringing orchestra and choir through the finale of the 'Ode to Joy'.

Con was drugged indeed, and the faces before him were drugged on his eloquence. Con's voice would drop, and he would select a single face from the sea of faces, and he would address a solitary, whispered, vibrant sentence to that one face, and then he would be addressing the mass again, building from small to bigger to biggest, ending with an appeal to live for Mother Ireland if they could not die for her, but the time for dying might come again and they must all be ready: ' . . . for this Ireland of ours is four green fields, and the northernmost field has been filched by the foreigner, and we shall have it back'.

Con would stop dead, fold his notes, and return to his place. There would be an instant of silence, and then the ovation, which would go on and on.

They would have followed him anywhere. The trouble was, Conor Emmet was not really going anywhere. He was a young man with a consummate power over words, but, when all was said, not a great deal to harness those words to.

Instinctively Con knew this, and it troubled him. He loved his Ireland: he was troubled about what he regarded as the lost province of Ulster, where he had been born and bred under British rule, but he had no blazing convictions on what to do about it.

He was shrewd enough to know he would never make a leader. He lacked the hard edge, the ruthlessness a leader must have. Eloquence – the power to entrance an audience – was only one of the attributes required in a leader, and Con knew he didn't have too many of the others.

And anyway, always the question, whither to lead? Or to go, for that matter?

Con was just an extraordinarily fine communicator. How did that differ from being an extraordinarily fine entertainer? Maybe that was all he was. A glorified joker.

Now, with Maeve Halloran it was different. She was in one of those republican clubs, and her eloquence came simply and solely from her searing convictions. She had few forensic or rhetorical techniques, yet her certainties gave her a startling persuasive power.

Con had once read about the difference between Emerson and Lincoln: when Emerson spoke, people said how well he spoke; when Lincoln spoke, people said, let's do it. Was Con cast in an Emerson mould?

But Maeve was the sort that lived to free the slaves. She was studying medicine 'to be a healer, not a money-maker'. Con believed her. And when she stood to speak in the Greek Hall, Maeve wanted only to shake people out of their apathy or cynicism, especially about Irish politics. It was southerners' apathy, she maintained, that allowed an unjust society to continue in Northern Ireland.

Con sometimes wished he had Maeve's certainties, her ability to live for things bigger than herself. But what could you do when you didn't have those certainties? Indeed, what was Con to do when the halcyon days of college life were over? Maybe he'd read law after completing his degree in Anglo-Irish literature, but it was all rather vague.

As the stars of the college debates, Maeve and Con found themselves thrown together a lot: they travelled on debating teams to Dublin, Cork and Belfast, and once to Liverpool. When Maeve was elected auditor of the society, she turned to Con to help plan debates and entertain the bigwigs who came to speak.

People thought them a handsome couple: lean, long Con, whose height and hatchet face and bent briar pipe lent him a somewhat unmerited air of mature authority; and Maeve of the red-gold hair, who was named after an ancient Irish warrior queen and who carried herself like one.

Maeve had grace. Her simple clothes hung well on her. She could hold her own in any company. She had an unerring instinct for when to come off the soapbox and be simply good company. Or rather, superb company, deriving from wit and a sense of fun, obvious breeding, an ability to hold well a moderate amount of gin, and a warm sympathy that went beyond charm.

Maeve could do a lot of things well. She was a fine swimmer and an excellent horsewoman. Her father trained horses in County Kildare and Maeve had been up on ponies since she was a toddler. At college she kept up her riding: a couple of times a week she'd cycle to stables run by family friends at Furbo, and would spend hours cantering through the fields above Galway Bay.

She began taking Con along, trying to teach him to ride. She would peal with laughter at his sorry seat on a horse. 'You look like Don Quixote,' she'd laugh, 'with those long old legs wrapped round the animal. Whyn't you tie 'em in a knot underneath? Hey, I'm Sancho Panza and I spy windmills. Come on there, Sir Knight!' And she'd gallop off, with Con trying to keep up.

Maeve could get away with things no one else could. On riding days she'd come onto campus dressed in her tweed hacking jacket and her superbly cut riding breeches in beige corduroy. The fellows loved it, and christened her Puss-in-Boots.

But in those days trousers of any sort were a strict no-no on campus, and eventually, inevitably, Maeve was hauled before. the Lord Almighty himself, Monsignor Paddy Browne, the famous and formidable ecclesiastic who was president of the university.

Maeve was afraid of nobody. 'Show me the rule that says you've got to wear skirts,' she said to Paddy Browne.

'Young lady,' he answered, 'you show me the rule that says you've got to wear clothes!'

Which was par for the course for Paddy Browne, whose way with words was legendary – he had once praised a vintage French wine as being 'like an angel pissing on your tongue'.

Old Browne, however, must have appreciated the sparkling colleen with the red-gold hair, or maybe he appreciated that the whole exchange had been conducted in Irish. Anyhow he didn't put a stop to Maeve, declaring that if one was engaged in a sport, one might dress for that sport, even on campus.

So Maeve continued to stride around campus in her riding gear, and on occasion even addressed the Lit and Deb in the boots and corduroy breeches, to the glee of the assembly.

Nobody thought it arrogance. Maeve was too simple a young woman to be arrogant. She was just doing, completely naturally, what she had done all her life – and doing it almost absent-mindedly, for her life seemed dedicated to things beyond herself. Besides, Maeve did everything with such unconscious style that people simply smiled and applauded.

And Con smiled and applauded more than any, as he found his thoughts and feelings straying more and more to Maeve Halloran. Besides, it was gratifying to be seen in the company of one of the most admired young women on campus.

Her face seemed always in his mind's eye – that face straight from a Renaissance canvas. It occurred to Con that those young-sters and angels and Graces in the paintings of Botticelli all had a remarkable family likeness, as though they were brothers and sisters, or at least cousins. Well, Maeve looked as if she had to be one of the cousins.

Indeed Con could be more precise: Maeve was Judith, on the way home after slaying Holofernes.

But a part of Maeve Halloran's life remained closed to Con. Like the far side of the moon, one was sure it existed even if if one had not actually seen it. There were young men of vaguely military bearing who had unquestioned access to Maeve and who seemed, in some subtle way, almost to condescend to Con.

Then there was Frank Flaherty, a class ahead of Maeve in medical school. Frank never patronised Con, and he had a cheery personality that Con liked. But Frank's acceptance by Maeve, even though the two rarely socialised together, and the intimation that there was something between them – something quite other than sex or infatuation or even love, and seemingly more important – left Con at times irritated and puzzled.

One did not challenge Maeve, or have rows with her – some-how one just didn't – and besides, what was there to have a row about, anyway?

Con contented himself with gently teasing Maeve about her 'republican club cubs' and her 'imaginary army', and Maeve would laugh and toss the red–gold hair and loosen the rein and nudge the horse with her legs and canter off among the higgledy-piggledy drystone walls of Furbo.

2

The two horses came over the hill at an easy canter, manes and tails flowing, nostrils steaming in the cold air, their riders tall against the clear October sky. The late yellowing sun caught the streaming hair of the girl, making it a flame against the metallic blue of the sky. The thump-thump of the hooves and the snort of the horses were the only sounds, save for the sigh of the sea.

Down along the low stone wall went the horses, Galway Bay a vast, dark blue below them, where white veins of foam marked the currents, and in the far distance the stone hills of the Burren were visible, dusted now with the evening's gold.

The horses wheeled at the bottom of the long field and their rhythm changed, and now the riders were rising to the trot. The rhythm changed again and the horses were walking. By the gap at the corner of the field the figures halted.

'You're doing great, Con,' Maeve said. 'But you're still pulling on that rein to ask for halt.'

'It's taking me a while, I know.'

'Try thinking that when you close your legs you're really telling him to move forward – but into hands that won't give, so he stops. You can see that's not the same as pulling on the reins, can't you? In fact they call it "into a still hand". Hey, would you look who's waiting for us!'

Beyond the gap, Frank Flaherty was standing. He came forward now, and held the horse while Maeve dismounted. 'You're to be up at the Kelpie this evening, Maeve,' Frank said. 'He's due in, on a flying visit. Not sure what time, so stay around.' Frank gave Con a friendly nod.

'The invisible army again, I suppose,' Con said.

The others only smiled.

An hour later Con and Maeve were sitting in the bar of the Kelpie, a hot whiskey in front of each. Frank Flaherty came over, gave Con an amiable punch to the shoulder and slid into the seat alongside Maeve.

'He's down in the back room now,' Frank said.

Maeve looked across at Con, then back to Frank. 'Do you think we . . . ?'

'Sure, why not?' Frank said.

Maeve stood up. 'C'mon, Con. There's someone we want you to meet. Take your glass with you.'

Con followed them through the dining area, down a corridor to a quiet room at the back of the building. He recognised a couple of Maeve's republican cubs among the ten or so figures seated around the table in the low lighting.

A figure stood.

'This is Conor Emmet now,' Maeve said. 'Commandant Sean Louth, of the Movement, Con.'

Con had an impression of close-cropped hair, a tanned outdoor face and a firm handshake. It seemed to him the handshake meant something – care, concern, goodwill maybe.

'I've heard quite a bit about you, Emmet,' Sean Louth said.

Within two weeks Con had taken the oath and become a member of the Movement, a secret, illegal organisation dedicated to driving the British from Northern Ireland and to uniting north and south in a New Ireland.

It was a changed life for Con. Weekends were given over

to training, mostly at a rundown farm in the wilds of Connemara, a couple of miles from the road in an area called Joyce Country.

The group had a handful of old Lee-Enfield 303 rifles – British Army, vintage 1917 – and a few Sten Mark 2-S machine pistols, which had been stolen the previous year in a raid on a Northern Ireland barracks. There was not a round of ammunition to practise with. So little was available it was to be kept for the 'real thing', whatever that was, whenever . . .

Basic drill came easily, as many of the youngsters had, while still at school, been members of the FCA, the part-time local defence force. Con had been an enthusiastic member during his final two years at Clongowes, and in his last year had been made corporal.

But the strategy and the tactics came mostly out of the skull of Frank Flaherty, or from tattered British booklets marked 'WAR DEPARTMENT/SECRET', containing step-by-step instructions for capturing a hillock, and sketch maps with directional arrows and tiny circles representing the men in V-formation supposedly sneaking around the side of the hillock to take the occupants by surprise.

It looked so easy.

Frank Flaherty was in charge for much of the time. His ideas were probably no worse than anyone else's. Ireland had been at peace for so long that there was really nobody to teach the fighting.

Sean Louth came up from Limerick when he could. And whenever he did come, Con saw what being a born leader really meant. It was Louth's conviction that made the old clichés take on a new meaning. He talked of the 'blood sacrifice', the idea that had powered the rising of 1916 – that only by the deaths of its patriots would Ireland awaken from its apathy and challenge foreign oppression. Patrick Pearse and the others had gone to their executions after 1916, and their deaths had indeed angered Irishmen so that a sufficient number of them took on the British, to ensure that, in the end, in sheer frustration the British had agreed to get out.

The only trouble, Louth explained, was that the British had never left the six northern counties. And Ireland was apathetic again. So the blood sacrifice might once again be called for – the 'terrible beauty' that Yeats had spoken of.

Neither Sean Louth nor his listeners bothered much with the considerable complication that a majority in those six northern counties wanted the British to stay, were utterly opposed to a united Ireland, and were well capable of a blood sacrifice of their own. 'What we have, we hold' was their slogan. They would yield 'not an inch'.

Louth sincerely believed that when the time came and the British sold out Northern Ireland, as they surely would, one million diehard unionists would cheerfully traipse into a united Ireland.

And, though it defied reason, listening to Sean Louth's burning words, Con found himself believing that that was indeed how it would be.

Meanwhile, Louth explained, occasional cross-border arms raids on police and military installations in Northern Ireland, which was all the Movement could achieve right then, would serve a threefold purpose. They would rub the wound of Northern Ireland, preventing it from healing. They would remind people the Movement existed, and bring recruits. And they would provide desperately needed guns and ammunition.

A new edge came into Con's public speaking. He no longer merely sounded like a leader. And where he led, there were some to follow.

Con felt a sense of responsibility, a kind of pride of ownership, towards these young men like Ciaran O'Boyle whom he invited to the back room at the Kelpie. They looked up to him in a way no one ever had before.

And when he strode through the Archway under the clock

tower of Galway University, freshmen students would nudge one another. 'That's Conor Emmet,' they would whisper.

It was humour that transformed Con's speeches at the Lit and Deb. As he matured in rhetoric he moved from the oratorical drum rolls that had made every occasion a Lincoln at Gettysburg or a Pearse at the grave of O'Donovan Rossa. His speeches became light and laced with wit; his irony gently probed and his mockery was almost kindly.

But people found themselves remembering points so deftly made and so effortlessly communicated.

And they flocked to listen to him. They would be crammed into the benches and choking the sloping aisles; they would be perched on the radiators and the windowsills of the Greek Hall, and there would be knots of youngsters clustered around the open doors, trying to hear what was going on inside.

It would have fed the conceit of many a man, but there was little conceit in Conor Emmet. He would take a bemused delight in his triumphs, and then fall to wondering how he could best use this talent.

Charisms were gifts God gave you, not for yourself, but to benefit others. He remembered a priest in a retreat at Clongowes had once spoken about such gifts in the Bible – like the power to heal, or the gift of tongues. In a way, Con had a gift of tongues, and he'd better learn to use it right.

Now that Con and Maeve were both in the Movement together, gone was the last trace of obstacle between them. They grew closer.

'But isn't life a cheat?' Maeve said to Con one day. 'Now that we want to be together more, we've got less time. I mean, with me in third med now, I never have a minute. And you training every weekend. Everything has a catch.'

'Everything has a price, rather. Oh I don't mean it in a bad sense, Maeve. I mean, whatever we choose to do, there's a price to be paid for it. And we've got to reckon, is it worth the price? In this case I think it is.'

The price was high enough, however: less and less time together as the months rolled by. They tried to fit in an all-too-brief session of horse riding once a week. They looked forward to it, and, as Con's riding skills improved under Maeve's tuition, they started hacking further afield, negotiating the rocks and cliff paths and little scimitars of strand along Galway Bay. Soon it was the high point of the week – after the Lit and Deb.

They never missed those Wednesday Lit and Deb meetings, and afterwards they would stroll down town, hand in hand through the damp streets where lamplight gleamed on the pavements, stopping on the bridge across the Corrib to watch the salmon weir glinting in the darkness, then wandering down to Lydon's to drink tea and maybe order sausages and chips.

Occasionally Con would slip across the street from college to hospital, to encounter an astonishingly professional-looking Maeve in white coat and stethoscope, and they would duck into the canteen for a cup of the sludge that masqueraded as coffee.

There might be a drink at the Kelpie on a Friday night, but it was early to bed, as a car would call for Con in the wee hours of Saturday morning to take him off to the training.

Yet as their time together grew less, something between them grew more.

The rarity of their moments together gave each a zest, an intensity. A walk along the Claddagh to Salthill, or a canter where the waves curled on the wet sand beyond Furbo – all seemed to be heightened experiences, with the skies a richer blue, the tang of the sea air sharper in the nostrils, the cries of the gulls almost music. Con perceived that Maeve too felt this quickening, and he could sense her joy in the way she tossed the red-gold hair and in how she stepped so lightly.

There were times when he experienced a sense of over-whelming affection for this gorgeous, joyful, simple creature. He found himself wanting to do things for her – anything – somehow to ease the burden of existence for her. Sometimes the longing to help could reach silly dimensions, as when

Maeve was overworked and Con found himself wishing he could do her studying for her.

They had a gentle laugh about that.

'There are things your dearest friend can't do for you,' Maeve said with a sigh and a smile. 'He can't learn for you. He can't pee for you: you've got to do it for yourself. And no one can do your praying for you. And no one can do your dying for you either. God, Con, 'tis a lonely old world when you think about it.'

She shivered, and Con wanted to gather her into his arms and kiss her and canoodle her and tell her he could and would do her dying for her.

He took her in his arms quite often now, more and more as the months passed. But the canoodling had its own discipline, which both tried hard to abide by. Buttons stayed buttoned and zips stayed zipped, and tongues mostly stayed where they belonged. That was the way things were, and they believed in the way things were.

Neither lovemaking nor getting wed were much talked of. 'We've got years and years ahead of us,' Maeve would whisper.

'And the things we'll be doing then,' Con would whisper back, and feel the chuckles vibrate in Maeve's body.

Yet, although Maeve was no tease, there were times when Con felt dizzy with the hunger for her, as his hands slid down her slender flanks and his head bent into the angle of shoulder and neck and he smelt the faint perfume of violets she wore. Throat would constrict and loins would tighten and brain would swim and breath would grow short with the longing. And the hunger grew with the months.

But if it was hunger, then that Easter was a famine, for they could not be together at all. Con had to spend the vacation with his father in Toledo. Maeve was tied down to her work at the hospital.

Con went through the experience perfunctorily, saw little of Toledo's famous Holy Week ceremonies with their masked and hooded marchers, and wrote to Maeve every day. It was a vacation of waiting – waiting to get back to Galway.

He got back a day early, by arrangement with Maeve, with the intention of getting a full day's trekking with the horses.

'There'll be precious little time for it this term,' Maeve had said on the telephone. 'With all my work at the hospital. And you never know what the Mov— what your friends may be asking you to do. There'll be something soon – though that's only a guess. So let's make this one day count: Sean Óg says we can have the horses for the whole day.'

'Tell you what, Maeve. Let's trek out Inveran way, and see how far we can get without wrecking ourselves or the horses. We can bring something to eat, in a saddlebag.'

'You're on,' Maeve had said.

It was one of those incomparable spring days when Ireland makes amends for the rain and the mists.

The day was yellow and blue – the gorse in bloom, so dazzlingly yellow it made you shade your eyes; yellow cascaded over the little stone walls, yellow blazed across the hillsides; great billows of yellow tumbled onto the track where the horses picked their way. The yellow, against the blue of a cloudless sky, was like a royal banner.

'Vermeer's favourite colours,' Maeve said. 'Yellow and blue. He put them together in all his paintings.'

'Sweden's national colours too. Maybe all northern lands turn yellow and blue in spring.'

You'd forget that Ireland was the Green Isle. On a day like this there were forty shades of blue. There was the delicate pastel of the horizon, deepening up the dome of the sky to the darkest indigo, lighter again at the back of the sun if you could manage to look.

The sea was cerulean, shading to turquoise in the shallows, and it winked in the sunlight.

The spring sun was warm on the skin, and the elusive scent

of gorse blossom hung in the air, stronger where the yellow was brighter.

'That scent,' Maeve said. 'It brings such memories, of picnics when I was a child. Easter picnics by the Hill of Allen, with my brother and me rolling eggs down the field. We used to gather handfuls of gorse blossom and put it in the water with the eggs to boil. D'you know, the eggshells would come out yellow, just like the blossom.'

The track took them down along the seashore, then back up through the gorse, then along the top of some low cliffs above the water.

They reached a spot where a cliff had crumbled, leaving a V where the clifftop sloped down to a platform of rocks, against which deep water sucked. The bottom of the V was a grassy hollow, begging to be picnicked in. They halted the horses and gazed down.

'And bowery hollows crown'd with summer sea,' Con quoted. 'Maeve, I never knew what old Tennyson meant until now. How could sea crown a hollow? But look down there: that triangle of sea that's peeping through the V seems high above the grassy hollow. Just an illusion, I know – it'll flatten out if we go down there. Hey, wouldn't this be the place to picnic?'

They dismounted and led the horses down to the hollow, where they let them loose to graze. A tartan rug was spread on the grass. They stood for a moment watching the sea, where each wave gurgled and foamed across a natural stone platform between two of the rocks.

'How about a swim?' Maeve said.

'But we don't have togs, do we?'

'Well, I don't mind, if you don't. Right? Last one in's a chicken!'

All of a sudden Maeve was scrambling out of her boots and breeches and shirt and bra and pants and was scampering across the rocks to where the spring tide foamed across the stone platform. There she hesitated a moment.

It could have been an eternity.

Time stopped. Con was looking at a scene outside time. Sparkles slowly winked and foam laced the edges of the waves that marched from the blue horizon.

The girl stood, facing out between two rocks, gazing over the sea, her body curved in a slender S, bright against the blue of sea and sky. The hair reached her waist, and the sea breeze lifted it to reveal the furrow tracing her spine.

The water frothed around her ankles.

She turned to look for Con. The right arm lay across the breasts; the left hand covered the fork of her body, where a reddish triangle peeped out. Her head inclined slightly, and the red-gold hair streeled in the breeze.

The birth of Venus. Incredibly. Almost precisely as Sandro Botticelli had envisioned it five centuries before. But living.

A wave slapped at the rock, and blue water and white foam soared upward, where it hung beside the girl's body, a shimmering stalagmite. She raised her hands to shade her eyes, as she sought Con against the sun.

Time moved. The girl turned to the sea, her body arced through the air and cut the water.

Con scrambled out of his remaining clothes, scrambled across the rocks and dived.

The cold knocked the breath out of him. But as he gasped for air and thrashed for warmth and felt the rich harsh ocean searing his nostrils, he knew the moment was not really gone, would never be gone.

The next day, as he strode into campus, Con got the order for the raid.

The following day Con, Frank Flaherty and Ciaran O'Boyle quietly absented themselves, and headed to meet the rest of the company at Dundalk, across the border from Newry. Flaherty would command. They were as trained as they would ever be.

The raid took place in the wee hours of Thursday morning.

Five days after the raid, a Mr Gleeson, heavy-set, of military bearing, called to the safe house in County Kildare where Con was hiding. He asked to see Con, who for days had done little more than sit on a chair and stare into space.

The papers had been full of the raid, and about the big funeral the Movement had arranged for those who had died. One of the dead was Ciaran O'Boyle, whose body had been found in the back of a van some miles out of Newry, at a place called the Flagstaff, overlooking Carlingford Lough.

There had been formal protests from the British government, with a note handed in at Dublin by the British ambassador. The Irish Prime Minister had gone on radio to warn that there was but one legitimate government and one legitimate army in the Irish Republic, and he and his government would not allow fanatics to usurp the functions of that legitimate army.

But the outrage on all sides was with an incident that had made headlines in every newspaper: how a girl of fifteen and two boys of eighteen and nineteen had been wantonly machine-gunned almost to pieces. Their bodies had been found at the Flagstaff.

'What in hell had you in mind?' Gleeson asked Con, pacing the room where Con sat gazing at the wall. 'What kind of goddam – what kind of cannibal are you?

'I'm talking to you, man. Have you any idea, any idea at all, how far you set back the Movement with this – this massacre? We're soldiers, man. Not butchers. At least we were, until the likes of you came along.

'I'm waiting for an answer, Emmet.

'Well, if you've nothing to say for yourself, I have quite a bit to say. First of all you should know there's been strong feeling at headquarters for a court martial. There won't be one, as a matter of fact; mostly because things have got too hot all round. So count yourself lucky.

'But we've had it loud and clear from the government to get you out. They know damn well who you are, and even where you are. And they want you out of the country now.

The Taoiseach's gunning for us, and we've got to go along right now. So it's America for you, boy. And count yourself lucky.

'Are you listening to me, Emmet? Because I'm only going to say this once.

'There's your passport. We picked it up at your digs in Galway. It's stamped with a visa – don't bother asking how we got it. There's tickets all the way to Chicago in this here envelope, and there's a hundred quid in dollars along with the tickets. We brought some of your clothes: they're in a bag downstairs.

'You leave today. You will see no one, speak to no one. And forget that girl. We're not letting her near a phone.

'When you get to Chicago, you take a bus – one of those Wolfhounds or Greyhounds or whatever they call them – to a place called Carbondale. There's an Irish-American, name of Dillon, teaching at a college there, and he's agreed to take you. He and his wife are in the Movement. Their phone number's on the envelope. Thanks be to Jesus they don't know what they're getting, or we'd never be rid of you.

'There you stay, till you get a work permit. We have our fellas working on that in DC, but it'll take time. And after that, you're on your own.'

Gleeson headed for the door. He opened it, paused for a moment.

'Emmet? One thing more. Forget about coming home. Ever. You'll be shot on sight if you do. That's official.'

3

At Carbondale, in the state of Illinois, everything that doesn't happen on the university campus happens on the town's main street.

Called Illinois Avenue, this long straight street is an artery through which at evening the lifeblood of the campus pulses. From 7 o'clock on warm spring evenings the sidewalks overflow onto the streets, the cars moving gingerly among the strollers.

The pace is that of the *paseo* in a Spanish town, except there is nothing Spanish about Illinois Avenue: the faces are Midwestern US; the sneakers and sweatshirts are all-American campus fatigues; the cars are cruising the Strip.

The Strip, or 'Illinois', as they call it (nobody ever bothers to say 'Avenue'), is where it's at. You can disco at Merlin's, share pitchers of foaming Schlitz at Jim's if you're old enough, or have your Cokes under an umbrella outside Pinchpenny's if you're not.

There are hamburger joints and doughnut joints and bookshops and boutiques and a Ben Franklin hardware store and a Christian Science reading room and second-hand stores and places to go for therapy and a train station and a bus station and a bowling alley, and hot-rod shops that will tart up your car so it looks like a spaceship.

A few decades ago the Strip was not much different. McDonald's hadn't come, to be sure, and Jim (whoever he was) had yet to found Jim's, so people drank at Bud's Place. The girls wore skirts and ponytails and the cars wore layers of chrome. Other than that – the same old Illinois.

That was when Conor Emmet walked it. Not that he walked it often, that first summer. But when he did, people turned to look at the long, lean figure who walked so slowly, with the slightly stooping shoulders, the hatchety face, the eyes that seemed to see nothing.

But the eyes did see something: the same thing all the time. Like those wisps within the eyeball's fluid that appear in front of the eye and move when the eye moves, so the image of a dying girl, blood ballooning from her throat, was always in front of Con's eyes. Or inside his eyes. Or inside his head. But there. Always. Behind her, dimly, two young men with machine-gunned guts.

The rest of him was numb. Memory numbed him, tying his heart, squeezing his lungs, locking his belly.

At least the numbness helped him live with his vision. A couple of times, when the numbness momentarily eased and he began to feel again, perhaps while wandering down Illinois or sitting with a beer outside Bud's, suddenly he would remember and his frame would convulse with an anguish that started in the gut and went through the body like a starburst. That's when dying seemed an option.

No, numbness was a long way better.

Dillon was an unobtrusive but compassionate host. 'No need to talk,' he told Con. 'When you feel like talking, Alice and I'll be here. That OK?' He was patient with the hours Con spent in a rocking chair, staring at the bedroom wall, listening to the moan of the air conditioning and interminably lighting his pipe.

Alice Dillon was delighted with someone to mother, in place of her two sons now grown and married. When her initial nervousness had worn off, she set about hanging flesh on Con's long bones. 'You're not just company,' she'd say. 'You're family. An' ah believe in feedin' mah boys!' Not indeed that either Dillon carried excess avoirdupois. Both were American Gothic, with the angles hardly rounded at all by campus life.

Occasionally of an evening Jack Dillon would take Con to Bud's Place, where a few of Dillon's rehab students would gather around. The pitchers of Schlitz would pile up and Dillon would hold court in his gentle way.

The students were warm to Con, and accepted his pipe and his silences.

Regulars were Wayne, a college footballer about Con's age; Mario, an ex-con down from Chicago, doing a master's in rehabilitation; and buxom Diane with a grin full of teeth, and a chuckle always at the back of her throat.

But Con preferred to be alone, and mostly they let him be. The summer grew hotter and damper, and Con stayed in the air-conditioned bedroom, and rocked to and fro on his chair nursing his pipe and his numbness, and cringed before his visions.

It was a long, hot, sweat-drenched summer.

But autumn was an artist's palette. Trees, the colour of Maeve's hair, blazed against blue skies; backyards rioted with colour; and the sky was full of wind and leaves. Dillon came into Con's room one afternoon when a mellow sun was pushing gentle fingers through the curtains, and a mild breeze rustled through the timber house. He turned a chair around and straddled it, chin resting on the high cane back.

Con was low in his rocking chair, filling his pipe.

'I was talking to the dean today, Con. He thinks he could arrange for you to take a couple of hours of English lit, if you wanted. Only if you felt up to it. And he'd look into getting you some credit for what you did at Galway. How about it?'

Con looked up bleakly. 'Mind if I think about it?'

'Sure, you think about it. Just an idea, Con. Something to be thinking about. It'll be there when you want, if you want.'

Dillon paused. 'Oh, and another thing. Bill Budslick tells me he needs some help down at Bud's. Evenings, behind the bar. Interested?'

Con roused himself. 'Now that's something I really might have a go at. Sure why not – I can't just sit here.' He ran a hand through his hair and stood up. 'Yes, OK. Tell this Bill I'll try it. But not to expect too much. An' Jack, I'll think about the college thing. Later. All right?'

Within minutes a relieved Dillon was on the phone to Budslick, and Con started work Monday evening at Bud's Place, down by the train station.

Con took quickly to bar work.

You learned easily how to salt a glass for a Tequila Sunrise and what the difference was between a Bloody Mary and a Virgin Mary, and how to put together a Harvey Wallbanger or a Purple Passion or a Rusty Nail. But mostly it was pitchers of Budweiser or Schlitz, and you just kept them coming.

Con found it strange there was no tap for Guinness, so there was no need to learn the craft of pouring a pint of stout.

Pub discipline was not that difficult. The day Con reported for work, big Stan Eckman gave him a few tips on keeping order. Stan doubled as manager and as cook over on the pizza side. He had learnt his cooking on an oil tanker, and unkind folks said that's where he got his cooking oil.

'If there's real shit – I mean real shit,' Stan told Con, 'you holler for me. OK? I'm such an ugly-looking mother, my face used to calm storms at sea. I just have to appear over at your side and it turns quiet. OK?'

Stan was being modest. True, he did have a god-awful face that any man could be proud of, but his calming effect derived in considerable part from the fact that he was six feet four and weighed close on 230 pounds. The sight of Stan Eckman's awe-some belly bearing down on a recalcitrant drinker was not unlike that of a supertanker bearing down on a yacht.

Con found that his own hatchet profile was effective for most of the everyday bar control.

He did not smile in those days. People who saw that face, and the pain lines in the face, drew few conclusions about Con's gentle nature or his lightly built frame.

Mostly Con only needed to come out from behind the bar, stand over a problem booth and ask quietly, 'Everything all right, fellas?' And that would be that.

The weekly punch-up between Gotto and Sullivan was no more than routine.

Both were part of the furniture, members of the chess-playing fraternity when sober. About midweek Gotto would tank up higher and faster than other days. He would lean across to where Sullivan was playing chess in the next booth, and mutter something inaudible, which people said was invariably about Sullivan's alleged prison record. Sullivan would bound from his booth and hurl himself on Gotto, scattering chessmen all to hell, everyone diving to safety.

Con would whistle for Stan, both would dive into the cloud of fists and feet, and Gotto and Sullivan would be deposited on the sidewalk to finish their fight in peace.

For the rest of the week both were amiable fixtures, often playing chess together.

The work was therapy, and Con grew to appreciate the nods of the regulars like Wayne and Mario, and the white teeth of Diane when she grinned a greeting.

The horrors moved to the edges of his mind during the hours he worked. They did not vanish: they lurked. And in the wee hours of the morning they moved easily back to centre stage. But at least the work hours were a relief, a breathing space in hell.

If the horrors moved aside during work, depression often took their place. It was almost welcome: depression is easier to bear than horror. As Con's seized mind began to turn over with a semblance of normality, he began to realise certain things. In particular he realised that Ireland had ceased to exist for him. He was an exile for the rest of his natural life.

A sadness would come down on him then, as he stood there polishing glasses or wiping down the bar counter. The sadness would enwrap him like those mists in Connemara that come down around the winter peak of Ben Lettery.

When an image of Ireland crept into his mind – maybe the purple outline of the Twelve Bens or the surf sucking at the Cliffs of Moher – he put the image from him, almost as he had been taught at school to banish what they called 'bad thoughts'.

There was no point in thinking of Ireland: for Con it was no more. But the sadness did not go away just because you pushed the thought away.

He tried not to think too much about Maeve. She was part of that Ireland that was gone. As good as dead. Dead to me. She can never leave the Movement, and I can never go back. Mustn't brood on it, dare not. Need my strength to cope with my horrors, when they come out in the grey hours before dawn.

But why did Maeve not write? Not even a card. As good as dead indeed. Both of us. But why? His heart shrank with the grief of it – not just exile, but to be utterly cut off.

Just do your job, Con Emmet, and try to avoid thinking, in the times between the horrors. I could write to her. Well, maybe. But what's the point right now?

Thanksgiving came and went. Con spent it behind the bar at Bud's. The nights lengthened and the days grew cold as winter moved over Illinois.

On one or two nights the horrors stayed away. Alice Dillon fed him and fussed around him, and rejoiced at whatever ounces she managed to hang on his spare frame. 'Finish the waffles, Con,' she'd say. 'Come on now. Ah cain't have the faculty wives tell me ah'm starving mah boy!'

Con got around to writing to his father, just to let the old boy know he was alive and well. Between father and only son there had been a measure of affection but no great communication, the efforts being covered with a sort of bluff heartiness.

So the letter said little more than where Con was, and that things were fine.

Old Doc Emmet rarely wrote letters, so Con was agreeably surprised to get a reply almost by return. There wasn't a scrap of news in it, of course, beyond details of the doc's arthritis, and no indication if his father knew anything of what had happened.

'Your affec. father' was how the letter ended.

A silver frost transformed the town the week before Christmas. Every twig on every branch on every tree became a tiny icicle that sparkled in the sun and tinkled in the breeze. The town was hushed, its cars and trucks banished from the glassy streets, its students gone home for Christmas to Chicago and Peoria and Springfield.

As he walked home from work Con's loneliness was palpable. The night wind cut his face and numbed his ears and he thought of Maeve. Write to her for Christmas. It's too late. Well, for the New Year then – but what's the point in writing?

No point. Write.

He walked carefully up the ice-covered path and let himself into the sleeping house. He tiptoed to the kitchen and switched on the light.

Something propped up on the table caught his eye – an airmail envelope edged in green and orange. An Irish stamp on it. Maeve's writing. He moved deliberately past the table to the counter, and his hand trembled as he lifted down the instant coffee jar. He hesitated, put it back, opened a cupboard and lifted out a half-full bottle of Jim Beam whisky. He poured himself a couple of fingers, carried the glass to the table.

Standing at the table he tore open the envelope. As he did so a faint scent of violets sought his nostrils.

There was a letter inside. As he unfolded it, something fluttered to the floor. Con reached down to pick it up.

It was a small black-and-white photo. Maeve in a white wedding gown. Flaherty beside her.

4

'You'll hafta go, Con. It's not working out,' Stan Eckman said.

Con nodded as he polished a glass. He did not reply.

'Look, it's jus' not the right place for you. OK?' Stan was trying to be kind. 'Not with all this liquor around. Shit, man, y'been your own best customer for the last three weeks – y'know that, don't you? OK? Y'come in here hung over, or else plain drunk, most afternoons. Y'couldn't begin to do your work. An' y'been drunk goin' home nights. Shit, y'paid for what y'took – I know that. S'not the point. I jus' don't wanna see y'destroying y'self. OK?

'Look, I know you're workin' through some shit inside your head – I'd hafta be blind not to see it. But liquor's not the way, Con. Willya take my word for it? I been around it a long time. OK?'

Con could agree that liquor wasn't the way. But it had eased the way during the last few weeks, and he was grateful.

A dam had burst inside him the night he got the letter. Grief deluged from him, tearing him asunder as it came. Tears tumbled from some vast, unsuspected reservoir. Shoulders heaved as his lungs lunged for breath. Fists bruised as they pounded table and wall. Ink ran in the tear-soaked letter.

Alice found him in the morning, sleeping face down on the table, letter caught damply between cheek and table. The bottle of Jim Beam stood empty beside him. She led him to his room and put him to bed.

He slept fifteen hours. Then Alice brought him soup and crackers, and he got up and showered and went out for a bottle of Scotch.

And that's how it was for three weeks, until Stan called him in and fired him. Then he stopped drinking. Or rather, the bout ended, and he became a normal drinker again.

Yet in some crazy way the liquor had helped. It banished the horrors by bringing blessed sleep – a sleep so deep even the girl with the ruined throat could not reach him. During the day, liquor massaged his temples and eased the numbness of his body. And when the numbness lifted and the embers of anguish would start to flare up in his belly, the liquor could get down in there and quench the flame.

And liquor made almost bearable the grief from Maeve's letter. She'd always remember the good times, the letter had said. And Con would always have a place in her heart. But they had to be realists: there was a chasm fixed between them. She was committed to Ireland and, by her oath, to the Movement.

So she must stay. And Con would be shot if he returned. Flaherty had asked her to marry, and it had made sense. And that was that.

Maeve hoped Con would be able able to build a life in America. And Frank sent regards.

The grief ran its course, emptying the breached dam during those three weeks. And then, astonishingly, Con recovered a semblance of his old self. Maybe it was the shock of being fired.

Even the horrors seemed to recede. The dying girl and the dead men moved back behind some grey curtain of mist. Were they gone? No. Just waiting. But for now at least they were not gazing at him. And Con began to perceive that, if Ireland was gone from him, America was for the taking.

Alice noticed the change, and fussed around him like a

clucking hen. In common with Irish and Jewish mothers, Alice had the conviction that much of life is about food. 'You just put plenty a food into a young man,' she would say, 'an' he'll start seeing life different. Take mah word for it. An' then he'll start doin' something 'bout life!'

Maybe it was the food – then again maybe it was the drink – but, not too long after getting fired, Conor Emmet started doing something about life. What he did would take him far.

'I met Jeff Stoller down at the *Chronicle* today,' Dillon said, about a week later over supper. 'He said he really liked that piece you sent him. Hey, I didn't know you were a writing man.'

'I'm not really, Jack. Just took a notion to try my hand at it.'

'Well, Jeff says the humour really got to him. He says you sure caught the atmosphere of working behind a bar. He's running it Saturday on the op-ed page – opposite the editorials.'

By meal's end Alice was clucking about Con not eating. He couldn't eat. Excitement filled him, and – for the first time in ages – joy.

The joy was keener when Saturday came and he saw his by-line. They say the sweetest words in any language are one's own name. If so, there must be few experiences quite as sweet as seeing that name in bold print at the head of one's first published article. Maybe it's not quite like the birth of one's first child, but it's of that order.

Con was like a child himself. He gazed at the page in an ecstasy of self-love. My article. My name. Me. I wrote that. Jesus, life could be fun. What'll I write next? Hey, I'm good at this . . .

He was of course modesty personified when the Dillons congratulated him. 'Well, thanks Alice. Really glad you liked it.'

'Liked it? Young man, ah haven't laughed that much in a month a Sundays,' Alice said.

'You're a pro, son,' Jack Dillon said.

It was a mini triumphal return when Con walked into Bud's

that evening. Stan Eckman took a proprietary pride in the new author.

'Hey, man! That was us, OK? And that dude behind the bar was me. Huh?' Stan dunted him gently with his massive fist. 'Hey, this one's on the house. What'll it be?' Then, *sotto voce*: 'Shit, wait. Mebbe you're on the dry, huh?'

'No, Stan. Not on the dry. But I'm over all that. I'm drinking like a normal Christian now.'

Stan chuckled: 'Not like a Christian, OK? Us Christians is the worst!'

The regulars crowded around Con, slapping him on the back, shaking his hand.

'Do I really fight like that when I'm wiped out?' Gotto asked. 'Heck, never knew I wus that good!'

'Watch it, Gotto,' Sullivan growled. 'He gave me equal billing. Didn'tya, Con?'

Diane put her arms around Con and gave him a wet kiss hard on the mouth. 'Nice goin', Irish,' she said.

The following Saturday's Carbondale *Daily Chronicle* carried another piece with the Conor Emmet byline, about kids cruising the Strip. The Saturday after that there was a piece about the joys of owning a convertible.

After the third article, editor Jeff Stoller sent for Con and offered him a job.

'You can write your fun piece for Saturdays,' Stoller told him. 'Rest of the time you'll be in the newsroom, and that means writing hard news.

'Hard news is the bottom line, Con. A guy who can't write it is no use to me. No use in newspapers. The profession is crawling with guys can write great feature copy, but can't or won't write hard news. And they wonder why they don't get jobs. So you go learn to write news. Hard news.'

Con found himself thinking that silver-haired, urbane Jeff Stoller was as hard as his news. Or maybe it was just a hard profession.

'And then when you can really write the news,' Stoller was

saying, 'when you're a competent journalist – paid your dues, so to speak – then you can build on that. You can be feature writer, commentator, columnist, you name it. But later. Right now it's news.

'Ask Joe Mays about the five Ws. Joe runs the newsroom. Trust Joe.'

'Christ A'mighty,' the city editor said. 'Why does Jeff do these things to me? You don't even know the five Ws?'

''Fraid I don't, Joe,' Con said ruefully.

'What. When. Who. Where. Why. An' don't forget How. Things you gotta have in every story. Obvious. Look, I send you out to an automobile accident. You gotta bring me back what actually happened. When it happened. Who got killed. Where they got killed...' Within half an hour that gentle black man Joe Mays had given Con a succinct and brilliant first lesson in journalism. Then he tossed two pink sheets of paper across the desk.

'OK. Now go write me these two obits. You'll find all you need in those pink forms. Mortician gets the relatives to fill them out: then he sends them over to us. Part of the service. It's all there: next of kin; where the guy worked; what he did in the war – that sort of thing. Use yesterday's obits for a model.'

Thus began Conor Emmet's initiation into newspapers. As hotel trainees start off cleaning lavatories or peeling potatoes, so Con was chained up in the newsroom writing obituaries, compiling lists of church services, calling the maternity hospitals for the births, writing up engagements and weddings from the inevitable filled-out forms: there seemed to be forms for everything.

'Margie, this bloody bride wore chiffon,' Con once yelled across to a woman reporter. 'What the hell's chiffon? And what's a corsage? A kinda corset? How could she be carrying a corset? Hey, Margie, willya help me? This is woman's work!'

'That's not even halfway funny,' Margie Skouros said coldly. 'Don't talk to me like that again.'

'I didn't mean it, Margie. Sorry. Honestly, I really didn't.'

And kindly, much-married Margie sighed and came across to help Con.

Writing the Saturday piece kept Con sane during those weeks. That and the comradeship he found at Bud's. In a way the folks there were his public: there his Saturday articles were analysed and dissected and praised. Back in the newsroom they were never so much as mentioned, and Con wondered if his colleagues were aware he wrote them.

He found himself looking forward to the evenings at Bud's, relishing Sullivan's growled compliments and Diane's husky chuckles at his latest printed witticism.

Within four weeks Con had his own beat; the tiny coal-mining town of Sidvale, fifteen miles from Carbondale, where he covered the school board and the miniscule city hall.

He became familiar with the exquisite tedium of school board meetings that went on for hours until everyone had uttered the same dreary commonplaces over and over, so that you'd be looking at your watch and wondering if Bud's would still be open by the time it was over.

But then nobody ever promised that democracy'd be exciting, Con would remind himself, as he climbed wearily into his beat-up Ford Fairlane that Dillon had helped him buy, and threw his notes on the seat beside him.

He decided that the politics of even the tiniest of city halls could be as ferocious as anything on Capitol Hill, with the Sidvale mayor glowering across the street at the police chief, and the police chief glowering at the sheriff in Murphysboro; and lobbies working over the city council about zoning ordinances and building permits; and cosy relationships between a couple of bar owners and the mayor, who happened also to be liquor commissioner.

'Stay friends with everybody,' Joe Mays advised Con. 'Remember, you're not out to get anyone. Cultivate your contacts – people like Joan in the mayor's office, and some of the good ole boys in the police. Christ, in a place as small as that, if you're open and friendly to everybody, they'll most all be your contacts.'

Mays was right, and soon Conor Emmet was a sympathetic ear for a lot of people on different sides in Sidvale. Gradually that ear assembled a corpus of inside knowledge hardly matched by any local pastor. Scarcely a scrap would have been printable, but that was not its function. Its function was to allow him to move with considerable delicacy, and report with astonishing accuracy, when anything printable did come up.

The months passed. Con continued to write his weekly humour slot for an increasingly appreciative *Chronicle* readership, while in Sidvale he was earning the attention of his newsroom colleagues and building a track record of straight reporting.

His gain in experience was not confined to newsgathering.

Every spring in Carbondale a remarkable social phenomenon occurs. A sort of spring fever.

Spontaneously, with no apparent leadership or announcement, all of a sudden, on the first warm afternoon of spring, the students pour out of campus in their thousands and swarm like bees on Illinois Avenue.

The city's police genially close the Strip to cars, and the street becomes a happy, laughing, swaying, shoulder-to-shoulder mass of youthful humanity, with bottles of Coke or cans of beer in every fist.

Not long after he took up his Sidvale beat, Con was sitting one evening with Diane at a table outside Bud's in Carbondale. It was that first warm day, the time of the spring fever, and they were watching the tide of euphoric students ebb and flow on Illinois Avenue.

It was a moment of smiles and laughter.

Con could feel the juices of spring stirring in his veins. The sun was just above the rooftops and its rays slanted across the street, warming the people at the tables and putting a rim of light around every head of hair.

The cluster of curls around Diane's face was like a halo where the sunlight drove through it. The light pierced the tall glass of beer in front of Con, and its golden shadow lay across the table, full of undulating arcs and parabolae of refracted sunbeams.

For the first time a future seemed conceivable. Con inhaled the warm spring air and felt his head swim a little. He reached for his beer.

'Hey, Irish!' Diane said. 'C'n I ask you something?'

'Surely. On a spring day like this, who could keep secrets? Ask of me what thou willst!'

'OK. Do you fuck?'

Con's beer spilled down his tartan shirt. He put his glass down. 'Aw now, wait a minute, Diane. P-people don't ask things like that.'

'Well, I'm people, an' I just did.'

'Yes, but I mean – Diane . . .'

'So do you? Or don't you?'

'Well, I – what I mean is – goddammit Diane . . .'

She clapped her hands like a gleeful child. 'Hey, I do believe I've got me a real live Irish virgin. All the way from Ireland.' She clapped her hands again.

Con was staring into his glass, and the back of his neck was on fire. Diane fell silent.

Then she touched his arm. 'Irish,' she said gently. 'Hey, I didn't mean to upset you. OK? Just don't be mad. OK?'

Con nodded curtly, and turned sideways, looking past her out into the street, clutching his beer glass in both hands. He was biting his lip.

He wasn't mad. He was in turmoil – a turmoil of shyness mixed with a deep and awful longing. Tell her yes. Just say yes. It's what you've always wanted. Tell her. Con had a fleeting image of what had just been proferred, and his throat tightened.

His old Jesuit school training plucked at him momentarily, about banishing sexual thoughts immediately from the mind. Instead he banished the Jesuit thought – later, maybe. I want her so much. I want this so much. He felt dizzy, and his mouth was dry.

But shyness had paralysed him. He drained his beer glass in one, and sat looking away from Diane, watching the revellers in the street.

'Look Irish,' Diane was saying. 'Forget what I said. OK? Look, I'll not ask you again. OK?'

Con's heart sank as the proferred experience slid away from him. He wanted to shout 'stop'.

'Whenever you feel ready,' Diane was saying, 'you just say. That OK?' Another chance. It was Chinese torture.

Con looked at his empty glass, then at the empty pitcher. Diane's eyes asked, More? He shook his head. The desire for beer was gone.

They stood, and Diane slung her bag across her shoulder. In silence they picked their way along the crowded, hectic street, Con gazing at the ground, Diane stealing an occasional glance at him.

His body was a cauldron of longing. Tell her, you fool. Tell her you want it. But his mouth was dry.

His voice was a croak when he spoke, and he looked straight ahead. 'Uh. What you said back there, Diane. Uh, you meant it? If you didn't, it's all right –'

He felt her hand coming into his. 'Let's go, Irish. My place, OK?'

The tightness in his throat almost hurt. He pulled her hand and they both started to run.

They scrambled up the outside staircase to Diane's small apartment, climbing across clusters of students sitting with beer cans on the steps. Diane fumbled for her key, then the door had clicked behind them and they were facing each other.

They stood for an age, breathing hard.

Con put out his hands and drew her to him. He pressed his

face into her neck. 'Promise me something,' he whispered. 'Promise you won't laugh at me. Promise?'

'You're no laughing matter, Irish,' she whispered. And then they were kissing.

Con lay for a long time in the soft light of the bedroom, gazing at the sleeping body beside him. She was the colour of whipped cream. Her back was to him, and he saw how dramatically the waist merged into the swelling hips. Like an inverted heart.

No man was ever like that.

It had been good. It had been very good. And no guilt at all. Instead he felt a splendid sense of wellbeing, of exhilaration almost, as a man might feel who had broken the sound barrier or run the four-minute mile. He would walk just a little taller down Illinois Avenue now, and would look other men straighter in the eye.

She had been kind, and very, very gentle. His mind went lovingly over the images: her joyous grin; the acrid hint of sweat; her legs locking his; and just how tender she had been.

Did he love her?

That would come. But he felt a profound sense of – of gratitude, maybe, to this young woman who had – who had helped him through this.

He sat up to look at her.

She sighed and turned towards him. His eyes moved over the sleeping body, over the long, strong legs, the sturdy hips, and then the surprisingly slender waist. His eyes wandered across her creamy shoulders, where a mole shone like a dark star, and his gaze rested on her neck. Her neck, smooth and pale, and when she stretched, the sinews moved inside it. Her neck. Her neck. Her *neck*. Oh Jesus, no, not that. Not the *neck*. Please no. And suddenly the horrors were back, and his body jackknifed and his head was on the pillow and his shoulders were shaking and the pillow was drenched in silent tears.

Diane stirred and her fingers sleepily caressed his face. They felt the wet of the tears and hesitated. They felt again, and Diane opened her eyes. Then she was hugging him. 'Don't take it like that,' she whispered. 'It has to happen to every guy. Be proud of it.'

She kissed the wet cheeks. 'Know something, Irish?' She kissed them again. 'You're beautiful.'

5

Joe Vogel, mayor of Sidvale, was standing at the window, glaring at the police office on the other side of the street.

When Conor Emmet entered the office, Joe beckoned him to the window. Across the street a curtain moved, and Con glimpsed the angry profile of police chief Mike Andersen just moving away.

'Thar. Y'see?' Joe growled. 'That's what I have to put up with. Just sits there, glarin' across at me, when he should be runnin' his department.'

He came across to his desk, and sat paunchily into the big, upholstered chair, gesturing with his cheroot for Con to take a seat. 'So what can I do fer you, young man? Guess you wanna know about this sum-bitch Andersen, huh?'

'Well, Joe, we're all a bit puzzled, if I might say so. I mean, first you tell Chief Andersen he's demoted to patrolman status, and in the same letter you tell him he's to continue acting as chief until further notice. Then yesterday you withdraw the demotion, and tell him he's suspended without pay for thirty days.

'And now this morning you tell him it's been reduced to five days, effective Monday. Now I'm sure you know what you're doing, Joe – it's just that we haven't quite – well – haven't quite been able to follow.'

The cheroot waved and the little chins wobbled. 'He's an insubordinate sum-bitch, Con, an' that's the bottom line. An' he hates my guts. Look, it's not just he won't enforce the early tavern closure on Sundays, like I told him to – that's only the tip of the iceberg. He frustrates me every which way, an' the sooner he gits his ass outa that chair an' moves to other parts, the better I'll like it.

'It's this goddam civil service commission I'm stuck with – they keep rescinding what I do. That sum-bitch has them in his pocket.'

An hour later Con was sitting down across the street with Sidvale police chief Andersen.

'He hates my guts, Con, an' that's the bottom line. He wants the locals mad at me, an' that's why he tells me to enforce the early tavern closure on Sundays. You'd think he'd have more to do than sit glaring outa that window across at me all day.'

'Are you not suspended right now, Mike?' Con asked.

'Sure am, Con. But then that creep says I gotta run the department anyhow. He's crazy, man.'

'Mike. What's it all about? I mean, really?'

Andersen leaned back in his chair. 'I gotta go across to the drugstore for a couple of minutes,' he said. 'Guess you won't mind waiting. Hey, by the way, that book on the desk is a charge book, that happens to be open at February 2 of last year. Classified, of course, an' I'm requiring you not to look at it. I'll be right back.'

He stalked out into the street, and Con leaned across to the big leatherbound volume on the desk.

A couple of days later, Con Emmet was once more in the mayor's office. Vogel finished briefing him on a zoning variance.

'Joe,' Con said, 'you remember that drunk-driving charge last February? When's it coming to court?'

The little red eyes stared at him. 'Jesus, how the hell d'ya know about that?'

'Arragh come on, Joe. You know we hear pretty well everything. Sooner or later. Always somebody in the newsroom has it. But sure we only publish a tiny bit of what we know,' Con added soothingly. 'Look, would you think of telling me the whole story, so at least we get it right?'

It all tumbled out then. Joe's problems with liquor. The cover-ups. Andersen wanting something done, but the good ole boys standing by Joe. The rookie patrolman picking Joe up on the highway and booking him. The court at 2 a.m., courtesy of old Judge Walker, with Joe pleading guilty and paying his fine.

'That goddam sum-bitch Andersen,' Vogel said through his teeth. 'Hasta be the one that leaked it. I'll see that bastard in hell yet.'

'You can never be sure who leaked it, Joe.'

'Oh I'm sure as hell sure, Con. You bet I'm sure. He thinks he's the only one can play that game – well he's got another think comin'. Hey, next time you see him, ask him is it true about Maggie Schmidt.'

'How d'you mean, Joe?'

'Just say that to him: Is it true about Maggie? Just say it.' He grinned and sat back. 'An' see what happens.'

Vogel leaned back and pulled open the bottom drawer of a filing cabinet. His hand dipped in and emerged with a fifth of Jim Beam, which it deposited on the desk. It dipped back in and came up with two glasses.

'I'm working, Joe,' Con said. 'I can't really.'

Vogel pressed a button on his desk. 'I'm in conference, Joan,' he said into the intercom. 'Not to be disturbed. Under any circumstances.' To Con, he said, 'Turn the lock on that door, son.'

Con walked across and locked the door.

'God dammit. Where in hell did y'come up with that?'

Mike Andersen's tall figure stood up behind the desk in agitation.

'Sit down, Mike,' Con said. 'Relax. They always know more in the newsroom than ever makes the paper. You know that.'

Andersen sat down and put his head in his hands.

Con leaned back and closed his eyes. 'Mike,' he said, 'could be we don't have the full story. Or that we have it wrong, which could be a helluva lot worse. Would you consider – only if you really want to, now – would you consider telling me the whole story? I mean, as it really is? It could set a lot of things straight.'

Andersen sat silent, then started pacing the room. Abruptly he sat down, leaning across the desk on his elbows.

'Y'know Maggie Schmidt? Shucks, everybody knows Maggie. Well, as y'know, her house is more or less the local, uh, cat-house for this here area. Hell, everybody knows that. You know that.'

Con nodded.

'Well, Maggie an' me, we been friends for years. Real good friends. An', like, coming up to Christmas Maggie usually has a bit of a present for me. Very generous lady. An' maybe something at Thanksgiving, an' around Easter. An' a couple of other times, mebbe.

'So, OK, Maggie calls me one night at home. It's real late. Says Randy Davis got hisself in a punch-up at her place, then keeled over with a heart attack. Leastways it looked like one, she says. An' he had no marks from the rough-house –'

'I remember Davis's death . . . a couple of months back. But there was no –'

'I'm getting to that. Anyway Maggie says will I help her, an' I tell her yes. So anyways, I come over in my car, an' Murdoch an' me, we get Davis in the back. We take him to Mack's Cocktails in Carbondale – I've done Mack a few favours – an' put him in the men's room there. In one a them closets, with his pants down. An' that's about it. Jesus, it was as much for his poor wife as for Maggie. An' it was a coronary – that's what they diagnosed in the hospital when he was brought in.'

'Was that much later?'

'They found him two hours after. Hold it – now don't go thinking we did him outa treatment. He was already getting stiff when we lifted him into the car. You hafta believe that.'

'I believe you, Mike,' Con said.

'Do you know something, young man?' Jeff Stoller leaned back with his hands behind his silver head. 'You have the makings of one extremely good investigative reporter. I absolutely agree we don't publish any of this' – he tapped the notes on the desk – 'but I must say I'm impressed with your facility for newsgathering. And with your way with people. That alone will take you a long way.'

Stoller paused to fit a cigarette into his holder.

He leaned back. 'Well, you're going to take the first step along that way. I'm bringing you in here to Carbondale. You'll take the police beat – that'll be routine – but I want you to spend the rest of your time checking out this strip-mine scandal. Do you know that in some states the coal companies are just walking away from worked-out strip mines – not putting back a dime's worth of topsoil? We need to know if it's happening here. There's a story in there – a big one – and there's a future for you in there too, as an investigative reporter –'

'Jeff.'

'And when that's wrapped up you can move on to –'

'Jeff! Jeff, I don't want that kind of future. Look I'm sure the mines need looking into, but I'm not the one to do it. Really I'm not.'

Stoller stared. 'Suppose you tell me why not,' he asked coldly.

'Look, Jeff. Let's say I can draw people out. Like Vogel and the Chief. But that's because I like them, and they like me. They're my friends. And they trust me – and half the time I don't know how to handle it.' Con ran a hand through his hair. 'Look, Jeff, the one thing an investigator needs is detachment. And that I don't have.'

Stoller said nothing.

'Maybe I'm wrecking my career before it's half started,' Con went on. 'But I have to say it now. Sure, I could do your investigating, and I know it needs to be done. But I'd do violence to myself – and I'd end up hating myself, or with an ulcer, or more likely boozing myself under the table. Anyhow Jeff, didn't you tell me I'd get to choose what I'd be doing – I mean, at some point?'

'Well, you can't just sit and write your column.'

'Jeff, I'm not talking about the bloody column. Look, you say I can draw people out, get their confidence. Well, I want to use that to find the good news – what the ordinary folks are doing that's worthwhile – who's helping who. There's a pastor down town starting a counselling service – I want to tell about that. That's as important as the bad news.'

'Ah. A good-news journalist – that it?' Jeff sighed. 'Heaven preserve me from good-news journalists. They're bad news. They all perish. Or mature into regular bad-news journalists.'

Con stood and leaned his hands on the desk. 'Jeff. I know we need the bad news. I know papers have to dig out the dirt. Somebody has to do it. But I believe they have to dig out the gold as well, find the good things going on in the community. That's news too, and it tells people life's still worth living – it's not all bad. Gives them something to live for. So people know there's help out there, or just know there's still good folks around. Jeff, I want to be a gold digger. And I want to go on writing humour. I believe it's one of the most necessary –'

'Could you handle the Saturday Personal Side?'

'Huh?'

'Sit down, will you. From next week, I'm giving you Satur-day's PS pages. You'll be editor, reporter, every goddam thing for those pages. Supposed to be the society pages – that's why they call them Personal Side – and you'll have to carry the weddings and the church services. But you can do what you want with the rest of the newshole. Try out some of those theories – God knows you can't do worse than Margie's been doing.' Stoller pulled open a drawer in his desk, then looked at Con. 'Ever handle a camera? No? Well, you start right now – it's part of your new job!'

He reached in the drawer and lifted out a heavy twin-lens Mamiyaflex camera. 'Take this to Margie, and ask her to show you how to use it. There's other lenses here when you get the hang of it. Any questions? No? OK, then go and convince me!'

For Conor Emmet it was a new lease on life. His role fitted him as a glove fits a hand. After barely two months, Personal Side had become the best-liked section of the paper.

With the encouragement of Margie, the world's least jealous person, who was delighted to relinquish the chore of editing, Con found himself transforming the PS section. Those pictures of society matrons presenting trophies to one another were banished to the inside pages. A single interview replaced them, dominating the section's front page, and usually topped with a half-page photo of the person interviewed.

Con relished those interviews. He did them himself, and found his subjects all over Jackson County, among the well-known and the very ordinary. He discovered what any journalist discovers in a small town: that there is a splendid story in every human being.

And much humour. There was the ancient doc, long past retirement age, who had whacked breath into half the people now grown up and running the town. The readers chuckled over his crusty views, and they shuddered at his remedies.

There was the pastor who had won a lifelong battle with the bottle, and was sharing the heartbreaking details so as to encourage others.

There was the attractive young mother of two, who was

going to pilot an ancient tail-dragger Cessna plane in the Powder Puff Derby, and the thirteen-year-old disabled girl who was organising the March of Dimes from her wheelchair.

There was no looking back after the interview with Delyte W. Morris, celebrated president of the university, friend of senators and industrialists, who was building Southern Illinois University – SIU – into one of the Midwest's most prestigious campuses. After that, a lot of people wanted to be interviewed by Conor Emmet.

And to be photographed by him, too.

For Con found he was a natural with the camera. He evolved his own techniques, photographing people against the light so that their hair glowed with a rim of light, placing groups ranged up along a staircase instead of lined up as for a firing squad.

He photographed Delyte Morris in profile, gazing out of his office window, so that the one-directional light from the window textured the massive forehead and nose and chin, leaving the rest of the head almost in darkness. Like a Rembrandt.

Soon the PS section carried its own picture page, always on a single theme: the loveliness of autumn at Crab Orchard, perhaps, or grizzled faces at the Veterans' Day parade. One big picture would dominate, with smaller pictures clustered around it 'like the moon and the stars around the sun', as Con was wont to express it.

Humour laced many interviews, and quite bubbled over in the Saturday column, 'Emmet, Dammit!', which Con continued to write for the op-ed page. Jeff kept him right up there beside Art Buchwald and Jack Anderson and the other big syndicated names. But Con kept his head: he was only in this one paper, while Buchwald was appearing in hundreds of papers all over the USA.

Even so, Saturday belonged to Con: people were buying the weekend paper because of what he put into it.

One day there was a call from Francis Xavier Kearney of the

Joliet *Independent*. Might they reprint the column each week? There would be a small fee, not a lot, but of course times being hard, and Con would understand . . . Con thought it over carefully for about two seconds, and said yes.

When a column begins appearing in even one other paper, a restraining membrane seems to be breached – some umbilical cord severed. The column is out free, and there is no telling how far it may go.

'So are you happy, Con?' Diane asked him one day. 'You have to know you're on the way up. You could go right to the top. You do realise that, don't you?'

They were lying together on the lumpy old bed in Diane's apartment. It was a Saturday afternoon.

'Happy? That's the big one, isn't it?' Con stretched and smiled. 'Bedad an' begorra,' he said in a stage-Irish brogue, 'sure don't I be after havin' me ups and downs, just like all the other fellas!'

'You have your downs, that's for sure.'

'Hey now, that's a bit – that's . . . All right then, how do you know when I'm feeling down?'

'Easy: it's in your eyes. You're only half with me. You sorta look past me, as if you're seeing things I don't see. Your face gets a look of – bleakness. An' you crack those knuckles more. An' I know where to find you those times.'

'Where?'

'You know durn well where. Down at Bud's, way at the back by yourself. Like I said, it's easy.'

'Jeeesus,' whispered Con, and fell silent. He climbed out of the bed, fumbled in the clothes on the floor for his pipe and tobacco, and got back in. He shivered slightly.

Diane was right, of course. He did have his downs, only he never realised they were so apparent. Maybe they weren't, really – maybe it was Diane had grown so close. She would perceive what others might not.

Yes, there were the down times, all right. There were the

times when depression sat on his shoulder like Cuchulain's raven, and he would brood about Maeve, or about the Ireland he would never see, or about his old father back in Newry, to whom he had never said goodbye.

And sometimes, still, the horrors came. Like that first time they made love – when Diane thought he was weeping for lost virginity.

Virgin killer. Killer virgin.

The horrors came unbidden. Sometimes it was the sight of a beautiful neck, on a girl coming towards him on the sidewalk. Sometimes it was a piece about Ireland, clattering off the Associated Press wire back at the office, that would call up the horrors. Sometimes they would come for no reason, at night when he was just dozing off.

But always they came suddenly, and his body would convulse, and anguish would surge through his arteries like some dreadful acid.

Still, they didn't come so often now. Perhaps they would eventually go away for good.

And there were times when the horrors let him be, but left in their place something that went gnaw, gnaw, gnaw, deep in his entrails. To gnaw and gnaw again – the 'again-bite of inwit' that poor old Joyce had known so well.

The gnawing might go on for weeks. You just carried it around inside you and went about your business. Sometimes the gnawing grew almost gentle: and sometimes whatever was gnawing would take a rest, and you could feel its inert weight like a tumour down there somewhere near the solar plexus. A drop of Scotch or bourbon helped. Not that it could dissolve the tumour or still the gnawing: but, for a brief and blessed while, none of it seemed to matter.

Curiously, the pain in no way affected the quality of Con's work. He could write sparkling humour even in the depths of depression, or when the gnawing was at its fiercest. It was as though two different parts of him functioned simultaneously – the humour subliming off the top of the mind, like wisps of steam from a ship's smokestack: the grief slurping around in the gut, like bilge water deep down in the wallowing hull.

Then too there were weeks, sometimes nearly a month, when the depressions and the anguish and the gnawing – the whole paraphernalia of pain – simply lifted off and vanished. Into thin air. Leaving not a trace. Those were the times when earth seemed heaven. Life seemed so – so conquerable then. Youth revived, and who cared that it wasn't to last forever? Have, get, before it cloy ... A whiff of Eden.

Like right now. This was one of those times.

'A penny for your thoughts!' Diane was smiling at him, hands behind her head on the pillow.

'Diane Schaefer,' Con whispered. 'Will you marry me?'

'Know somethin', Irish?' she whispered back. 'I thought you'd never ask!'

6

Conor Emmet and Diane Schaefer married on a bright June morning, at the Jackson County Courthouse in Murphysboro, Illinois. It was two days after Diane's graduation from SIU.

Con was to remember the months before the wedding as among the happiest in a lonely life.

The horrors hardly came. They lurked, but at a discreet distance, so he was often free of their torments. Depression mostly stayed away. Sometimes he even felt euphoria.

Merely to breathe air was a rich experience. Sunshine and blue skies brought sheer physical joy, as he strolled with Diane by the campus lake at Thompson Point, or sat with her watching the sun sparkle on Little Grassy Lake.

'I know now what the Indians meant by Laughing Water,' he said to Diane on one of those afternoons.

Diane grew on a fellow. Maybe Con had begun by looking to fill the void left by Maeve, but Diane existed in her own right now. She was nobody's substitute, with her earthy humour and her throaty chuckle, and her way of saying outrageous things with an innocent grin. Diane might not make *Playboy*'s centrefold (and thank God for that), but there was a lot that was beautiful about her.

Did Con love her?

What does that mean, anyhow? When you're both happy to be together all the time, and you think maybe it can work for all of the future, well, what the hell else is there?

And Diane was gentle and loyal and patient. Patient even with Con's drinking. Anyway he only drank for joy now, and relatively little. Little, compared with the bad old days.

The bad old days were gone now.

Other Illinois papers started running the column. A couple of months after it started in the Joliet paper, it began in the Collinsville *Echo*, and shortly afterwards it began in the Kankakee *Daily Mail*. Soon eight papers around Illinois were running it, and one across the river in Missouri.

Of course it didn't just happen. It was made to happen, and much of the drive came from Diane.

'Now you listen to me, Irish,' she said one day to Con. 'If folks here like what you write, an' they like it in Joliet, stands to reason they'd like it over in Collinsville. Thing is, you can bet the *Echo* editor never heard of "Emmet, Dammit!" Well, you an' me – we're gonna make him hear about it. OK?'

'You have that look – that look you get when you're going to make me do something.'

'Dead right I am. Don't you worry: we'll do it together. First, we pick your five best pieces an' Xerox them. Then we do a brochure about the column – you can put in some of those letters from readers. Brochure quotes a nice low rate. Then you do a handwritten letter to each editor – we pick out about twenty editors to start with. And we mail the packet off to them. Look, if only one or two bite, it's worth it. OK?'

And that's how 'Emmet, Dammit!' really got going. A couple of editors did bite, and then twenty more were circulated and a few more took the bait. And so on. That spring Con won the Sigma Delta Chi award for best newspaper column in the state.

By then Con had developed a rhythm in his column writing, and more ideas kept bubbling in his mind than he could ever use. He carried a notebook, and jotted down each seed of an idea as it occurred. Sometimes he might develop it then and there; other times it would remain a few words or a sentence or two. On Thursdays before he sat to write the column, he would thumb through the notebook. Usually one of the ideas would get him going, and within minutes his fingers would be dancing around the keyboard.

His columns matured into tightly written pieces, where each sentence was lovingly sculpted and every word selected so that no other word would have done. Mostly they were comment on the American (or just the human) scene, from the viewpoint of an Irish onlooker. It was a viewpoint leavened with whimsy, humour, sometimes outrageous exaggeration, and occasional dead seriousness. Some columns were tongue-in-cheek, some were fiercely in earnest, and part of their fascination was that no one knew what would come next. Con gently mocked, for instance, the American penchant for ice in drinks, which, he said, only froze the taste buds and took up the space that should have gone to the drink, thus saving money for the bar. Back home in Ireland, Con said, ice was something you walked across to get to the pub. It might stick to your boots, but it never got into your glass.

'If any proof is needed of the brainwashing power of American commercial interests,' Con wrote, 'it lies in the fact that a whole nation has been made to salivate at the tinkle of that malign substance that sank the *Titanic*, that wrecks automobiles and makes murderous the nation's highways, that locks away the riches of Antarctica, that bursts waterpipes and ruins the engine of my car, that causes grief to my teeth, that lures little children onto ponds and gives way beneath them, that closes harbors and airports to lawful commerce and engulfs Alpine villages in avalanches.

'And those evil crystals are piercing the souls and chilling the bodies of 250 million Americans.'

People loved it. They cut out his columns and taped them to their fridges. They looked for the first time at the ice in their drinks and wondered what it was doing there. And they looked in a new way at their chrome-laden, oversized automobiles, at their reverence for business breakfasts, and at their green beer on St Patrick's Day. And smilingly started to wonder at it all.

It was arrant nonsense, most of it. But at least it was a relief for folks to turn the page on the dreary insanities of the Cold War, to the harmless lunacies of 'Emmet, Dammit!'

There was a brief letter from Maeve that year. She said Con had never been publicly connected with 'what had happened outside Newry that night'. The Movement had gone quiet after those events: people did not want to know any more. The members were holding together, of course (it wasn't a thing you quitted). Lying low until times became more opportune. And given the discrimination in Northern Ireland, those times would come, she said.

Meanwhile Maeve and Flaherty were pushing ahead with their medical careers.

There was also, about two weeks before the wedding, a letter from one Mark Carey of the *New York Times*: would Mr Emmet consider coming to New York to discuss with Mr Carey the possibility of nationwide syndication of the 'Emmet, Dammit!' column, through the New York Times Syndicate?

The Golden Fleece, the Holy Grail, the End of the Yellow Brick Road for every man or woman who ever wrote a column in America. Now offered to Con.

Of course the invitation was not just out of the blue: once again Diane had mailed samples of the column, 'for the heck of it'. And once again the column had worked its magic.

It was agreed that Con and Diane would fly to New York after the wedding, combining a brief honeymoon there with a meeting with Mark Carey at the *Times*. So, after the open-air reception at Margie's home (the reception was her wedding gift), the couple would drive the eighty miles to St Louis, overnight there, and fly next morning to New York.

There were only four people at the wedding ceremony.

Stan Eckman, who like a benevolent deity at Bud's Place had presided over the growing intimacy of Con and Diane, was best man. Now, as he walked with Con up the steps of the Jackson County Courthouse in Murphysboro, he was more like a benevolent orang-utan.

While waiting for Diane and Margie, Stan kept dunting Con in the shoulder with his great fist. 'It was me brought you guys together, OK?' he kept saying. 'Jeez, I'm real prouda you guys. Don't you guys ever let me down, OK?'

Stan's joy was infectious. During the ceremony, when old Judge Exeter was short-sightedly muttering his way through the marriage ceremony, Stan dunted Con in the shoulder. 'Give her a kiss,' he whispered. Con obliged, and discovered the judge was not as short-sighted as he seemed.

'Young man,' the judge said, glaring up at Con over his glasses, 'there'll be no kissing in this here courthouse until I give the word. Izzat clear?'

Con snapped to attention, as though Exeter was once again the marine sergeant he had been years before. He thought he detected a twinkle within the judge's glare, but he wasn't banking on it. The judge resumed his peering and muttering.

Rings were exchanged and the brief ceremony ended.

'You may now kiss the bride, young man,' the judge said, and this time the twinkle was apparent.

There was time for a snack and a bottle of champagne at the restaurant across the street, and then they headed for Margie's to get things ready for the fun.

Margie had done the inviting, and had invited everyone.

Each guest brought something to eat or drink: a salad or a cooked dish, or a plate of brownies or a bottle of wine. By

4 p.m. the trestle tables on the lawn were groaning under the dishes and the wine.

Con was finding, as he mingled under the warm June sun, how many Carbondale folk cared for him. And for Diane. Jeff Stoller was there from the paper, along with Joe Mays and everybody from the newsroom. Half the advertising staff and most of the back shop were there too.

J.J. Hall had come, with a couple of colleagues from the journalism school on campus.

Chief Andersen was there along with his mayor, and they seemed to be the best of buddies.

Bud's Place had emptied itself for the occasion, some of its more permanent denizens blinking in the sunlight as if it was the first they had encountered in a long time. Gotto and Sullivan were sitting on the grass, peaceably playing chess.

For everyone Diane had a grin and a word and a chuckle, as she walked among them with Con, wearing her pink summer dress which was both wedding dress and going-away outfit.

'Go easy with the liquor, Con,' she whispered. 'Remember we drive eighty miles tonight.'

'I'll watch it,' Con promised. 'How about I stick to the beer? No more Scotch. OK?'

'I love you, Conor Emmet,' she whispered back. 'Jeez, how I love you.'

Margie was beaming with that purest of joy that only a generous person knows, in the presence of another's happiness.

Stan was dunting shoulders galore. Jack and Alice Dillon had the relieved but bemused look of parents whose problem child has unexpectedly made good, and Alice was telling anyone who would listen about the nutritious foods she had fed Con.

It was almost dark, and Margie had the garden lights on, when Con and Diane climbed into the old Ford Fairlane. A last dunt from Stan, a tearful kiss from Margie, and Con swung the car down the avenue and out from the driveway, and accelerated fast up along the narrow country road.

Around the bend came the lights of an articulated truck at high speed on a collision course, trailers weaving and klaxons blaring like a freight train. Con shot the car into the left-hand grass verge, and the rig roared past. The car mounted the slope, flipped over as neatly as a ploughshare turns a sod, and with a screeching of steel on asphalt slithered on its roof back onto the roadway, hit the far margin and rose up on its side. It teetered momentarily, then collapsed back on its four wheels.

Con found himself still at the wheel. His mind was blank, and a numbness in his left knee was giving way to agonising pain. He sat there.

Then he thought of Diane, and turned to the seat beside him. She was not there. She was not in the back. She was not in the car at all.

He tried the driver's door and found it jammed. His hands were starting to shake. He threw his shoulder against the door but it would not yield.

He smelled petrol and groped for the ignition key.

He manoeuvred himself across the seat to the far door and found it would not budge. He lay flat on the seat and put both feet against the door and kicked and shoved and kicked with all his might. The door gave, and he staggered out.

His left knee would not hold him and he grabbed for the car and went dizzy with the pain.

Far down on the other side of the road, under a street lamp, figures were gathering around something pink that was lying on the grass.

7

Great bloody party, Margie. Who's giving it, anyhow? No, don't worry about me. You know I like being by myself – just watching it happen. Gives me ideas for the column. Sure y'know me by now, Margie – Emmet, the Great Loner. Thanks, sweetheart. You too – have fun.

Oh hey, Margie, before y'move off – do me a favour. Willya fill my glass for me? Shot of that Jameson – see if there's any left. If not, Scotch or Jim Beam'll do. Thanks Margie, you're a dear, Margie.

Great bloody woman, Margie Skouras. So – sensitive. Understanding. Never gets mad, even when I'm in one of these gawdawful moods. Yep, I know I'm in a gawdawful mood. But ole Margie understands. Knows when I wanta be alone.

Like now.

Jeez, that woman helped me through the bad patches. So many. Like when Diane died. Thought I'd go mad. Did, I suppose. For a time, anyhow. How long's it been? Can't be six years. Sure, it can.

I miss her. Never got a chance. Could've been the start of something – something really good. Never got a chance.

Wonder what it'd be like now? Would it a been a good

marriage? What's a good marriage, anyway? Maybe even kids? What the hell. Wonder does God know those things – what might've been, that sort of thing?

That's if there is a God. Which I doubt.

My ole dad woulda loved grandkids. Told me once in a letter. One of the few times ever wrote his feelings. No letter-writer, my ole man. Not too good meself either.

God, I ought to write to him. How long since I . . . ? Well it's not my fault: I'm writing columns all the time. Shouldn't blame myself. Mebbe get him here on a visit. Yep, that's it.

Naw. Tried it before. Always kicks for touch when I suggest.

Hey thanks, Margie, Jesus ya didn't exactly fill it up, didya? OK, Marge. No sermons. Please. OK?

Fabulous aroma from Irish whiskey. Much more than Scotch. Y'can breathe it, sorta like cognac. Wonder what gives it the aroma? Great when y'heat it, like in a hot whiskey. Aroma goes all over the house. Funny, sometimes I find it hard to imagine Diane's face. The way it really was – not like after the accident.

Was it drink did it? Mine, or the lorry driver's? Was the lorry on the wrong side? Or me? Nobody saw it. Was I confused and took the Irish side of the road? I'll never know. Couldn't even ask the lorry driver – never even stopped. Probably never knew there was an accident.

And Andersen saying he fixed it so I wasn't checked for alcohol level. One decent man. Though I was probably OK.

No, ma'am. Don't you worry about me. Often sit alone like this at parties. No, I enjoy it, actually. Really I do. And I do appreciate that you invited me. I'll join the others in a while.

Well yes, I s'pose y'could freshen it up a little. Some of that Irish whiskey, please, if there's any left. Straight, and no ice. Ice is extremely dangerous, ma'am. Y'know it sank the Titanic, *don't you? Well, there you are.*

Yes, you can fill it right up. Did y'ever hear the saying, 'There's no such thing as a large Irish whiskey'? Now there's a proverb for you.

Stupid cow. Why can't she play hostess somewhere else and stop bothering me? No, that's not fair. She's really quite kind, and they say she's a bloody good prof over on campus. Why do I think so negative? Must start thinking positive.

Though some of these hostesses can be a pain in the arse – the ones that only want you because you're famous.

What was it *Time* said about me? 'One of the best of that rare breed of humour writers . . . Sparkling Celtic insight into the workings of the Anglo-Saxon mind.' Something like that, anyway. Column's in how many papers now? Over four hundred, last time I bothered to count.

Strange how life is: lost Diane, gained the world . . . It was Margie made me go to New York. Couple of months after Diane died. Said life must go on. Funny how I remember those big revolving doors at the *Times* – West 43rd, wasn't it? Why do they choose such grotty places? Maybe they didn't – just got that way. Later. Big revolving doors, and all that polished brass.

An' me standing there thinking this could be the doorway to a new life . . .

Mark Carey coming out from behind his desk, taking my hand in both of his, saying how sorry he was. How he wished he'd had a chance to know Diane. I felt he really meant it. Same as Sean Louth really meant things.

Carey was a gentleman – one of the real ones. Not too many.

Then down to brass tacks.

How's this we started? Ah yes: him telling me how they had over 700 clients – seemed sort of small, then I realised they were newspapers, not just readers. And me asking if I'd have to come and work at the *Times*, and feeling sorta hurt that Mark had said it was the last thing they'd want. They wanted the column's flavour of small-town America – and I'd lose that fast if I came to the Big Apple. Wonder why they call it Big Apple? Said the last thing they needed right then was another Winchell or Dorothy Kilgallen, who were steeped in New York and knew nothing else.

So Mark says, just you carry on in Carbondale. And here I am, six years later, carrying on . . .

Not that Carbondale was the same after that. Different when you've got money, and when people know you're getting famous. There's the old friends, of course. Like Margie. And Andersen. But some of the others think you wouldn't want to bother with them, and they back off. That's what's sad.

Or maybe they feel your new lifestyle's too costly for them to join in with.

So either you have to cut back and not use the money, or lose the friends. Can't just give them money to keep up with you: lose them twice as fast that way. Can't buy friends.

Yet if you cut back they think you're stingy.

Just as well I didn't have fancy tastes. Except maybe the convertibles. So nothing much changed, really. Only now I could afford the liquor, instead of getting more in debt. And – I don't care what they say, or what the hell Margie says (interfering oul so-and-so, anyway) – the liquor does help when the horrors come.

And they come whenever they want now. Since Diane died. Seem to have lost control of them. Must get them back under control one of these days –

Jock Hall! And how are you, my dear sir? And how are things on campus? Please don't mind my squatting here in a corner – I'm in one of those solitary moods. But I'll be joining you shortly, if I may. Doris with you? Good.

Wait, I'll walk across with you and get myself a drink. By the way, I really like your new bunch of students. They're bright, and they want to learn. And some of those women are fabulous – do you choose them for brains? Tell me the truth, now . . .

Funny thing, that's the part I like best. More than the money. Recognition. Like being Visiting Prof over on campus, and the journalism students looking up to me as a success. And, like, when I sign my name in a restaurant and the waitress says are you *the* Conor Emmet, the one in the papers?

And the lecture circuit, when people crowd around afterwards, and think I have an answer to everything. God help us, and me with just a smart line of questions.

Sometimes I start half believing I'm special. The horrors mostly put a halt to that gallop: so I'm special, am I, with three kids rotting in an Irish graveyard, one of them a girl with no neck . . . Here we go again. Swallow that whiskey and think of something else quick. Quick. Yep, being famous, that's always an easy thing to think of. Being a writer's the best – not like a actor, where everyone knows your face. Could never handle that.

Someone like Richard Burton, he's stuck with his fame. Stuck with his face. Face is his fortune. People say there goes Richard Burton. No privacy. Must get so fed up.

But me – I can switch on and off being famous, whenever I like. Nobody really knows my face – that thumbnail sketch on the column wouldn't help anyone. So, like, when I lectured up in Chicago I could go into those Rush Street bars and be free as a bird – nobody bothering me. Until I choose.

Can switch on being the big cheese whenever I want. Not that I'd go up to somebody in a bar and say, wanna guess who I am? Probably punch me. Got to be subtle. Air of modesty. Shrinking violet. I like that – ole Emmet a shrinking violet. Wasn't that Maeve's perfume? Violet? Hardly shrinking, though. Do I shrink? I need a shrink, that's for sure.

No, I'm-the-greatest doesn't wear well. Look at Cassius Clay.

That night on Johnny Carson. Wrecked my privacy. But people forget so quick. Never touched TV after that: too close for comfort. They all think I'm just modest.

Well, let them. Maybe I am.

Being famous. Funny, you fart just the same when you're famous. Never thought they did, really – Queen of England, the President, Marilyn Monroe, James Joyce. Oh, he farted, all right. Couldn't stop telling us.

Imagine, the Pope pisses.

Reminds me, better get to the can soon. Yep, being famous – it's just something in other people's minds. But money's different – it's something in your own pocket. Means a lot, if I'd just admit it. Like, after always wanting a convertible, and suddenly being able to have any convertible I want. That first open Mercedes – never forget it. And hitting the button and the whole roof lifting right off from above your head. And lying back and just looking up at the stars – from the comfort of a car. Jeez, it's still something marvellous.

And the smell of new-mown grass from the roadside as you're cruising along: smell is one of the best things about convertibles. People who never had one don't know that. And then wishing Diane could be in the seat beside me, with the smell of the grass in her nostrils. Oh dear God, if only . . . Hold it: that line of thought gets you nowhere. Well, Maeve, then. Think of Maeve. At least she's alive. Least I think she is.

Strange how there's hardly been a woman since Diane. Couple of pathetic affairs. Led to nothing.

But at least the fling with Margie left her and me sort of permanently intimate – funny how two people can understand each other and even respect each other better just because they screwed a few times years ago. So much goodness in ole Marge, so much care.

Thing is, when you've booze on board you don't really feel interested. Jeez, haven't even jacked off in ages. When did it last stand up and salute? Can't remember. Must check sometime, to see if I can still make ole Mickey stand to attention.

Arragh, sure who cares? Ole Mickey's going nowhere. His master's busy. Drinking.

I know I do a lot of drinking. But hasn't done me a whit of harm. Physically I'm fit as a fiddle. People say my columns are better than ever, and they're always out on time, three times a week, never a miss.

The whiskey's been a help, actually. Not for everybody, of course – can be bad for some folks. But it's been a friend to me – I need something to push back the horrors.

That's what the booze is for – functional, sort of.

The horrors are part of everyday life now: just weave in and out of my existence like a sort of black aurora borealis. A sort of black pain wells up inside me.

Such agony.

I need the whiskey just to ease the pain a little. Nothing else works. Just the whiskey. Oh God, Oh dear God, where is it all going? Better head for the can.

Well, hello Jack. Listen, see you in a minute. You're lookin' good, anyhow. All that travel. Must be agreeing with you. Catch you in a minute.

Different man, Jack Dillon, ever since Alice died. Giving himself completely to the Movement. Lecturing and collecting all over the States. Funds must be piling up in Ireland. Guns, more likely. Just waiting for things to blow up, in the North. Won't stay quiet forever.

Steady now. Feet wide apart. Careful aim. Our aim, to keep this place clean; your aim will help. The old joke. Urinal, what a pompous name. Remember some nun visiting Clongowes, accidentally barging into the urinals. 'What lovely showers for the little boys,' she sez. Story the fellows told, anyhow.

Used to call it the Square – place where all the urinals were. Wonder why? Because it was square, dummy.

Shake well after use. Another old joke. Where's my tobacco? Ah yes. Wish my hand wouldn't tremble. So goddam tired – only happens when I'm tired.

Where'd I leave that glass? Never mind – take another one, fill 'er up, carry carefully back. Carefully, I said. Far too precious to spill.

Helps me cope with the bad moments. Be honest, now – even in the good moments, liquor is fun. Fact is, I enjoy gettin' pissed. I enjoy every goddam sensation of every goddam stage of gettin' plastered. Like the point when you get that massaged feeling around your temples, like as if Maeve's fingers were strokin' your head ever so gently.

An' then the point where everyone at the party suddenly seems beautiful, and everybody seems to be moving so slowly, an' everybody seems so kind and good, an' you feel you love America an' you want to weep for all America has done for you.

Land of the Free.

And then you're sort of up there above yourself watchin' yourself at the party – well nearly. That's the best bit. Gettin' like that now. Beside myself. Jeez that's funny. Beside myself.

An' then there's the bit where the room starts movin' in a circle around you and you're sort of at the centre of the universe and everything else is revolvin' around you.

Payin' homage, sort of.

Want to – want to get to that stage now. Can't, not with this empty glass. Know what, I'll just bring the bottle over here beside me. Jameson. Nobody'll mind – they're all drinkin' that bloody bourbon. Or Scotch. Don't know what they're missin', do they?

I said, don't know what they're missin'! Am I right? Tell me, everybody, AM I RIGHT?

Ssh, pipe down, Emmet. Folks are lookin' at you. People might think you're pissed. Hah, thas a good one – people might think Emmet's pissed. They'd be right, too. Hey, bloody great – ole room's startin' to move around me. Into orbit, here we go. Fasten seat belts. Oh Christ, here comes Margie.

Hya, Margie. Come to take me home, Margie? Just because they took away my licence? Fasten seat belt Margie – things are startin' to move. Startin' to go round. Margie's goin' round. Around and around. Away alone a last along the riverrun, Margie. Around and around. Here we go round the mulberry bush, the mulberry bush, the mulberry bush . . . Arragh dance with me – come on!

Fasten seat belts, Margie. That you, is it? Fasten fuckin' seat belts, Margie. Margie, Margie, quite contrary, how does your garden grow? With silver bells an' – an' cockle shells, all in a fuckin' row. Singin' cockles an' mussels alive alive-O. One for the road, Margie. Aw come on, don't be a drag, Margie – just one for the road. One for the fuckin' road. Where's me glass? Arragh fuck it, drink outa the bloody bottle. Open mouth, insert bottle, head back. Jeeesus I nearly fell. Nearly fuckin' fell. One for the road, Margie. Motherin' me again, Margie? Mother Mary Margie. Reverend Mother Margie of the Holy Order of Motherin' Fuckin' Meddlers.

Sorry, Margie. Didn't – didn't mean that, Margie. Take me home, willya, Margie?

8

Once Conor Emmet's fortunes began to dip, they went right to the bottom. His journalistic career became like the trajectory of a mortar shell: an astonishingly swift and steep rise; a momentary pause at the top of the curve; then the downward plunge.

Relative to his many bleak years, Con's time at the top, the time of success, fame and money, was pathetically brief – hardly more than the illusion that attends a pole vaulter when the upward thrust is in momentary equilibrium with the pull of gravity.

Liquor could only accelerate the downturn. That time at the top was a time awash in alcohol, and sooner rather than later the liquor bill would be presented, payable in the customary currencies of health, career, or sanity.

Once the downward plunge began, its pace was so dizzying and its curve so steep that, when he looked back on it in later years, Con could not easily distinguish the various stages.

It began with a letter from Maeve, the first in some years. It was addressed to Con, care of the *Chronicle*.

My dearest Con,

I am sorry to have to tell you, but your father is very seriously ill. He has been asking to see you. I understand he does not have a great deal of time. He is in St John's Cancer Hospital.

You should go through channels over there and try to get permission to come. But NB do not, repeat, DO NOT attempt to come without permission. It could have the most serious consequences for you. Please just take my word for that.

I hope all goes well with you. We occasionally see your column when an American paper gets over here, and we feel very proud of you. You have done well. Frank works at the Mater Hospital and I am in private practice here in Dublin. Things are quiet. But people are starting to march for civil rights up in Northern Ireland – I think they got the idea from that Selma thing you had over there.

I am sorry to have to tell you about your father. But perhaps we will all get a chance to see you now. I hope so. Frank sends his best. And so do I.

Affectionately,

Maeve

The letter left Con thinking and thinking about the kindly, shy old man in tweeds who had spent a lifetime looking after the sick and dying of Newry, and who himself was now dying without a relative in the world. Except Con. Con, who had so neglected him these last years. 'O father forsaken, forgive your son.' Con found a measure of consolation in the words of poor James Joyce, written when Joyce was half blind and mad with grief at the death of his own father, whom in thirty years Joyce had never gone home to see. Con repeated those words over and over and over as if they were a prayer or a mantra.

Con would go. No question about it. The Movement would allow it: the Movement had its human side when it came to things like that. Channels? Jack Dillon would know.

'You'll have to go up to Chicago, Con,' Jack told him. 'There's a guy works in the Irish consulate there, name of Moore. He's sort of dogsbody, general secretary really, to O'Hagan the consul. No one in the consulate knows he's our man in Chicago. Movement's area organiser. He's the one to go to – the only one could get through to Ireland and get you permission.

'No, Con, telephoning is out. I know it'd be faster, but it's simply out nowadays. Remember there's trouble brewing in Ireland, and that means the FBI are sniffing around us more than usual. You'll have to go up there in person.'

Con met Moore in a quiet Chicago bar, a block from the Wrigley Building where the consulate is located. Moore was Irish-American: Con had somehow expected an Irishman, perhaps a northerner. Moore carried an umbrella and looked like a corporate lawyer in his dark grey bespoke suit and blue-and-white-striped button-down shirt.

'I'll do my very best, Mr Emmet,' he said. 'And I'll stress the urgency, that I promise. However, please do understand that it just may take a little time: a lot of things are happening over there right now that have not made the papers. It's this civil rights thing, and it's tying everybody up. Please understand that.'

'My father is dying, Mr Moore. He's got very little time.'

'I do understand, really. And I'll stress the urgency, that I promise,' he said again. He got down from the stool and threw his Brooks Bros coat over his arm.

'When I get the green light, I'll send you a cable. It will simply read, DAD EXPECTING YOU. You can move immediately you get it. Oh, and in the unlikely – the very unlikely – event of a refusal by Dublin, the cable would read, DAD UNAVAILABLE. But, as I say, that's not on the cards.'

He shook hands. 'Goodbye, Mr Emmet. My deepest sympathy about your father. And the best of Irish luck.'

Moore walked out, leaving the cedar scent of Dunhill in his wake. Con signalled to the barman.

Ten days later, Con was at the end of his tether. There had been no word from Chicago, and no further word from Maeve.

'There's nothing you can do, Con,' Dillon told him. 'Except wait. Moore's a good man.'

Con tried a long-distance call to St John's Hospital, and got the runaround from some disembodied female voice. 'A call from where? Speak up please. The United States? You're ringing about who? Who? Will you please speak up. There is no Doctor Emmet on our staff. A patient? Why didn't you say so? Hold the line please.'

After ten minutes: 'Hello: are you a relative? A relative of Doctor Emmet? Yes, there is a patient of that name here, but are you a relative? A son? Well, you could have saved a lot of time if you had said so in the first place. Doctor Emmet's condition is stable. That's all the information I can give you over the phone. You'll have to come round if you want more information. Listen, it's not my fault if you're outside the country. No, I'm sorry – you cannot speak with the patient. There is no phone by his bedside.'

Con felt he deserved a large Bushmills after that. Then he tried international enquiries for Maeve's telephone number. It seemed to be unlisted. He lacked the will to fight Round Two, this time with the Mater Hospital where Frank worked. Instead he settled for another drink.

A few days later, Dillon and Con were walking home together from Bud's Place.

'I'm not waiting any longer, Jack,' Con told him. 'I'm getting my ticket to Ireland in the morning, and bugger the consequences.'

'Give it a couple more days, Con,' Jack said.

They said goodnight. Con went in, poured himself a drink, and switched on the late television news. Something about Northern Ireland, somewhere called Burntollet Bridge. Scenes of riot and uniformed police wielding batons. Voice-over asking something about whether Britain's dormant volcano was finally erupting.

The telephone shrilled. It was a woman from Western Union. 'I have two cables here for a Mr Emmet,' she said. 'I'll read the first: FATHER DIED THURSDAY STOP DEEPEST SYMPATHY STOP MAEVE. Are you there, Mr Emmet? Hey, I'm sorry. He was your dad? I really am sorry, mister. Well, here's the other cable. It just says DAD UNAVAILABLE STOP. There's no name. Goodnight Mr Emmet, and all my sympathy.'

The following three weeks ever afterwards remained a blank in Con's memory.

A great dark stormy emptiness, lit with occasional lightning, revealing perhaps a strange bar with the barman shaking his head, or Margie reaching in towards Con from some enormous distance, or a huge amber glass of whiskey and a girl refracted in it and blood pumping from the girl's neck, or the cramped agony of a park bench and a policeman shaking Con's shoulder and the whole of St Louis waterfront behind the policeman and the lights of the docked riverboats dancing on the dark Mississippi water.

Then a warm hospital bed and Margie sitting there and sometimes Jack Dillon or Stan Eckman or Jeff Stoller. And injections of sodium something-or-other and visits from some sort of therapist who seemed kind and patient.

And Jeff Stoller again, silver head nodding with earnestness. '... covered for you with the syndicate,' Jeff was saying. 'Told them you were seriously ill. Which is no more than the truth. They reran some of the early columns – they were real decent about it.

'Now look, Con. Now that you're on the dry – and I thank God you are – you badly need a change of scene. Would you consider spending a while in the Northwest? Managing ed of the Portland *Post* is an old friend of mine. Name of Ed Morris. And an admirer of yours, by the way – he's been running your column on his Forum page for years.

'Well, Ed's willing to take you, if you'll try it. It's Portland, Oregon. It would mean we'd no longer be home base for the column – but the way things were going there'd soon be no column. I really recommend this, Con. And I've friends in Portland who'd give you a real welcome.'

'Would I ever get back here, Jeff?'

'Just as soon as ever you want. Look, you don't even have to go, Con. You can stay on here if you'd rather try that way. But if you do decide to go, I'll keep a place here for when you're ready – I promised that to Margie. Look, Con, why don't you give it a try? For a little while?'

'It's an honour to have you aboard,' Ed Morris told Con. Ed was a comfortable, fatherly man, with a kindly smile and not many words. 'By the way, I'd like you to work on the copy desk, if you're willing. I think it would be good for you – help keep you in touch. Right? Try it, anyhow.'

It was providential that Con had work at the *Post*'s copy desk (or perhaps it demonstrated Morris's foresight), because within six months Con no longer had a syndicated column to write.

He was drinking again, after the first three weeks in Portland, and drinking heavily. Whereas in earlier times his drinking had not interfered with his creative production, now it did. There were times when Con's thrice-weekly column did not get written, and some long-forgotten early piece had to be dusted off and mailed out. Indeed, that yellowing file of columns from earlier years became a treasure trove, to be pillaged in times of need.

For the first time, too, the magic was dwindling in the columns that Con did write. He was using old ideas warmed over. The sparkle had dulled and the humour was brittle.

Missing were those sardonic observations on everyday life: perhaps if one is no longer a part of everyday life, one can hardly observe it.

The change was noted in New York. Also noted were the cancellations that were coming into the syndicate from all across the United States. Then Con disappeared for a couple of weeks. His colleagues covered for him once more, and the cuttings file was plundered once again.

When Con eventually went back to his desk, red-eyed and wretched, his fingers had to fumble open a long white envelope with 'New York Times Syndicate' embossed in the corner.

The syndicate deeply regretted that, from the end of the month, it would no longer be in a position to distribute 'Emmet, Dammit!'. Two further cheques would be forwarded shortly. The syndicate would like to express its appreciation for all Mr Emmet had done over the years. With every good wish, etcetera.

Sic transit gloria . . . Con went missing for ten days, and ended up in a detox centre at Lake Oswego.

Two months later he was back at the paper, dried out and as thin as a stick of beef jerky.

And so it went on for nine wretched months, with Con lurching from dry to wet to dry, and back to wet. Until finally he found himself listening once more to the words he had heard from Stan Eckman years before: 'You'll have to go, Con. It's just not working out.'

But Morris was not simply tossing him out in the cold. He wanted Con to try a clinic across the river in Vancouver, Washington. It was connected with Fort Vancouver, the military camp, and had a singular record for successful treatment of alcoholics. Morris would pay.

'And Con, if you can make it through, and really dry out this time, I'll find a spot for you on a weekly paper. I know an editor across the river in Weston who'd give you a chance. Wages wouldn't be great, but the pace'd be easier.

Con, what you don't need right now is a big hectic metro like the *Post*. We'd be the death of you – nearly were already.'

And so, five months later, a new start at a new paper, and an income only a tiny fraction of what syndicated columnists earned.

This was what they called 'community journalism'. The Weston *Weekly News* covered the doings of a tiny town on the banks of the Columbia River, and was locked in combat with its rival paper, published in the mill town of Camas a few miles downriver.

Weekly News publisher-cum-editor J.B. Morel was a great hater. He hated everything in the rival town of Camas, especially its weekly paper which he saw as a rival for scarce local advertising.

And especially he hated his new staffer, Conor Emmet, for the success that Con had once enjoyed and for the drunken ways that Con all too soon resumed.

Con's time at the *Weekly News* was mercifully brief. After a pathetic attempt at sobriety, Con spent more and more time in his cups, head bowed before the abuse of the hating little bantam cock of an editor. It ended with a ghastly scene at Weston High School's commencement ceremonies, when an inebriated Con, fumbling with a camera and supporting himself with camera tripod, endeavoured vainly to record the event in front of outraged parents and snickering students. He finished flat on his face in front of the dais, with his camera smashed.

'Just get outa my sight.' Morel was dancing with rage the following morning. 'Just pick up your money and collect your things and get outa here right now. How could Morris ever a sent ya? Out, an' don't let me see your face again. Ever. D'ya hear?'

9

Being on skid row in a small town is not the same as being on skid row in a city. Bums are few so you have no rivals. People in small towns still care, and still have time to notice others, even the occasional resident bum.

An affable bum, with a bit of personality, can be accepted as a 'character'. Con became a familiar figure in Camas: folks got used to the tall, stooped silhouette and the hatchety profile and the mostly unlit pipe. Con spoke hardly at all, but was perceived as a friendly if harmless fellow.

He settled into the routine of the small-town drunk. Life in a tiny room under the roof of Kelly's place in Camas, a block from the main street. Welfare, after the unemployment ran out. Deserted downtown to prowl at night: an empty shell, apt abode for the empty shell of a man.

The black moods still descended. The horrors came and went, as the rainbow comes and goes. But there were long walks among the Douglas firs and hemlocks above the town, and along the swerve of the Columbia River shore, with a bottle of Thunderbird or sherry in a brown paper bag. The almost interminable walks Con indulged in, day in, day out, winter and summer, helped keep his body in some sort of condition, long after it should have been pickled in alcohol. And the scenery through which he walked still worked occasional magic on his bloodshot eyes, and sometimes on his soul.

One day, wandering alone along the swerve of shore by the Columbia, Con sat on a tree stump to rest. He was gazing across at Mount Hood, rearing Fuji-like beyond the vast expanse of river, its snow-clean pyramid piercing the sky and reflected in the dark blue water. He found himself murmuring one of the psalms he had learnt as a boy at Clongowes. 'I will lift up mine eyes unto the hills, from whence cometh my help,' he murmured. 'He that keepeth thee will not slumber.'

Then he was saying to himself the last brief verse: 'The Lord shall preserve thy going out and thy coming in, from this time forth . . .' He realised he was weeping.

Once a week Con got a couple of hours' work, bundling newspapers at the loading bay behind the Camas newspaper building. The folks there accepted Con. The few dollars helped towards sherry and tobacco, and paid for the occasional bowl of soup at a local lunch counter. Con ate little – he preferred his nourishment out of a sherry bottle.

In spite of his cast-off jeans and logging shirts, Con strove to stay clean. Cleanliness is the last habit a man discards, and Con would be struggling with an icy sponge on winter mornings, and carting his pathetic bits of clothing to the laundromat over by Safeway.

He sometimes gave in to the temptation to play on being Irish. In American lore that meant being a bit of a character and being fond of the drink. It did no harm to hang around outside the Shamrock tavern near the paper mill when the workers came off a shift. Somebody might buy a beer for 'Irish'.

The police gave him no trouble. They recognised a man who would give them none either. Indeed they seemed fond of him. Patrolman Stevens sometimes brought him into Fran's for a coffee, or a bowl of soup on a cold day.

Eventually Con was leading a life as routine as that of a

monk in a monastery, however different in content. It was peace, of a sort – at least it was when the horrors kept their distance. There was no reason why this life should not have gone on and on until Con's health disintegrated. Which might not have been all that long, anyhow. As it was, it lasted almost two years.

Then one day came Momma, complete with one doberman, two dachshunds, and three chins.

It was a cool evening in early autumn. Con was walking home from Safeway with his bottle of Thunderbird in its brown paper bag. Parked outside Con's rooming house was a red GMC pick-up with a wicked-looking doberman glaring down from the back. As Con edged past, the doberman showed him the whites of its eyes, and the whites of its teeth as well.

'I wanna word with you, young man,' said a voice from the pick-up's cab. 'Climb up!'

It was a long time since anyone had called him 'young man', and Con rather liked the sound of it.

'Well, are y'comin'?' the voice demanded.

Con climbed up to find an astonishingly large lady filling the cab, and to encounter a cacophony of yapping dachshunds and the puzzle of where to deposit the bottle in its paper bag.

An offer he couldn't refuse: 'Y'wanna come to m'paper up in Rainhaven? Gotta job for y'there. But first y'gotta go an' dry out – somewhere I send ya.'

'Where would that be, Mrs . . . Mrs . . .'

'Van Beck. Sharon Van Beck. I own the *Daily Record* up in Rainhaven. I'm offering y'a job. Start y'small, but if y'can handle it . . . By the way, I know quite a lot about ya. Friends a yours wrote me from Illinois.'

'Then you'll know just how many times I've been dried out before. What's the point in going through it again?'

'There's a place in Seattle cured m'husband. I want fer ya to try it. It's run by a nun. A li'l nun called Sister Clare.'

'A nun, huh?'

'Look, young man. I'll make y'an offer. You go to this nun an' dry out. Then stay dry. Then come an' work for me. If y'don't stay dry an' I fire ya, I'll pay yer rent an' likker fer six months. That fair?'

Indeed, it was an offer one couldn't refuse.

10

Con spent almost fourteen months at Evergreen Lodge, that rather unorthodox facility for alcoholics in Seattle run by an equally unorthodox nun called Sister Clare.

Much was a blur when he tried afterwards to remember it, especially those early months. His recollections were of isolated incidents, vignettes, strung together like sequences in a badly edited film. Of his first days at Evergreen Lodge he had no recollection whatsoever.

Con's first memory was of a comfortable bed and the unaccustomed softness of fresh, clean pyjamas. Someone in white was giving him an injection. He liked the way she smelt.

The next thing Con remembered might have been a few days later. About six men of varying ages were seated in a circle, so that Con's bed was part of the circle. A dangerous-looking man with a bushy red beard was saying he felt very down and wasn't sure if he could go on. 'I'm just eaten up by the things I did to my folks, way back,' he was saying.

From the circle of men warmth seemed to flow. A thin black man beside him put a hand on Red Beard's arm.

'Man,' he said, 'Ah know your pain. You know Ah got cancer, Al, don't you? Well, the pain Ah have with this cancer is nothin' – nothin' compared with the pain a bein' an alky. Ah know your pain, Al. Remember, Ah got both.'

'Al,' said a tousle-haired youngish man, powerfully built, who seemed to lead the group. 'Al. What you done is only a speck, when you think a what you're gonna be able to do for God. Sister's always sayin' that. An' I believe it.'

'Not me. I'm no good. I'm just shit.'

'God never made no shit, Al,' the black man said. 'That's another thing Sister keeps sayin'. Well, she sez junk, not shit. She says, even if y'lose everything, y'still got your immortal soul –'

'Hey you guys,' said the tousle-haired man. 'Look who's sittin' up an' takin' notice! Hi, Con. Remember me – Chris? I'm the guy met you when y'got here last week. Remember?'

'Afraid I don't, Chris.' Con smiled ruefully.

'No? Guess not. Most of us don't, those first days. Anyway, Con, meet the guys – we all got beds in this here room. Con, this is Gary. An' this is Al. Wesley. Don. Clayton. Ken.' Each of the men warmly took Con's hand. A couple of them whispered a word or two of encouragement. 'An' don't forget, you guys,' Chris was saying, 'last man in that door is the most important man here. An' that means Con.'

'You'll stay with us this time, Con?' the man called Wesley asked. 'I mean, you won't walk out on us again?'

'How d'you mean?'

'You don't remember, Con? You don't remember bein' here a couple of months back? After four days in that same bed, you yelled for your clothes and shot out that door like a cork out of a bottle, an' we never seen you again. Not till you walked in again this time. Five days ago.'

'I just don't remember. None of it. Did I come back all on my own?'

'Sure did, Con.' Chris spoke up. 'I met you at the door.

You'd took a bus all the way to Seattle – dunno where from – an' you took a trolley all the way up Fifteenth to here. An' you walked in that door and you said to me you weren't walking back out until you had it licked.'

'I said that?'

'You bet. An' that's what counts. You'll have Sister's help to get through it, and don't forget that. An' you'll have our help – all the help we can give you. An' you'll have God's help.'

'Well, we'll see,' Con said, embarrassed at this easy reference to a God that probably wasn't there.

As he dozed off the men were saying some kind of prayer about serenity and accepting the things they couldn't change . . . and courage to . . courage to . . .

Next morning they were together again, Con's bed part of the circle. These ward meetings took place each morning for about half an hour.

The man called Chris seemed to have a singular warmth. He vibrated concern. He was trying to reassure Al.

' . . . I feel like quitting,' Al was saying. 'There's so much jealousy in this place. It's sick – everybody's jealous of everybody else.'

'I'm one of the jealous ones, Al,' Chris said. 'An' you know what? – I never even knew it till lately. Remember when you broke out an' hit the bottle? Well I was real mad at you: I resented all the attention you were gittin' from Sister. I felt you were takin' her away from the rest of us. I was just jealous, Al, but I didn't know it until Sister threw it right in my face. I'm sorry, Al.

'You guys know I came real near to breaking out again, just to git Sister's attention? But Sis knew, an' she threw in my face what I'd likely do if I hit the bottle again.'

Chris turned to Con. 'Con, these guys are sick hearin' about it, but I'll tell you what I was like – what I am like – when I'm drunk. I used to come back home an' the first thing I'd do is, I'd pull the telephone right outa the wall. So's they wouldn't git to call the cops. Then I'd smash the TV. Then I'd git to work on the glass in the doors an' the windows. Then I'd go after my son, Dave – he'd be in bed pretendin' to sleep and I'd haul him out an' beat the shit outa him. D'ya know, he still has nightmares, even though he's sixteen now. An' once – I hope it was only once – I tried to screw Lynn. My daughter. That's when they left me. Con, I lost my wife an' my kids an' my job an' my house – an' Con, they all still hate me, an' they'll go on hating me till their dying day. An' I can't blame them.'

Gentleness, kindliness, emanated from the man who was telling this. Had they been two different people?

'Tell you what, Al,' Chris was saying. 'You wanna go back to bed for a couple of days? Look, nobody's gonna say you're shirking – you jus' need a bit more rest. Hey, listen. You do that, an' I'll bring you your meals. I'll look after you. OK, Al?'

Al nodded. 'Thanks, buddy,' he said.

Evergreen Lodge was like a rather seedy hotel. Or so it seemed to Con as he shuffled along its corridors during those first couple of days out of bed. Yet a sense of tranquillity seemed to hang in the air. And a sense of hope.

You could see it in the faces. They seemed a living contradiction: gaunt faces etched with despair, yet the eyes showing hope and the lips sometimes smiling in defiance of the lines around them. People stopped to chat, to introduce themselves, to give a word of encouragement. They gave only first names: family names seemed to be out. Con had never seen so many people smoking so many cigarettes in any one place. His own pipe was going like a puffer train.

There were a lot of women, and some young people in their early twenties. A couple of ten-year-olds went scampering past. God almighty, not that young, thought Con.

'What are you kids doing here?' he asked a flaxen-haired

child in yellow sweatshirt and blue jeans as she ran back along the corridor.

'We're visiting with our mom,' she answered. 'Mom's coming home next week. We been here with her since Friday.'

'Where do you stay?'

'Sister gives us a room upstairs.'

'You come often?'

'Every weekend. Lotsa kids come. It's a real neat here.'

A rabbi walked by, bearded and skullcapped, deep in conversation with a frail-looking young man. Dark eyes smiled a greeting.

Evergreen Lodge was an amalgam of three of the big timber houses that line Fifteenth Avenue where it runs along Capitol Hill. The houses looked as if they had been battered into one: a couple of timber corridors connected them, and there were wooden single-storey buildings at the back, also connected by corridors. The grounds were extensive, with well-tended flowerbeds and rock gardens in every nook and cranny.

At almost every turn Con encountered religious pictures and plaster statues of the kind he had never liked. Most portrayed the Virgin Mary, and none of them flattered her.

Framed notices on the walls carried exhortations or brief prayers. Some were crudely lettered, some crafted with care and love. One of them read: 'I have come here to change myself – not anyone else.'

It occurred to Con that he had not thought about a drink in over a week. It occurred to him he would like one very much. He put it from his mind.

Monday morning everyone came to the house meeting. Con guessed about thirty were there. The meeting was about running Evergreen Lodge. It was chaired by Susan, a handsome woman in her thirties, who face showed some of the ravages of alcohol.

A new team was assigned to the cooking, and another team got the task of washing up. Complaints were voiced that the lavatories were not being properly looked after, and somebody said that a bottle of Thunderbird had been discovered behind a statue of the Virgin. That brought a hush.

'Listen, you guys,' Susan said. 'That's the only real rule Sister has, an' you better hear it again. You bring likker in here, you're out on your ass. Period. Don't say you didn't know.' She pointed to Con. 'This here's Con, for anybody hasn't met him yet.'

Some people said 'hi' and smiled, and a few people nearby leaned over to shake Con's hand.

'So what you want to start on, Con?' Susan asked him. 'There's a place on the cooking team, or there's work to be done in the garden.'

'Can I do a bit of both?'

'Sure can, Con.'

'I don't understand,' Con said to Wesley over a coffee in the smoke-filled coffee bar. 'This Sister. She's like God: everyone keeps talking about her and quoting her, but you never see her.'

'That's easy enough,' Wesley said. 'She's away. Off raising money, as a matter of fact. To run this place. You know, we're pretty well broke here all the time.'

'What's she like? What's so special about her?'

'Dunno, Con. She just seems to have more – more God in her life. She has this terrific faith in God. And after you talk to her, you have hope. Hope, maybe for the first time in your life. It sorta rubs off her.

'She cares, Con. It all boils down to that. It boils down to Sis having an awful lot of love.'

'Faith, hope, and love, these three . . .'

'Huh?'

'Scripture, Wesley. By the way, do I detect a trace of Belfast underneath that American twang?'

'Belfast it is, Con. Though I been over here for donkey's

years. Would you believe I'm a Protestant? 'Course it's wore a wee bit thin by now.'

'But this is a Catholic set-up.'

'That's what I thought too. I walked in here and seen all the statues, and I says, fuckit I got it wrong again – this is strictly for Papishes. But it's not, Con. Sis takes all kinds – Jews, Prods, Arabs, Jehovahs – as long as they're members of the drinking fraternity. She says we all have a God we can turn our lives over to, whatever name we call Him. Or Her. Even non-believers, she says, can find a power greater than themselves.'

'This Sister. What's she look like?'

'I was a week here before I met her. She was off at her dad's funeral. Then I seen her walking down a corridor, and I knew immediately who she was. A little nun walking like a steam train. She's not thin and she's not fat – she's fit. Full of energy. She's the one person whose time is so much in demand it's unbelievable. How she deals with so many little things without blowing her top ... But then she does blow her top sometimes, and Jeez that's something worth seeing. Vesuvius isn't in it!

'You know that her left hook is famous? I seen her give a man a clatter across the face. I seen her pull the trousers off a man and throw him onto the bed and tell him to stay there till he was fit company for decent people.' Wesley chuckled. 'D'you know, I once seen her bring a man down with a foot-ball tackle, and his bottle of T-Bird smashed all over the floor. Listen, that woman's something else.'

'Is she good-looking?'

'She must have been gorgeous when she was a wee girl. And she's still a fine-looking woman, even though she's the wrong side of forty.'

'So what's she got?'

'Haven't a bloody clue. That faith, mebbe, I told you about. There was a man dying here once, and she got on the microphone to get us all to say a prayer with her – I think they called it the Memory or the Memorare or something. That's her – she uses prayer as a sort of practical tool. Instead of pie in the sky.'

'Weren't you embarrassed? I mean, that's a prayer to the Virgin Mary.'

'I was scared I'd look an eejit. I mean, when I came first, with all these virgins and statues and stuff. But they don't rub your nose in it, and you can just ignore it. But, y'know what? it's restored my faith in my own God. I don't think religion's got a damn thing to do with it.'

'Tell you something, Wesley,' Con said. 'That's the thing has me worried. I'm not sure I can put up with all this praying.'

Con appreciated the routine of Evergreen Lodge. He'd had a routine on skid row, but Evergreen Lodge was a lot more comfortable. In the rhythm of existence there, during those first couple of months he hardly thought about drinking.

One could easily grow institutionalised.

It was nice to get up for breakfast about 8 a.m. and to have hot water and showers. The brief morning prayer in the chapel after breakfast could be skipped, and Con skipped it religiously. It wasn't compulsory: besides, some of the other denominations held their own prayers in other parts of the house.

The morning ward meetings helped. It was good to hear people sharing their problems, although Con for a long time didn't open up, and stayed almost silent. But they encouraged him and he was gradually talking a little bit about his alcoholism.

But he never as much as hinted at that night outside Newry.

The horrors were actually staying away. It might have been the rhythm of the life, or it might have been the prayerful surroundings or the atmosphere of hope that kept them at bay. Con wasn't sure, but he was grateful.

Everyone worked until lunchtime. Con would be in the kitchen, peeling potatoes or chopping the meat for stew, or dipping the fish in batter for frying. The work was relaxing, and Con enjoyed the banter of the kitchen, though he rarely contributed to it.

After lunch there was usually a therapy meeting. Sometimes people would talk; sometimes it might be a tape, maybe about remorse, or about guilt feelings or resentment.

Con worked in the garden until supper. Father Kowalski, himself an alcoholic, acted as Catholic chaplain and would sometimes offer Mass before supper, or one of the local Protestant pastors would come in to hold a service.

After supper there was about ten minutes' optional evening prayer, and then time in the TV room or the ever-open coffee shop.

Twice a week, at 8 p.m., people from Alcoholics Anonymous groups in the city would come in and hold meetings, and on other nights there would be a film on some aspect of recovery or on AA. Then TV or the coffee bar, then bed.

Every two weeks there was a dance, and relatives and neighbours would come in to join the fun.

In a way it was like a monastery. Or a convent: Con thought maybe Sister had got the routine from some convent where she must have started. Con couldn't see how such a routine could wean anybody off the drink, but there he was, dry.

'So how is it going, Con?'

Con looked up from the rockery he was weeding. A nun was smiling at him. He knew she was a nun from the skimpy sky-blue veil. She was dressed in lay clothes, quite smart ones. She had a nice face.

'Here, let me give you a hand,' she said, and promptly sat down beside him.

'Hold it, Sister, you'll get your – you'll get yourself damp sitting on the ground. Here, sit on this plastic bag.' He looked at her. 'You'd be Sister Clare?'

'And you'd be our new Irishman! You know, I must have read every line you ever wrote.'

'Times past, Sister,' Con said.

They weeded in silence, sitting rather than kneeling. She's just an ordinary woman, thought Con. I can't seen what the fuss is about. Though she sure looks fit. The nun caught him looking at her and smiled. Wait, those eyes are special. The way they look at you. And such vivid blue, almost shining.

'Are you at peace, Con?' she asked.

Con shrugged. 'Well, I'm dry, Sister. That's about all I can say.'

She looked at him. 'Don't forget Father Kowalski's here if you ever need to talk. Or, if you don't mind talking to a woman' – she smiled – 'I'll be around. I'll not be going anywhere for a while.'

When the horrors came, they came with such ferocity that Con felt he must die. They came one evening when he was watching television – it was something about Ireland – and all of a sudden they hit him and his body coiled and his gut was an engine and his brain was an anvil. And the girl and her two young men were thrashing again in that last agony that was never the last.

And Con thrashed with them all night.

He was grey in the face when dawn came, and his hand shook as he tried to hold the razor steady. It shook at breakfast when he tried to hold his cup of coffee. At the ward meeting he sat with hands locked to stop their trembling. When the meeting was over, he headed out the door and down the street.

The first bar he came to was Bloch's, on the corner of Fifteenth and Mercer. He started on whiskey and he stayed on whiskey. When they put him out in the early afternoon, he went across the street to the Canterbury.

By nightfall he had woven his way through several more bars and had reached Pioneer Square. But someone must have spotted him and told Clare.

Then she was sitting beside Con on some park bench and

it was dark and Con didn't know how she got there or even if it was really she at all and then she was helping him into a car and there was somebody with her and he didn't know where they were taking him and he hoped she wasn't mad at him and he didn't fuckin' care whether she was mad at him or not and why didn't she mind her own fuckin' business? and then she was undressing him gently and putting him to bed.

When Con's body crept out of bed seventeen days later, his soul was in hell.

Even the horrors hardly mattered: Con's soul was part of a world without end that was totally, absolutely empty. The body that shambled through the corridors of Evergreen Lodge was a thing, not a person. The eyes saw nothing, and lurked in the caverns of his skull. The hands trembled and clasped each other so as not to tremble more. The mouth twitched. The gut and the bloodstream and the brain shrieked to God for alcohol.

Yet through that vast, empty hell ran the slenderest, frailest of threads, to which Con clung like a lifeline – a promise he had made to Sister.

She had sat by his bed for much of those seventeen days and nights. She had held the basin while he vomited; she had held his shoulders while he blasphemed God; she had held his head in her arms while he wept.

She had whispered to him, as he sat up gasping in the darkness, that there was something out there greater even than the evil that enwrapped him, a power that could free him when he was utterly without power himself. And when Con had wept and groaned that he believed in no such power, she had begged him to believe at least in her belief.

And then, somehow, Con had promised he would not drink again.

There is no bottom to hell.

Even below that desolate landscape through which Con

shambled, there waited still lower depths, and that grim ground opened beneath his feet and he slithered down into a sewer of self-loathing, where his deeds and his very being reeked to heaven.

Con saw that the only memorable thing he had done with his life was to take the lives of three young people.

He saw all the liquor he had swallowed in the course of a lifetime, and it was a sizeable lake. He himself was a loathsome pissing machine, taking every precious gift of God and turning it into liquor and turning even that into piss. His life was a lagoon of piss and the steam from that piss ascended unto the nostrils of God and God turned away shuddering.

And Con loathed himself with a hatred hot from hell.

Dante was wrong: there is no bottom to hell. Even this false ground opened beneath Con's feet and he plunged to a region where hope had no place. The emptiness through which he had walked was as nothing compared to the blackness that now opened before him – rather, that opened within him.

Even in the most awful desolation there remains at least the tiniest, faintest shimmer of hope, perhaps unnoticed, like that faint sky glow that abides even on the darkest of nights. Starlight: it is there even when the stars themselves are hidden behind impenetrable clouds.

Now the stars went out.

Lasciate qui speranza, voi ch'entrate. Once upon a time the stars had gone out for Judas. Now in that same impenetrable darkness, Con's hands were groping for the exit Judas had taken. Yet as he fumbled in the darkness, his fingers kept encountering one gossamer thread – his promise to Sister that he would not drink. Almost perversely, meaninglessly, he held to that promise.

In after years, when Con would look back, those months seemed an almost physical blackness. Like death. There was nothing to remember: nothing illuminated those seemingly interminable days and nights. Occasionally, very occasionally, he might sense Sister's presence there in the darkness, but that was all.

One tiny thing might have been a turning point – Con never was sure if it had been. It was some words he noticed one day, on a cloth banner hanging in the chapel: 'Turn your face to me O Lord, and give me peace.' Nothing dramatic, no big change in a man not given to prayer or chapels. But Con had found the words running through his mind, and sometimes they seemed to help.

Eight months later, Con sat in Sister Clare's cubbyhole of an office. They were drinking coffee.

'It was prayer brought you through,' Clare was saying. She smiled: 'You find that hard to take, I know, Con. But many of us here, the Protestants and the Catholics and the Jews and the Mormons, we stormed heaven for you. You were one of the worst I've seen. Sometimes I wondered if you'd make it through.'

'Have I made it, Sister?'

'You have a ways to go. But I'm not sure you need to stay here to do it. I think you've got to learn to care about people again. I guess one time you used to care, but somewhere along the line you switched off. And you stopped showing feelings, even to yourself. Stopped having them, maybe.

'It'll take time, but you'll have to start caring again. And some day you're going to have to talk about whatever happened to you – whatever it is that's still gnawing deep down inside you. Maybe you have to carry it as a cross for the rest of your life – I don't know. But you're going to have to talk about it, and maybe some day you'll talk to God about it.' She smiled. 'It's called praying, Con. But listen, if you don't talk about it, you could find yourself drinking about it. Remember that.

'Now I'm going to ask you a favour. Would you stay on with us three more months, to help us with some of the others? Chris asked if you would. There's a man here right this minute, going through very much what you did. Would you help us to help him?'

'I'll do that, Sister,' Con said.

Three months later, almost to the day, Momma, the dogs and the red pick-up were at the door, to take Con to Rainhaven.

11

Where the Pacific Northwest meets its ocean, the water and the wood of the region work together to make a landscape that is incomparable.

Water rolls against rock and cliff, piercing the forest in a thousand pellucid inlets; water sweeps from pewter Pacific skies in curtains of rain; water builds the high cumulus clouds of spring and autumn; and, as delicate maritime fog, it softens the silhouette of lighthouse and beaked promontory.

Where the water ends, the wood begins. Backdrop to every seascape is some dark hill, sawtoothed against the sky, where evergreen trees give serrated edges to every high horizon. Driftwood like pale antlers piles high on the beaches, making haunting shapes in morning mist. Logs float down the rivers, bobbing like matchsticks in the wake of the tugs that pull them to the sea. The smell of fresh cedar wafts from shakemills.

From the waters of every harbour and river rise cable-lashed wooden posts and pilings: perches for proud gulls, ties for log booms, or crumbling remnants of ancient docks.

Inland the trees march to meet the Olympic temperate rain-forests, where they measure rainfall in feet, and where moss and tendrils entwine everything that grows, creating green Gothic cathedrals under the trees.

Coastal Washington has a subtle loveliness, where hilltops look flat and pearly grey in morning mists, paler each behind the other like an oriental silk painting, and where wooden pilings rise from mirroring harbour water in sharp foreground silhouette.

On such mornings you could almost see some phantom schooner from bygone days move silently by from its berth in the Rainwater River, to be glimpsed for a moment and vanish forever into the mist.

This is a region of rocks and cliffs and lighthouses and crying seabirds and swirling mists and log booms, and buoys with haunting bells, and boats with silent men and creaking oars, and water dripping from rustling live wood in the forest and dripping too from creaking dead wood on crumbling old waterfront docks.

The people of that coastal strip are as unique as the land they inhabit. The quintessential Northwest man wears a checked shirt, jeans held up with brightly coloured braces (they call them suspenders), drives a pick-up truck – preferably a four-wheel drive – with a doberman prancing around in the back. They are an outdoor people, earning their livelihood by logging the forests or trolling the seas for salmon.

Or if work in sawmill or office keeps them indoors, they emerge at weekends to fish or hunt or prowl their forests in their four-wheel-drive vehicles.

They call their land an Eden, and – for those who do not mind a lot of water in paradise – perhaps it is.

For some time, however, there had been shadows in that Eden, and by the time Conor Emmet came there, those shadows were lengthening.

The salmon were dwindling. There was bitterness between Native Americans and whites over Judge Bolt's award of half of all salmon catches to the coastal Indian tribes.

The timber industry was hurting from the shrinking Japanese market, and unemployment was growing.

And big-city violence was, as one victim had put it, 'only a car ride away' – meaning that criminal elements in Seattle and Portland had become aware of the easy pickings only a couple of hours away in the little coastal towns.

Rainhaven, where Con was to settle, was still grieving over the murder of a Rainwater County sheriff's deputy by a trio that had moved into a motel to plan a heist at Rainier Bank; further down the coast, at Hoquiam, a city policeman had been shot through the heart when he flagged down a car from Seattle.

Nothing is perfect, of course, in an earthly paradise. And starting off in Rainhaven, Con encountered his share of good and ill. Sometimes indeed it was hard to tell which was which.

First there was Momma.

Everybody called her that. Maternal; massive. She was one of the good things – well, mostly. Generous in praise – indeed generous in all but paycheques.

There was a quiet, pipe-smoking, boozy, salmon-fishing, whatever-you-say-my-dear husband, who had sold out his logging enterprises and sawmills to the Smith Pulp Corporation, but retained the 25,000-circulation Rainhaven *Daily Record*, which his grandfather had started.

Momma ran it. Or rather, she ran the people who ran it. And popped her husband in and out of detox centres until she thought she had him cured. Sister Clare had nearly succeeded.

Momma – State Representative Sharon Van Beck to you – always just about to run for the senate at Olympia, but never quite getting around to it; journalistically illiterate, but with a genius for nosing out talent (and then paying it wretchedly); in whom motherliness and stinginess vied inconclusively.

Then there was the Rainhaven *Daily Record*.

Surviving by paying miserable wages and keeping out the unions; staffed by youngsters on the way up, like Barrett, or folks like Conor Emmet who weren't going anywhere.

Everyone was really waiting for the ailing and ancient

managing ed to retire: things were in a holding pattern. But Kane simply soldiered on, and Momma was too kind to fire him.

Citizen Kane, as they called him, lived in an Aeolian whirl of paper and crises, grumbling and tugging at his mournful moustache and daydreaming about the retirement cabin by the ocean and about dumping the managing editorship off onto younger shoulders like maybe those of Marty the city editor – shoulders broad enough to bear Momma. Kane was well over seventy, and could hardly bear her much longer.

Momma went with the job, and she existed to infuriate Kane. Everything she did rendered him near-apoplectic. She infuriated him by sitting in at the morning page-one meeting whenever she felt like it. She infuriated him by attending the weekly staff meeting and making some worthwhile suggestions. She infuriated him even more by foisting on him a dried-out Irish has-been.

Yet the low wages and the realities of small-town journalism were muted and softened by the grey sea mists and the loveliness of an evergreen land. It wasn't so hard to be poor when you had only to head a few miles up Rainwater River for the best steelhead fishing in Washington State.

And the small miseries of an understaffed newsroom took on a new perspective when one walked a logging trail at evening under the cumulus clouds of the Northwest.

Conor Emmet was Northwest editor and assistant city editor – an ambiguous pair of titles devised by Momma, which left him surprisingly free to explore the minor marvels of Rainhaven and to probe, by way of interviews, the myriad occupations and interests of the healthy outdoor people who lived there. And to help out in the features department, which was also part of his duties.

Each morning, up to the 10 a.m. deadline, Con's duties were to taste and select from the regional wire news that deluged into the computer from Associated Press in Seattle.

He had to edit the stories and position them on the paper's three Northwest regional pages. This he did with pencil on scaled-down blanks or 'dummies' of the pages, which had the column outlines marked.

Everything else he did directly on his computer screen, all the time watching the hands on the clock creep around to the 10 a.m. deadline.

There were video screens on every desk, networked to a central computer. The system had been installed shortly before Con arrived, and the older staffers still regarded it as a cross to be borne.

There was also the cross of Momma's three dogs.

It was not quite a condition of employment, but it was a matter of the strictest expectation, that members of the newsroom staff should accept these creatures into their homes whenever Momma went travelling, which was often. Con usually got one of the dachshunds, if only because they hated each other and both enjoyed the hating.

Plato was a loathesome little creature. He started, about three inches above the ground, with a long, cold, snobbish nose, shaped extraordinarily like the nose of the F-4 Phantom jetfighter.

The opposite end was less impressive: it had a blunt, chopped look, comprising two little bandy legs, a foolish-looking tail, and a lot of ridiculous plumbing equipment so close to the ground that it hurt Con even to look at it.

The two ends were connected by an astonishing length of brown, cylindrical body, which made Con realise, in a blinding flash of intuition, where the Americans must have got the name for their hot dogs.

When Momma had asked Con, with her undoubted charm, to take Plato unto his bosom, Con had said OK. After all, he told himself, he would hardly notice a wee thing like that around the house, and he might even train him a little.

That first night, Plato set about training Con. The beady eyes watched from the dog basket in the corner of the bedroom until Con went to sleep.

Training began at 2.07 a.m. First came three shrill yelps. 'Christ,' muttered Con. He climbed out of bed and, within two steps, his foot encountered one of Plato's turds. Bad enough when one's shoe encounters it: but there is a kind of silken horror when one's bare foot slides into it and it creams up between the toes.

As Con got the light on, the inevitability of it became apparent. In the random pattern of mines in a minefield, eight turds lay in wait.

4.45 a.m. Yelp, yelp, yelp. Same again. Always the training was reinforced by the deposition of puddles and turds from Plato's inexhaustible lode. By morning Con was fully trained.

That evening Con made one half-hearted attempt to recover his role of dominant male. Plato had for the tenth time carried a lump of his loathsome pink TV-recommended dog food into the middle of the carpet, in defiance of orders. This time Con took a rolled-up newspaper and thumped the carpet beside Plato.

A bloodcurdling series of shrieks brought the couple from next door running over to see what was wrong. Con could only stand red-faced with the rolled-up *Daily Record* in his hand, a bully caught in the act. The neighbours stared in through the open door, silently, accusingly. Pluto lay on his side in the foetal position, licking nonexistent bruises, and his eyes glittered.

It was then Con realised he was not really up against a dachshund puppy with five months' experience. He was facing something several million years old, with the accumulated experience and cunning of aeons of training mankind to minister unto it.

Plato was no more than the current embodiment of that ancient thing that masquerades as man's best friend.

Those first years with the *Daily Record* brought Con once more in contact with people.

The interviewing brought him perforce to meet interesting

characters around the county. Some became his friends, like old Chuck Watkins, who had built up his small fleet of Hiller helicopters around the needs of the forestry companies to lift out cedar, and who was the presiding deity at the small local airfield that had grown up around his fleet.

Con wondered sometimes why most of his friends were older folk like Chuck. Not that he didn't like the youngsters in the newsroom – with the exception of Barrett the Canadian (whom nobody liked on account of his arrogance). Con got along fine with them, and they liked him and his wry remarks about Kane. But their talk was of the journalism schools at Eugene and Pullman; their virtues were fanatical adherence to the *AP Stylebook* and a passion for exactness in reporting that made Con feel slightly ashamed; their vices were beer parties and the occasional joint.

Con looked in vain for the fire in the gut that had burned him up in his early twenties. In spite of its appalling consequences for him, he still respected it in others, forgetting perhaps that a dispassionate but thorough report could still stir souls to action. Con missed the enthusiasm of the Galway days: here only a couple seemed to have it.

Barrett was a sincere young man, but he had what reporters call the killer instinct. Get the story no matter who gets hurt. He was forever yakking about some great investigation he was doing, but never brought to a conclusion – something about pinpointing former Nazis in the Northwest. He was doing it in conjunction with some AP and metro fellows up in Seattle, or so he told everyone.

'The place is swarming with Krauts,' Barrett was always saying, in his slow Canadian accent. 'It's a matter of figuring which of them did the war crimes.'

Pete Barrett was every inch the hard-nosed reporter, inasmuch as he always tried to live up to that image. The hard nose would wrinkle, rodent-like, as he nattered on the telephone with his metro buddies. Funny how the profession attracted the very compassionate or the very egotistic. Barrett was a prima donna if ever there was one.

But, like it or not, he was a young man with a future. Maybe that was what Con really disliked, Con told himself shrewdly. That, and the fact that Barrett hardly thought it necessary to pass the time of day with him – treating him, in the arrogance of hard-climbing youth, as a 39-year-old has-been.

Paz sat at the desk across from Barrett. Slender young Anna Maria Paz, troubled perhaps with too much compassion, struggling sometimes to find a balance between compassion and objectivity.

What a fine line they all walked between pity and cruelty, trying to remember that simple truth-telling – the conveying of information – was a social service more valuable than any other. 'The truth will set you free.' Hadn't scripture given journalists their mandate two thousand years ago? Long before journalism.

Paz wore her hair pulled severely back – it reminded Con of that bust of Nefertiti – the dark hair ending in a ponytail that bobbed up and down as she walked. She had the neatest ass Con had ever seen. Having the City Hall beat, Paz had to spend much of her time on stories of solid-waste sludge and other similarly fascinating matters, but her newsie's heart was elsewhere.

Those files of hers contained enough allegations (and some proof) on exploitation of illegal aliens to make certain forestry and tree-thinning contractors look very bad indeed. A few more calls, Paz kept saying, and a few more nails would be hammered home in the coffin of one Antonio Gómez, grown fat on the sweat of hungry, frightened, homesick Mexicans.

The fellows teased Paz in a gentle way, mostly about her feminist sympathies.

Shinn, the wire editor, would pick a couple of gorgeous, barely swimsuited beauties from the pile of photos on the laserphoto machine, give Con a nudge, hold the pictures and say, 'Hey, Paz. Which do we take for page one today?'

Paz would grin and say, with a trace of California in her

voice, 'If you guys don't know your job, I'll sure be glad to help you along.'

Why did they call her Paz, instead of Anna? Con couldn't really say. Something to do with women's lib, maybe? And behind her back they sometimes called her 'the Nun'. But affectionately. Someone said she had been a nun once, but nobody knew for sure, and she never mentioned it. Well, she'd make a damn good-looking nun, that was for sure.

Paz sometimes chided Con for his apparent lack of commitment. She could not know how the fire in the belly can burn a man out, or how it can shrivel into the dull red cinders of remorse, or how the attempts to quench its angry glow can leave a man washed-out and alcoholic.

'What's with you, Con?' Paz was forever asking. 'Don't you care?'

'Ask me that again when you get to my age,' Con had once replied. Only once, for Paz had exploded in wrath, telling him he was using age as an alibi and that he was still a young man, and that he was a lazy creep that just wanted a cushy life and to do as little as possible to get by.

'What are you trying to hide from, anyway?' she had asked him. Con had shrugged and lit his pipe, but his gut had jerked itself into a knot and stayed that way for a considerable time.

It was at times like these that a Celtic black urge to drink would descend on Con. He left the drink alone, but grew silent and more gaunt, and the rare smiles were rarer still and the wry humour scarcer. People walked carefully around him then, not that they feared unkindness, but rather they sensed layers of nameless substances under the crust of Conor Emmet.

Old Max Stern, a compositor in the back shop, was the one who seemed to understand. People said Max was one of the few Jews to have survived Treblinka concentration camp, and perhaps he had learnt there just how many kinds of torment there were.

Not that he ever spoke of that part of his life.

At 10 every morning Max and Con stood together at the slanted paste-up counters, where Max, wielding his scalpel like a surgeon, would bring together the multitude of scraps of paper carrying columns and headlines and pictures that made up the pages Con had designed that morning.

This was the best part of the newspaper experience: there was a joy in conceiving a newspaper page with pencil and ruler on a small sheet of paper, and then seeing it become a reality an hour later under Max's scalpel.

'So,' Max would say, and pin each of Con's pencilled dummies at eye level above the counter. On the steeply sloped counter would be a full-sized blank newspaper page with faintly ruled blue lines indicating the columns. On this the wax-backed headlines and columns of print would be affixed. This was paste-up.

'That Olympia piece's not going to fit,' Con might say. 'We'll drop the last two 'graphs. And let's centre that nuclear waste head and put a two-point hood around it. Oh, and air the piece on Trojan – it's half an inch short.'

And Max's scalpel would slide in among the columns and headlines and slit and cut and discard and move and align and press down the waxed scraps of type, and Con would watch a newspaper page come to be.

It was a small daily miracle that brought a small daily joy to the heart. It looked so easy: paper seemed so much simpler to manipulate than wood or metal or canvas or paint.

Standing beside a man day after day like that, working a little daily miracle together, you could grow close. Con and Max did. Little was said in those early days, but Max seemed to sense the occasional tautness in the long, stooping figure beside him. A trust grew between them, although the few shared words were mostly about work.

One morning – soon after the sharp words from Paz – Max must have noticed the white knuckles on the counter beside him. Positioning a three-column story under its headline, as the scalpel moved across the page the older man said gently,

'My friend, I too have my memories. And my guilt, as you do. Let us leave them with our God, and do today's work well.' And he tapped the page with the tip of his scalpel.

Con's eyes widened, but he said nothing.

The work went on and the pages grew under the scalpel. By 10.30 Max was rolling the pages flat. He carried each camera-ready page to the rack across the room, to be photographed and made into printing plates. Con gathered up his dummies and headed back to the newsroom.

Max would clear the waxed cuttings from the counter and brace himself for the mumbly-grumbly arrival of Kane with his page one dummy. Page one had an 11 o'clock deadline and was usually a crisis, more because of Kane himself than any breaking story it might be carrying.

Two days later, as they were finishing the paste-ups, Max asked Con if he ever fished.

'A tiny bit in Galway, years ago,' Con said. 'On the Corrib.'

'I have a small boat up at Falls Lake, Conor, and tomorrow at six in the morning I go there to fish for trout. Would you care to come?'

'Why not?'

'Good. So today you go to Blaszka's and purchase yourself a licence. No card for steelhead – you will not need it. We fish for trout. And get two jars of salmon eggs.'

'But a rod? I don't have one.'

'I will provide for us both. None of this greased line or fly-fishing stuff. Simple rods and lines. There will be a Thermos of coffee and some cheese sandwiches, and we can pick up a fried chicken on our way if we so wish. You will have observed by now I am not into kosher. And afterwards, in the evening, we eat with me – at my home. Agreed?'

Falls Lake that Saturday morning was smooth and windless. The curve of evergreen trees around the shore were mirrored like shark's teeth in the water, and the boat rocked gently as Max reeled in his line. The Olympic Mountains glinted white beyond the trees.

Con could feel the warmth of the morning sun caress his shoulders.

'Just let go, my friend,' Max said. 'Let everything go.'

Con stretched his legs and drew the morning air deep into his lungs. He leaned his back into the V of the prow, and his fingers touched the water.

A bird was wheeling in lazy circles high above. A pulse still puttered somewhere down in Con's gut. Leave it be: it's not really hurting, and maybe it'll die down if I forget it. What kind of bird is that anyway? Do the Olympics have eagles? Or a vulture? Maybe thinks I'm food – thinks I'm dead. Get a shock if he comes down to look. Man, this sun is – warm . . .

Max was shaking him by the shoulder.

'Come, sleeping beauty. The prince has kissed thee. Time to drink coffee!'

Con struggled to a sitting position and looked at his watch. 'Christ almighty, it can't be three-thirty. What's been going on?'

'You have been sleeping like a child, and I have been catch-ing trout – three of them, to be exact. Come, drink your coffee and let us see what kind of fisherman you are. We have yet one hour.'

Con caught one miserable specimen that had to be thrown back, and Max caught two more, before they started the outboard and headed for the landing.

Driving back to Rainhaven, Max turned to Con. 'Today you felt the peace which the Northwest can give – if you allow it to do so. And now we go to my home for trout and parsley butter. A fitting end to this day.'

It was a simple but delicious supper, and Max showed how to grip the tail of a cooked trout and, with a flick of the wrist, pull out the backbone cleanly, leaving a pile of pink flesh with nary a bone in it.

As they faced each other over mugs of steaming coffee, Con thumbing tobacco into his pipe and Max with a cheroot,

Max reached across to the sideboard and placed a chequered board between them. From a wooden box he tossed out a set of handsome chessmen, and looked at Con enquiringly.

'Not since I was eleven,' Con said. 'With my father.'

'I recommend this, Conor. It will steal your tensions away. If you so wish, I shall teach you. But only if you wish it.'

'Why not?' Con said.

Con found he remembered most of the moves. They agreed that Max would play to win, but would explain each of Con's mistakes as they went along. After three games Con felt he was getting the hang of it.

They met to play again on Sunday afternoon, and three more times the following week. On Saturday Con won his first game, carrying off the queen in a neat fork movement of the knight, mopping up Max's remaining pieces, then using queen and rook to force the king to the edge of the board for mate.

By then Con had grasped what a superbly cruel game chess is. A game without mercy, without quarter, where you force a man into a corner, then deprive him of hope by closing off one avenue of escape after another until there is nowhere to go.

And what a perverse joy it is. Indeed Con found a surprising deal of emotion in chess, where imperturbable old Max could be pushed to mutter '*scheise*', and where Con found his heart thumping as he waited for Max to see through his strategy.

But the most marvellous thing was the way a chess game could suck out a man's tensions, pulling them down to a board where every chess piece seemed to emanate vibrating lines of force until the board was a network of such lines, that only the player could see.

So that when the game was over, win or lose, Con would lean back with a sigh of contentment such as he had not remembered in years.

Thus began a friendship that revolved around fishing and chess, few words, and a shared sense of pasts that were somehow unspeakable.

They shared silent hours in the boat on Falls Lake, and during the steelhead season they were a familiar pair on the banks of the Rainwater River – a gaunt silhouette ambling along beside the stocky, elderly, foreign-looking figure in high black waders. To the locals they became known as Mutt and Jeff, but the name was bestowed with affection rather than ridicule.

Con was a frequent visitor to Max's neat bachelor bungalow set among the trees in the hills above Rainhaven, and he grew familiar with Max's one great passion: a deep and heartfelt longing for European unity.

'It is the antidote to war, my friend. This European Economic Community is only a step – a first step. But *hör mal*, when political unity comes, even your problems in Ireland will be solved. I promise.'

He would send Con home with the latest issue of *Europe* magazine, with an article by Simone Veil, the beautiful French Jew who had spent her girlhood in a Nazi concentration camp and was now a French politician and ardent apostle of European unity. Max worshipped her image as others worship film actresses or sports stars.

From Simone Veil, Max had learnt about forgiveness. This Jewish woman was teaching Christian Europe that its salvation lay in forgiving and forgetting – forgiving even those monstrous things done by one side to the other, like the wiping out by the Nazis of Lidice or Oradour-sur-Glâne or the Warsaw ghetto, or the wiping out of Dresden or Hiroshima by the Allies. And after that, Max said, those who had perpetrated such evils must learn to forgive themselves.

'You too must learn that, my friend. Since long ago, God, or the cosmos, whatever you wish to call it, has forgiven you whatever it was that you did. But you have not forgiven yourself. Do so, and peace will come.'

Then, Max said, Con would no longer be gazing inside himself but would find himself extraordinarily free – free to be useful to others. That was what life was about, not for looking at your navel.

Gradually Con became aware how much old Max Stern quietly did for people.

Max had been one of the moving forces in starting the Crisis Hot Line, and people close to self-destruction had often found an anonymous, foreign-accented voice at the end of the telephone line to give them hope and a sense that someone somewhere cared.

People at the paper, men and women, drifted into the back shop to see Max when they had problems.

Letters came to Max from Latin America, with photos of dark-eyed waifs and laboriously penned letters, all curiously similar, saying thanks to Uncle Max for all he had done for them. Max smiled at the similarity of the letters.

Yeats had talked of a place where peace comes dropping slow, and perhaps Rainhaven, at least with Max around, was such a place.

Certainly, by the end of a couple of years, an intermittent peace had descended on Conor Emmet, so that his knuckles whitened less and his gut tightened only occasionally, his spare frame gathered some flesh, and he began to feel some contentment with sparse victories over trout or steelhead, and sparser ones over a mean chess opponent.

He started noticing the skies and the mountains and the waters and the woods, and even took to lugging along on his fishing trips one of the old Nikon F-2 cameras from the newsroom.

The old humour flickered more frequently around his lips, and lust was beginning to flicker around his loins. And his eyes were beginning to notice Anna Paz.

12

For many years the popular image of a newsroom had been of a dingy, Dickensian place where cadaverous figures in eyeshades crouched over clacking typewriters under pools of yellow light – a windy kingdom of Aeolus where scraps of paper whirled about in the breeze that moaned through the cracked windows, a place of vertical spikes on which editors impale unwanted stories and, perhaps occasionally, unwanted journalists.

That was the kind of newsroom Con remembered, but it had disappeared from the Rainhaven *Daily Record* shortly before he got there. Gone were the spikes; gone too was most of the paper; gone was the clack of the typewriters and the clank of metal from the caseroom next door. Since the coming of the computer, the *Record*'s newsroom had looked more like the control room for a moon shot. People peered into video screens, fingers plucking at quiet keyboards. The newsroom had grown hushed. People whispered instead of yelling. The tension of a newsroom coming to deadline was still there, but it was a silent urgency that could seem almost menacing.

Even now, after two years of the new technology, the

newsroom had not reverted to the old rattle and hum. Con missed it, but it was gone forever.

But Con didn't let any newsroom pressures worry him: he clung jealously, with a sort of quiet desperation, to a contentment that was intimately bound up with an open-air existence and with the waters and the woods of the Northwest.

Depression, guilt, angst, lurked just beyond the periphery of his existence, and he tiptoed around anything that might shake his composure. Above all he stayed away from controversial journalism. He resumed his column, just for the *Daily Record*, but put no sweat into it. Soon the Portland *Post* picked it up again for its Forum page, and a few other Northwest papers followed suit.

Con stuck doggedly to a nice, bubbly humour: it threatened nothing and no one, and any small controversy that ensued was no more than the froth blowing off the top of the brew. And Con's tongue stayed securely in his cheek.

It wasn't easy to stay uncontroversial, with Anna Paz so committed to her causes, and doing her best to involve Con. Like the day he invited her to Rosita's Mexican Diner for lunch, at the end of a heavy morning.

Rosita greeted them with a hug each. 'Don't mind me if I yell at the cook,' she said. 'I'm on one a them diets again. Think it's working?' She pirouetted for them.

'It's certainly doing something for you, Rosie,' Con said evasively. Rosita was not quite another Momma, but she was getting there.

'Hey you guys, I got *chilli rellenos* today,' Rosita told them. 'Y'wanna try some?'

'Sounds good,' Con said. 'Paz?'

'Me too.'

They sat down and Paz leaned across. 'Con, if I asked you to do something for me, would you?'

'You make me nervous,' Con said. 'I always get scared when you start like that! So what is this something?'

'Well, y'know I'm working on this raw deal they give the Mexicans – y'know, the illegals? An' y'know I'm trying to get the dope on that creep Gómez? He's one of the biggest exploiters round here.

'When I have this sewn up, I'll be doing a head-on interview with Gómez – I'll confront him with all the facts and see what he has to say for himself. But that's at the very last, otherwise he gets wise to us and gags all our sources. Old rule of investigative reporting: leave the big fish till last.'

'Fascinating I'm sure. But what's it to do with me?'

'I want you to interview Gómez. But now.'

'But you just said –'

'Listen to me. What I need right now is a bland, up-front interview: well-known businessman, leading citizen, that sort of PR stuff. Not touching the dirt – not even hinting at it. An' that's your kind of story anyway, so it wouldn't arouse suspicion. Whereas I'm a known muckraker.'

'But what use would it be?'

'It'd give me things to follow up. You'd find out where he's from, what he did before he came here, where he did it. Where he met his wife, what's his range of business interests. All the usual stuff. He'd probably tell you a lot: he's a conceited bastard, and his suspicions aren't aroused. And if he's the creep we know he is, he'll have left a mighty dirty trail. An' then I can check it out. Figures, huh?'

'No, Paz.'

'Huh?'

'Leave me out of it. Paz, I don't want to get involved.'

'Con. Come on. Do me this favour.'

'Look Paz, you want to go stirring things up, that's your business. Fine with me. It doesn't mean you drag me into it. You want to do it, go do it.'

'Con, this creep is an exploiter – you know that.'

'He's not exploiting me – Momma does enough of that, thanks. See here, Paz, I'm looking for a quiet life, and you're obviously not. So let's each do our thing, shall we?'

'You. You are so smug.'

They ate in silence. After some time Paz reached for her briefcase, and took out a hefty file which she plonked beside Con's plate.

'Con. Would you just read this – that's all I ask you. Would you do that for me?'

'Sure, I'll do that for you, Paz.' Con smiled, signalling peace.

'Tonight?'

'You don't give up easy, do you? Tonight, then. But remember –'

A slender, dark young man was standing by the table, with two winsome small girls in his arms. He smiled shyly at Paz. *'Buenas tardes, Señorita Anna. Qué tal?'* He gave a friendly nod to Con.

'Hola, Manuel. Cómo te va? Con, this is Manuel Sánchez. From Mexico – he's one of the guys I was telling you about. Conor Emmet: Manuel.'

Manuel attempted to shake hands, the children still in his arms, and the two men ended up laughing. Con gestured to a chair. 'Join us for a bit?'

Manuel bowed and sat down, resting the children on his knees.

'His English is not good, Con. Hey, you mind we talk Spanish for a couple of minutes?'

'Be my guest. I'll talk to the kiddies.'

A torrent of Spanish poured across the table, and Con turned to the doll-like little girls, whose huge dark eyes gazed at him unblinking. These elfin creatures, watching him so solemnly, seemed to Con quite breathtakingly lovely. They must be about three and four years old, he guessed. He put his hands in front of his face, then peeped out at the children. The older one smiled shyly, then the little one smiled too, taking her cue from Big Sis. Con crossed his eyes and made a horrid face. The little ones laughed for joy, and it caught Manuel's attention.

'Lucita,' he said, nodding towards the older one. 'Y Lupita.'
He nodded at the other.

'Well then, ladies, now that we have been, as it were, ahem,
uh, properly introduced,' Con intoned, 'I suppose we might
feel free to speak to one another. Well indeed, haven't we got
lovely names – Lucy and Loopy. They're for short. You like
that, Lucy and Loopy?'

The children chuckled, and Con felt an unexpected warmth
for these splendid, dark-eyed creatures. 'Hey kids. Wanna see
me crack my knuckles? Listen.' He pulled his middle finger
from its socket and there was a noise like a tiny pistol shot.
Eyes grew wide with wonder, and the children cackled
heartily.

'Wanna see another?' Splat went an index finger. 'Hey, I
can crack my toes too –'

'For shame, Conor Emmet. Teaching bad habits to the kids.
Manuel saw you too.' Paz's smile belied her tone. 'Anyhow,
Con, guess we better get back or Kane'll have the dogs out.'

As they stood to go, Con whispered to Lucita, 'I – love –
you.'

'I love you too,' came the prompt reply.

'Well, I'll be – she speaks English?'

'Sure does,' Paz said. 'We got her into kindergarten with
the local kids.'

Driving back to the paper, Con felt an unaccustomed
elation, as though the children had touched something deep
inside him.

'What y'think of Manuel?' Paz asked him as they turned
into the *Record* parking lot.

'I liked him. I don't often say that, as you know. And those
kiddies – they're something else.'

'Tell you something. Manuel's our great white hope –
among the Mexicans, I mean. He's got a bit of education. He's
even trying to learn English – just starting, of course. But he's
got drive, real drive, and a lot of determination. It's hard to
have that after you've been kicked around the way these

people have. And he's got political savvy: he wants to do something about things, to do something for his people.' Paz climbed out of the car. 'You watch,' she said. 'That Manuel's going places.'

'Does he work in the forests?'

'Used to. That's a story in itself. He got an absolutely shitty deal and there was a fight.'

'So what does he do now?'

'Wheeling and dealing, mostly. Used cars, scrap, second-hand stuff. To tell the truth, I worry about him sometimes – those scrap dealers can be crooked as hell, and I wouldn't want them leading him wrong. But Manuel's got a lot of savvy – so I don't worry too much!'

That evening, as Paz was leaving the office, she laid another thick file on Con's desk. 'That's the rest of the stuff,' she said. 'Just in case you don't have enough! You promised you'd read it, OK?'

'I'll read it,' Con said with a sigh.

He opened one of the files and sifted through the typed notes, newspaper cuttings, interviews, signed statements, scraps in Paz's handwriting, and letters from people Con had never heard of.

Four hours later he was still reading, fascinated. He looked up to find himself in a mostly darkened newsroom. At the far end he noticed Barrett, plucking silently at his computer keyboard under a narrow cone of light.

It was a tale of callousness that cried for a terrible trampling where the grapes of wrath are stored. Paz must have built up her documentation over a considerable time, and it was from all over the Northwest.

It was a modern version of an old, old story.

For generations Mexico's burgeoning population had been spilling northwards across the US border, hoping that whatever they might encounter had to be better than life in their home villages in Sonora or Durango.

It rarely was.

Yet still they came, and the tide of migrants pressed inexorably northward, from California to Oregon, then to Washington State. The work changed as the tide moved northwards: in California it had been in vineyards and citrus groves and lettuce fields; in Oregon it was fruit picking in strawberry fields and apple orchards; in Washington it was planting and thinning trees in the forests.

As the work changed, conditions worsened. In California, leaders like César Chávez and unions like the United Farmworkers had begun to win some fairness for the migrants. But in the vast forests of the Northwest the Mexicans were so isolated, and their numbers relatively so few, that exploitation was more virulent than ever.

Big money was involved. Paper companies like Smith Pulp Corporation owned massive tracts of forest in and around Washington State. Here the most back-breaking work – and consequently the lowest-paid – was tree planting and thinning. Thinning was the hardest of all: the cutting out of every third or fourth tree in a cluttered stand, so the other trees would have space to mature. A clipping from a northwest newspaper described thinning as 'dirty, demanding and difficult – stoop labour that most Americans disdain'.

The work was handled by private contractors. Some of the big companies might not know how these contractors operated. Which left the operators a free hand, and by God a few of them took it.

Some contractors kept their bids low by the expedient of hiring undocumented, illegal migrants who had nowhere else to go, paying them pennies, then running them into the ground. 'A situation that amounts to slavery', was what Joe Telford, director of the state's Mexican-American Affairs Commission, called it. A report in the files from another reporter, with whom Paz had evidently been in correspondence, itemised the slavery:

Brought in by out-of-town contractors, illegal aliens commonly are crowded into shabby trailers and tents, left for days without adequate food or supplies, and cheated out of their wages, according to workers and public officials.

Document after document spelled out the grim details. And figuring prominently was the name of Antonio Gómez.

If a man complained about his treatment, he was told the immigration authorities were 'just a telephone call away'. If he complained again, he was dragged out of his hut and beaten unconscious. The rare individuals who protested a third time, at least in Gómez's camps, were simply led away during the night. Some said they were buried under the newly planted trees; others said they were rumoured to be back in Mexico. But nobody really knew, and the terror of this *Nacht und Nebel* strategy brought a singular discipline to the forests.

The migrants had nowhere to turn. They were prisoners, not so much of the contractors, as of their own illegal status. Any approach to the authorities, in search of a fair deal or to register a complaint, meant you were rounded up with all your workmates and shipped off to Mexico. Often it also meant a term of five months and twenty-nine days, for immigration violations, in the concrete blockhouses of Safford Federal Prison Camp in Arizona, before being dumped back in Mexico.

The ultimate cruelty was that the contractors themselves sometimes blew the whistle on their workers.

Gómez was adept at it, according to Paz's documents. The timing was always spot on – the very day a contract job was to finish, immigration officials would be mysteriously alerted to the presence of undocumented workers in the area. They would move in, round up the workers and ship them out – before the contractor could manage to pay them their several months of accumulated wages.

It even saved the contractor the cost of transporting them from the site.

Government officials were aware of the practice. Ken Giddings, of the US Border Patrol in Bellingham, had gone on record that certain contractors had a reputation for blowing the whistle. 'You get a call that there are a bunch of illegals working up in the mountains,' he had said in an interview for a Northwest paper. 'So you go up there and the contractor's nowhere to be found.

'It happens to you once; it happens to you twice; maybe three times – and pretty soon you start thinking maybe you're being had.'

Years ago, in religion class at Clongowes, Con had learnt of the 'sins that cry to heaven for vengeance'. One of these had been 'depriving a labourer of his wages'. Now, for the first time, he understood. He rubbed his eyes and looked at his watch. Good God, it's nearly midnight.

Under his cone of light, Barrett was still plucking away at his keyboard.

Does he ever sleep? Con thought. Well, who am I to talk? Haven't even eaten yet.

Con gathered up the papers, put them back in their files and locked them into his desk. He took his jacket from the back of the chair, slung it across his shoulders and headed towards the exit.

Barrett looked up as he passed, rodent nose awrinkle. 'Hey, Con,' he said. 'Whyn't you get your Jewish buddy to give a hand with this Nazi thing I'm working on? Y'know – where-are-they-now? – that sort of shit. Wasn't ole Max in Treblinka or somewhere? Bet he could give us a bit of local colour if he chose to. Whatcha think?'

13

Before sleep came that night, Con found his mind turning over and over what he had read.

The saga took on a personal dimension from the fact that he now knew Manuel. He tried to imagine that slight figure toiling on a forest mountainside, seething in frustration as he saw himself cheated, then threatened and probably savaged by goons. He thought of Lucy and Loopy. Those little creatures too had been exploited, without ever having been on a mountainside: their father's deprivation could mean hunger and cold or a bleak future for them too.

Con felt an anger redden inside him – the first anger he had felt in years. As he lay there he seemed to see the two elfin faces gazing at him. Then the faces puckered into smiles, and Con smiled back just as he dozed off.

By morning, Con's more practical self was back in control.

More comfortable that way, he thought, as he sat working towards deadline. Easy to get worked up over the Mexes when you're lying in bed after reading all that stuff. Sure, they're getting a raw deal. But who isn't? and you can't take the whole bloody lot on yourself. Could go off your head that way.

Anyway stop daydreaming – gotta get a paper out. Christ, look at that clock. Come on, Emmet. Move. Forget Lucy and Loopy. Where's Paz? Not at her desk.

'Hey, Marty. Where's Paz?'

'Day off, Con. Due a couple of days.'

'Jeez, I'd forgotten. Gone anywhere special?'

'Not that I know of. I think she's at home. Or around town, mebbe, following up that Mexican lark.'

After deadline Con faced up to a heap of letters to the editor. He was working his way through them when the phone rang.

'Con? It's me, Paz. How about Rosita's tonight?'

'Why not?'

'Six-thirty OK? Catch ya later, then.'

Con selected from the pile of letters on his desk a couple of the more malign ones to run in the paper. He dummied the next day's editorial page, did a couple of chores, and headed across the street for a sandwich. Nothing much, because Rosita's would be later. Need space for that Mexican food.

After lunch there'd be an interview with the schools' superintendent, then back to the newsroom.

Paz wasn't at Rosita's when Con got there. Rosita came over.

'Hi, Con. Your friend Paz left you a note. Hey, know what? That girl, she really likes you.'

'Now then, Rosie, you back off. Do your matchmaking somewhere else. We're just good colleagues.'

'Time will tell, Con. Have I ever been wrong? Huh? You tell me that, huh? Hey, you try the *enchiladas* – they're real good today. Gotta get back to the kitchen.'

The note was in Paz's minute handwriting: 'Had to call at hospital,' it read. 'Xplain later. Go to Max after you eat. Catch you there.'

As Con ate, he found himself studying the faces around him. Fierce, moustachioed Pancho Villa faces, with the keen Indian eyes.

What quiet people they are – look like they could tear the place apart, yet there's hardly more than a murmur of conversation. And what's this about aliens having to hole up in the mountains for fear of Immigration? Nobody's hiding here. Must ask Paz.

No sign of Manuel or the kids. Kids got to you, didn't they? Getting soft, Emmet. Watch it, or those bloody Mexes'll have you by the balls. You'll be running all over trying to fix things, like some goddam social worker. Like Paz, for God's sake. Jumping through hoops for the Mexes, when she'd be better off covering her beat. Said to meet her at Max's. Better be getting up there.

Paz was not at Max's. Con was surprised to find Max sitting at his big dining-room table with about nine young Mexican men and women.

'English class, Conor. Conducted by a German speaker, alas. But please not to laugh. You care to join us?'

Con sat in at the table. He noticed Manuel, and leaned across to shake his hand. Manuel indicated the small-boned, dark-haired young woman beside him. No doubt whose mama she was. Pregnant again, by the looks of it.

'*Mi esposa, Consuelo,*' Manuel said. '*Señor Emmet.*'

Con shook hands, and Consuelo smiled a Lucy-Loopy smile. Manuel introduced Con around the table, and Con shook hands solemnly with everyone. He turned to Max, lifting an enquiring eyebrow.

'She will be here, Conor. She called to ask will you please wait. She is up at the hospital with María Álvarez, who is having a baby. Anna sits by her to translate for the doctors and nurses. She had been there most of today.'

'I see. And this' – Con's gesture took in the English class – 'I take it this is her lark as well?'

'It is her lark, as you call it. She has taught English to these people since several months. She lately asked if they could meet at my house. It is but once a week. I said yes, and that

I would help with the teaching.' Max smiled. 'I think she may be asking you to help as well.'

'You can be sure of it, Max. It's like a bloody spider's web. You find yourself getting caught and you struggle a bit, then another strand wraps you round. Max, that woman's a menace.'

'But a rather beautiful menace, *ne?* Anyhow, do you care to sit and watch our class?'

'Well, I declare, Max,' Con said, after the Mexicans had left, 'you should have been a teacher. That was quite impressive.'

'Anna Paz taught me to teach,' Max answered simply. 'That young woman has taught me many things. I do not know where she learns them herself.'

'Tell me something, Max. Why does she get herself involved in all this? They're not even her people – I mean, apart from her name, she's an all-American girl. Why does she do it, Max?'

'I truly do not know, Conor. How do you say it? – I do not know what makes her . . . tick. But these people had no one to care about them until Anna began to care. Remember they are non-persons: officially they do not exist. And they dare not admit they exist, so how can they ask for help?'

'Max. I ate at Rosita's tonight. Nearly every man, woman and child there was Mexican. They didn't look as if they were trying not to exist.'

'Yes. But remember, Conor, there are Mexicans who are legal, who have papers. They go to Rosita's, naturally. There probably were illegals there also. I will tell you how the system works. You have heard of . . . the blind eye? Well, the authorities turn it, for months at a time. Then, when all are relaxed, they pounce. Like a shark who swims quietly among the little fish – until he feels hungry. It is a game that saves the authorities much trouble.'

'And you're telling me the game is spoilt if some illegals start looking for, say, legal aid or welfare?'

'*Genau*. It forces the authorities to recognise that these illegals exist. Then they have to take them away.' Max paused. 'And even that is not all of the story,' he said. 'Sometimes an illegal can be quite visible, yet not be touched. Yet all know he is illegal. You will even find illegals making a claim in court and sometimes even winning. And that person is not touched.'

Max turned to face Con. 'When that happens,' he said, 'almost always you will find Anna Paz in there somewhere. Involved. Perhaps she has got around the sheriff to back off. Or she has persuaded an attorney to give his time for nothing – you will even find her in the court acting as interpreter.'

'So when does she get her work done, Max? I mean, her newsroom work?'

'You tell me, my friend. Does she get it done?'

Con pondered the question. 'Well, Kane hasn't fired her,' he said.

'There you are, then. So far she keeps her job and does all of this also. That is quite something, *nicht wahr*? I will tell you more. Tonight María Álvarez brings a child to the world, up at the hospital. María is illegal, yet she will not be arrested. No illegal who goes to that hospital is ever reported. You wish to guess who got that arranged?'

'Don't tell me. Paz?'

'Anna Paz indeed. You know, they truly love Anna there at the hospital. Sometimes they call her to come up and help a Mexican person deal with documents. Or help with anything – today they called her to interpret for María who is having her child –'

Wheels scrunched across the gravel outside. A car door clunked. There was the sound of the house door opening.

Paz came into the room. Her dark eyes were shining.

'Baby come yet?' Both men spoke, almost in unison.

'Sure did. An' he's big, well over seven pounds. An' he's all together, too!' She threw herself into an armchair. 'You guys should've seen it happen: it's the most beautiful thing in the world.'

'I'd hardly call it exactly beautiful,' Con said.

'That's because you've never seen it, Con. Honestly, you can't imagine. I've watched it a couple of times now, and it gets more fantastic every time. This time was the best. I wouldn't have missed it for the world.'

'You had a long wait this time, Anna,' Max said. 'You must be tired now. And hungry.'

'Got a chicken sandwich up there, thanks Max.' Paz looked at her watch. 'Hey! Well, it sure didn't seem that long. It just passed like that.' She clicked her fingers. 'The first few hours we just sat in the labour room, and sort of talked about her home, and cooking, and folks back in Mexico that she remembered, and stuff.

'When we got to the delivery room, I found myself doing the breathing along with her. I had to tell her the progress. The nurse would say, push. I'd tell her, *Empucha*. Take short breaths. Push. Harder. Now don't push – *no empuches*. *Empucha* – *no empuches*.

'Then when the baby was out, the doctor said to tell María it was OK. And to tell her it was a boy.

'But would you believe? Right away the baby held out his arms to his mother.'

Con had never seen Paz so radiant. Happier than he'd ever seen her in the newsroom.

'But do you know what was the biggest surprise?' she went on. 'That the mother's stomach was so noisy. I never noticed it the other times.

'They put some sort of microphone here on the mother' – Paz tapped her abdomen – 'and it's connected up. That was in the labour room, and there were earphones I could use.

'Well, I could hear everything inside. There was the baby's heart going boom, boom, boom. Or the mother's, I'm not sure. But what absolutely amazed me was, you could hear the water – it's all water in there round the baby – an' d'you know what? It sounded like waves washing on some seashore.

'It was a strange kind of feeling, hearing that. A wonderful feeling. It was just a magnificent thing. No wonder they call it the miracle of life . . .' Paz trailed off and closed her eyes, remembering.

They sat in silence, thinking about the bringing of a child to birth: the woman remembering how it had been; the men remembering how she had told it. It was as though something rare and wonderful had reached into the room and touched the occupants.

Max stood up quietly and went to the kitchen to make coffee. Con broke the silence. 'Do you do this often, Paz?' he asked. 'This delivering babies, I mean.'

'Not delivering, Con. Interpreting. Only a few times so far. But they been asking me more lately. Maybe it's a Mexican baby boom!' She smiled tiredly.

'Max here was telling me all you've been doing for the migrants. I must say, I didn't know the half of it.'

'Somebody has to do it, Con.'

'And thank God somebody is. But something's bothering me, though. Not sure if I can express it. Look, maybe I'm being devil's advocate, but these folks are illegal. And they're illegal for the very good reason that they're taking work from Americans. Well now, you're American, not Mexican. So, what I mean is, by helping them aren't you harming your own country? There, that's it.'

'But the point is, they're not taking jobs from Americans. There's jobs Americans won't do: like this tree thinning; like fruit picking, slaughterhouse work, sweatshop work. They won't do it, period. So employers have to find workers somewhere – and the Mexicans are ready and willing. So who's getting hurt?'

Max spoke as he put down the tray with the coffee: 'If these people are needed for this work, Anna, why cannot we make them legal? Perhaps allow them in where work is needed, and let them return home when it is completed?'

'Did that years ago – right up to the mid-sixties in fact.

Called them *braceros*. And it really worked: it helped us and it helped Mexico. But the unions got it stopped: said they were losing jobs to the Mexicans. And now they can't get Americans to take the jobs.' Paz sipped her coffee. 'I'd love to see the *bracero* thing get another chance. So would a lot of farmers. And I bet the paper companies would, too. Y'know, I think after we nail Gómez, we should get a campaign going to bring back the *braceros*.'

'You mean, if you nail Gómez,' Con said quietly.

'You gonna help me?'

'Never let up, do you? Look, I'll do that interview. I'll call Gómez in the morning and set it up. All right? But Paz, it's a one-off thing, to help you this time. I'm not getting involved, and I want you to understand that. Right?'

'Fine by me, Con. And I really am grateful. It'd be such a help. Sometimes I feel so godawful tired.' She sighed.

'You should go home and sleep, young lady,' Max said.

'We should all go home and sleep,' Con said.

Driving home, Con found himself thinking about Lucy and Loopy. Their faces floated in his imagination, and then the faces of Manuel and Consuelo. The haunting, Aztec features of that little family were coming to symbolise all the illegal aliens.

And Paz's face floated in and out of his mind too, that face so splendidly alive as she recounted the birth of a child. Such energy. Was Con letting himself get sucked into these madcap schemes of hers? Or getting involved with Paz herself?

Or was he being conned by the whole bloody lot of them?

How about this evening up at Max's? Could it have been a set-up, just to get him involved? Showing him how involved Max was? Hardly. But in a way it did remind Con of that evening years ago in the Kelpie in Galway, when they took him to meet Sean Louth.

Con got his interview on the Saturday afternoon. It took place in the Gómez residence, an imposing pseudo-Frank-Lloyd-Wright structure standing alone on a hill above Rainhaven, with a superb view over the bay. A Mercedes pagoda-top convertible and a late-model Continental stood in the driveway. The sound of baying hounds came from the grounds behind the house.

Gómez opened the door. 'Mister Emmet. You are more than welcome: *mi casa es tu casa*. Please do come in.'

One bloody handsome man, that was for sure. Tall – not quite as tall as Con, but carried himself straighter – iron-grey hair that contrasted with the keen, bronzed face. He wore a well-cut jacket in Scottish or Irish tweed, and beige cavalry twill trousers with knife-edge creases. A cream handkerchief nestled in the breast pocket. A beige knitted tie made for a somewhat European military look.

He took Con's arm as he led him to a room with a huge picture window overlooking the bay. 'You will drink a little something with me, Conor? May I – may I call you Conor? I am Tono, by the way. Short for Antonio.'

'I don't drink, Tono. But I would take coffee or tea,

if I might. It's Con, by the way. Short for Conor.'

'Tea is already being made, Con. Let us both take it.' Gómez went to the door and called: '*Guillermina! Queremos tomar el té ahora, por favor.*'

Con was at the big picture window, drinking in the view. The bay spread below him, blue and flecked with foam. There was no sign of the town, which was tucked away under the hill on which they stood. The hills around the bay were dark with evergreens, and the trees marched to the water's edge.

A tiny yellow tug moved across the bay with logs like matchsticks bobbing in its wake. Save for the tug, it was a scene as untouched as anything explorers Lewis and Clark might have encountered on reaching the Northwest coast a century and a half before.

The Pacific was a blue-grey line to the west.

'I see you have an eye for beauty, Con.' Gómez was standing beside him. 'That is really something, eh? You know, the sheer beauty of this scene has refreshed me, and kept me going, so many times when I just wanted to give up – to quit and walk away from everything.'

Con turned to look a him. The man spoke with such warmth. Con had to pinch himself mentally: stay objective, you dummy. 'You've felt like giving up?' he asked.

'More time than you can imagine. Listen, when a man sets out to help his countrymen, as I have chosen to do, he is not always thanked. The contrary, in fact. May I speak off the record for a moment?'

Con nodded.

'I am referring to what they call the illegals – my compatriots who have no documents or work permits. For a long time I have being trying to help them as much as I can. That is what is off the record.'

'I see,' Con said. 'Look, let's stay off the record a bit more. I'd really like to learn more about this. It'd help me understand you as a man, even if we can't print it.'

'Fine with me. But remember, what I am doing is illegal,

so do not let me down. Back in Mexico these people have nothing – and I mean, nothing – so I try to help them to come here and to have work waiting when they arrive. I pay big money to the *coyotes* – the smugglers, Con – to get these boys safely into the States, and to get them up to the Northwest where I can give them work.'

Gómez led him to a sofa. 'Trouble is, once you get into anything illegal, even for the best motives, you can make enemies, you have trouble with the law, and you are a sitting duck for threats and blackmail.'

He smiled sadly. 'Even your own *pollos* can turn against you.'

'*Pollos?*'

'Chickens, Con. It's the word the Mexicans use for the people we smuggle in.'

'They turn against you?'

'Sometimes, Con. It is very sad. Maybe a man feels I have given someone else a better deal. And he gets angry. Or maybe someone resents that I am a US citizen. Or wants me to pay him more. Or resents that I seem to have money.

'Con, I don't deny I make good money. But if you knew how much of it I spend on my people, you would be amazed. It costs a small fortune just to get them here. Then I have to lend them money to buy their chain saws. And chain saws are not cheap, Con. And I have to look after my people's needs while they are here. Even their spiritual needs.

'Which reminds me, Con. There is a Mass in Spanish being said for them, here at my house this afternoon. Why don't you stay?'

'Perhaps I will, Tono. And thanks. Tell me, do many turn against you?'

'It's not how many, Con. It's the fact that any do – that's what hurts. And it's what they do. I've had my life threatened more than once. This window has been smashed. And what some of them say – you know, I have even been accused of calling Immigration so I don't have to pay them. Now that hurts.'

A dark-eyed girl entered, carrying a tea tray. She wore a black dress and white apron, like the maid Con remembered in the house in Newry when he was a child. She smiled as she put down the tray.

'*Gracias, Guillermina*,' Gómez said gently. '*Nosotros nos servimos.*'

The girl smiled at Con and withdrew.

Tea was in the Irish manner, with milk and sugar, the jug and sugar bowl matching the flower-patterned cups and saucers. Bone china, Con observed. He raised his teacup to sneak a peep at the imprint on its base.

'Royal Doulton, Con.' Gómez was smiling at him, and Con felt slightly caught out. 'I know,' Gómez went on, 'I do like to have fine things around me, as you will have observed, good newspaperman that you are. But' – he shrugged – 'the money is there, and I say to myself, why not, if it harms no one?'

'Why not, indeed?' Con said. 'Look, I suppose we ought to get back on the record. What you've told me is fascinating, and some day maybe we can write about it. But right now I need a story I can print – you know, about you as prominent local citizen, maybe running for city council, your views on the salmon fishing, and so on.'

'Fine by me. And, let me say, I always read you in the paper, and I like those interviews that you do. I feel I trust you. So ask me whatever you want to know. OK?'

'Well then, let's start – at the start. Where you were born. How you got started. That sort of thing.'

For an hour Gómez talked and Con's ballpoint danced. It was a straightforward story. Gómez had come from a family of some influence in Guadalajara. He had graduated in engineering from the city's university, and had got a job with a San Diego construction firm with interests south of the border.

Those were the heady days when big companies were falling over one another to sign up young engineers just out of college, and visas and work permits presented little difficulty to a graduate. As did citizenship, after the requisite number of years. By then Gómez had married an Americal girl, anyway.

'I'd love to meet her,' Con interrupted.

'She's not available right now, Con,' Gómez said, offering no further explanation.

Back in Mexico the family hit hard times, and Gómez had to look after some of their needs. He needed more than a single professional salary. He tried a number of things, and finally found himself as a subcontractor to the paper companies, first in Oregon, and later in Washington State.

And, God be thanked, things had gone well. Gómez had been able to help not only his family but many of his country-men (only Con would please not write that, given that so many are illegals). Gómez was involved to some degree in local politics, aiming for a seat on the Rainhaven City Council. He might consider eventually running for Olympia.

'It's a good life, Con. Apart from – from what I told you. The threats and the trouble. But I'm not complaining.'

They went on to Gómez's views on local issues, such as the nuclear plants being built down at Gray's Harbor County, and Gómez's aspirations for the region.

It was a good interview, but Con's mind was in a whirl by the end of it.

Not for the first time he found himself echoing Pilate's 'What is truth?' Not a flaw in Gómez's story. Nor in Gómez himself. Likes the good life, but who doesn't? An amiable fellow, and seems to have good instincts. An unlikely bad guy.

Could Paz have got it wrong – ballsed the whole thing up? How good a journalist is she, really? Has she ever done a really good piece of investigation? Ever see a really good story by her? Not really.

So where do I go from here? Con asked himself. Sometimes wonder which end of life is up. What if the good guys are really the bad guys: like Max a bad guy, and Manuel a bad guy, and myself – Jesus, I am a murderer. I'm not what I seem, either. So why not the rest? Maybe nothing's what it seems. Pilate was right –

' . . . and the Mass will be in the dining room,' Gómez was saying. 'There's Father Felipe now. Shall we go meet him? Con? Con, are you with me?'

'Huh? Oh, sorry, I was just running over my notes for a moment. Yes, I'd be glad to meet him.'

During the Mass Con watched the lynx-eyed, quiet priest from Seattle. Very Mexican Indian. He wondered what the priest really thought of Gómez. Did he see him as a rascal? If so, then was Father Felipe selling out for a fat donation? Or hanging in there for the sake of Gómez's workers? With a man like that you'd never know.

Con looked at the faces of Gómez's workers gathered around the table. They looked ill at ease in the gracious surroundings, but what they really thought Con could not begin to guess.

He resolved to get the priest's phone number: it could be useful.

At the Sign of Peace, Gómez, who was serving the Mass, went around to embrace everyone, as did the priest. When Gómez embraced Con he whispered to him: 'God bless you, Con. And may He give you peace.'

On the way home Con felt the old journalistic juices flowing. He had kept his promise to Paz, had done all she asked. But now he wanted to do more. For Paz? Maybe for himself.

He stopped off at Rosita's to ask where he might find Manuel.

'Probably not at home right now, Con,' Rosita told him. 'But Consuelo'd know where he is. Whyn't you go over there?' Rosita directed him to a run-down A-frame across the tracks. Manuel's family shared it with two other families, she said.

Lucy and Loopy were playing on the porch with some children, and came shyly to meet him when he got out of the car. Con knelt and submitted himself to wet kisses and hugs from sticky hands.

Consuelo waved from the door, and shouted inside, '*Manuel! Alguien te quiere ver.*'

Manuel came out, drying his hands on a towel. When he saw Con he smiled, handed the towel to Consuelo, and came down to meet him.

'Will you walk with me a little?' Con asked. 'We need to talk.'

'Sure, Con. We walk. OK?'

They strolled along the sidewalk and Con said: 'You worked for Gómez, didn't you, Manuel? I'd like you to tell me about it.'

'Gómez?' Manuel shook his head solemnly. 'Is bad news.'

'How long were you working for him?'

'Oh yes. Is very bad news.'

'Manuel. Can you understand me? How long did you work for Gómez?'

'*Es ladrón*, robber man.' Manuel drew a forefinger across his throat. Con was unsure if the gesture meant Gómez would cut your throat for a penny, or that Gómez needed to have his own throat cut. The conversation began to languish.

Con had an idea. 'Tell you what, Manuel. Let's go to Rosita's for coffee. Nearly there anyway. *Café*, Manuel? Rosita's OK?' He made a drinking gesture.

'*Sí*,' Manuel said, and grinned.

At Rosita's, Con ordered coffee and telephoned Paz.

'Paz? It's me. Could you spare me half an hour?'

'Right now?'

'Right now. I'm over at Rosita's with Manuel, and I need an interpreter.'

'So what are you guys talking about?'

'Give you one guess.'

'I'll be right over. Give me a couple of minutes. OK?'

Minutes later Paz slid into the seat beside the two men, with a questioning look at Con.

'We're trying to talk about Gómez,' Con said.

'Guess you're really getting interested.'

'Don't bet on it. I did that interview: let's say I want to hear both sides. Journalists are supposed to.'

'OK. Shoot.'

It took a lot more than half an hour, but Manuel painted a somewhat different picture from the one Con had already got. With Paz translating, the conversation moved swiftly.

'Gómez? King of broken promises,' Manuel said. 'Liar too, a thief, a cheat, a savage bully – and probably even a murderer, if it could only be proved. He sucks his compatriots dry and grows fat on it. That man is bad news, Con. He's a vampire – only he prefers sweat to blood. And he often ends with blood, too.'

Manuel had been working in the Oregon strawberry fields when he heard of Gómez.

'I was in this tavern in Woodburn, and this guy asks me to come north to work. I say, Canada? No, he says, Washington State. He offers me not-too-bad money for each hour. As well as free food and a place to sleep

'I say OK: Consuelo can wait in Woodburn. Next day the man puts me in this van with no windows – fourteen men already in it. He drives non-stop up Interstate Five – we nearly choked, we were so crowded – and then miles into the mountains to this Gómez work camp somewhere south of Glacier.

'Work camp? Hah! Con, it was a couple of filthy trailers next to some leaky army tents beside the track. Already there must have been forty men in them.

'Driver charged us sixty dollars each for the ride, and we said we couldn't pay it, so they said they'd take it out of our wages. I asked what our wages would be, and you know what? it was only a third what the man promised.

'I started to yell, and two men grabbed me and marched me up the track to where a tall man was standing with two big

German shepherds on chains. He let go the chains and the dogs came and knocked me flat on the ground. I thought I was going to die, and then there was a whistle and the dogs went back to the man.

'The man said nothing, only walked away with the dogs. Later I learned he was Gómez. I was shaking with fright for two days.

'I tried to stay quiet. I was scared. There were two men did a lot of grumbling, and they were taken away one night and we never saw them again. But in the end I had to say something.

'They cut our food money from the wages we were going to get. The two men who ran the camp would take off, and one time they left us without food for three days. We were miles into the mountains, didn't know where we were, and had no money. And no wheels either. So we had to wait. The men only laughed when they got back.

'Then they told us we'd have to pay for our chain saws: they were going to cut that from our wages too. You know, they never even showed us how to use the saws right. Men lost fingers – it was like going to war.

'But the last straw was what happened to Raul Espinoza. His chain saw slipped and caught him in the abdomen. He screamed and screamed when they threw him in the jeep, and he was dead when he got to the hospital. It's as well he died.

'The men got very angry, and I guess that's what brought Gómez back up the mountain. I was getting the men to sign a grievance list, saying to stick by the terms we got in Oregon, or pay us off and let us leave.

'Gómez had his two dogs on chains when he got out of the jeep. He stood there while his men came for me. He looked at me as if I was some sort of roach.

'Then he says, *Largate, pollo.* Start running, chicken! I take off down the track. Then the dogs are on me. The terror is worse than the pain, Con. And I can remember the wet dog smell. I went unconscious and woke up in hospital.

'The dogs must have been trained not to go for my face or neck. But look. *Mira.*' Manuel rolled up his shirtsleeve to reveal a number of scars that looked like curved, pink zip fasteners.

'*Y mira.*' He opened the top button of his pants and tugged out his check shirt. He pulled up shirt and undervest to reveal an abdomen scarred in the same strange way.

'*Y mira esto.*' Manuel stood up, and Con was unsure whether he was going to drop his pants or roll up his pants leg.

'It's OK, Manuel,' Paz almost whispered, and pulled him back gently to his seat. 'It's OK. Con's seen all he needs.'

1 5

The following Saturday Con went fishing with Max. By noon Max had caught three trout and Con had got two photographs.

Dawn had been grey when the men got to Falls Lake. Then the sun broke through, laying a golden pathway across the gunmetal water. 'Like Monet's *Impression of a Sunrise*,' Max had said.

A canoe with three figures moved over the lake. Con waited, camera focused on the pathway of sparkles, until the dark outline of the canoe cut into it. He squeezed the shutter, catching the curled prow just athwart the shimmering pathway. He let his breath out and felt his body relax.

Immediately the muscles tightened again under another pictorial challenge. 'Max,' Con said, 'I need the same shot again with a wide-angle lens. To get the trees in. Could we get that canoe in line with the sun again? Sorry, old man.'

'The things I do for friendship,' Max sighed, pulling in his line and starting up the outboard. 'Or perhaps I do them for art.'

The boat puttered across the lake and the sun's pathway kept pace with them until it caught up with the canoe and Con got his silhouetted shot.

'Thanks Max, really. Now we fish. All right?'

'So kind of you,' Max murmured, with the ghost of a smile.

'Go jump in the lake, old man,' Con replied, and they settled down to fish.

Punctually at noon Max pulled in his line, took a Thermos flask from under the seat, and unwrapped the foil from a couple of sandwiches. 'Smoked salmon today, Conor,' he said.

They munched quietly until Max said, 'So you have fallen for the young lady?'

Con choked on a crumb. 'Where the devil – did you – get that notion?' he wheezed.

'Your whole body calls it out, my friend. The way you move today. Even how you sit. And your eyes, your eyes. The windows of the soul, remember?'

'Max, she wants me to get involved with that social work she does. Y'know, with the Mexicans.'

'These are two separate matters, Conor, and the young lady will have to realise that. She is too simple: love me, love my hound. She cannot demand it of you, even if you love her. She can be somewhat overpowering in these enthusiasms of hers – you see how she also drags me in from time to time. And you, my friend, are not the world's strongest personality.'

'I suppose not, huh?' muttered Con, slightly hurt.

'You are a communicator, Conor, not a leader. One of the most effective communicators I know. But you are like the engine of one of those, ach, bulldozers – someone must point the bulldozer at the right object and then it can do wonderful work.'

'You're suggesting I need Paz to run my life, Max?'

'You would never allow her to do so. And you would be right not to. No. I am suggesting that perhaps it is time you began to care – about people, what they do to each other. About people who suffer wrong.'

'Max,' Con said, 'I've already been that route.'

'Yes, I know. And someone got killed –'

'Goddammit, Max.'

'Calm yourself, Conor. Calm yourself. No one knows. I guessed only because I have been around death so much. I have seen what it does to those who kill. Sometimes their sufferings are the worst of all.'

He stopped. Con's head was in his hands, and he was bent almost double in the prow of the boat. The hands were trembling.

Max fished in silence.

Con raised his face to Max. He dropped his head again, and through the cupped hands he said, 'I have never spoken of it to a single human being since the night it happened. Max, how can I start now?'

'Conor, you do not have to start. I do not wish to know. But it is true, *nicht wahr*, that you carry some memory, like a cancer, inside you?'

Con nodded.

'But you have begun to forget, here on the lake, here in your life in Rainhaven? At least sometimes? A kind of peace, *ne*?'

Con nodded again, head in hands.

'And you are afraid to lose that peace by getting involved – by starting to care again?'

Con was gazing at Max now, hands cupped below his chin.

'So that is why you write those amusing columns,' Max went on. 'You can be the brilliant communicator but be free of things that really matter. That is what has troubled Anna Paz about you, all these months. It is not the Mexicans, Conor. She just wants you to care about something – anything. But you are afraid to care. Except to care about yourself.'

'You're a fucking bastard, Stern,' Con said.

There was silence between the two men. Max rinsed his cup in the lake, and screwed it back on the Thermos. He took Con's cup and rinsed it too; he scrunched the foil from the sandwiches and put everything into the rucksack. He took a couple of salmon eggs from the jar, baited the hook, and cast. Con followed suit. They fished in silence.

'Sorry I said that, Max,' Con said after some minutes, without turning his head.

'*Macht nichts,*' Max said.

The lake was now a deep, dark blue, devoid of sparkles from the high-riding sun. Not the ideal weather for fishing. Still, a trout leaped from Max's net and thumped around under the seat with the hook still in. Max groped for it.

'So how does a fellow start caring again?' Con asked casually, still gazing over the lake.

'You want to know what I think, Conor? Truly?'

'Uh huh.'

'I was wrong. I think you already do care. Perhaps too much, and in the wrong place.' Max thought for a moment. 'Remember Cain. He said, Am I my brother's keeper? He killed, but worse than that, he did not care about the man he killed. But you care. The problem is, you care too much. You care so much that you have no care left for those alive and around you today. It has paralysed your life.'

Con was gazing across the lake towards the swerve of evergreens beyond which the mountains gleamed. He said nothing.

'Conor, my dear friend, let go. Let go of those you killed – one, two, I do not know. Leave them to God: that is where they belong now.'

'Max, all my life I have been trying to let go. To forget. It doesn't work.'

'Conor, if I tell you to concentrate on not thinking of monkeys, you will think of them all the time. But if I tell you to think of parrots you will forget the monkeys.'

'So?'

'So you grow to care so much about those around you that there is no room for useless, negative remorse. Do not your scriptures speak of hungering and thirsting after justice? I am sure that means justice for other people. It is easy to hunger for justice for ourslevles: we do it all the time. The secret is to hunger for others. Conor, a hungry man has no other thoughts: he does not fool around.'

Not for the first time Con wondered at Max's grasp of the Christian scriptures. 'But Max,' he said, 'I'm no social worker. I'm a journalist. Remember?'

'Conor, a dealer in second-hand cars – could he hunger for justice? How would it show in his everyday life?'

'I s'pose he'd sell a car at a fair price? And not cover up defects?'

'Precisely. And a doctor would hunger to heal, not to grow rich. And a poor old printer like me? I must do ordinary things extraordinarily well – even Kane and Momma deserve a fair deal from me. We do not have to be social workers.

'And you know something else? If all of us did hunger after justice, and did our work as it should be done, and lived our lives as they should be lived, there would be no social workers. They would all be out of a job.'

'A journalist, Max. How does a journalist manage this, uh, hungering and thirsting?'

'Call it caring, Conor. That is all it is. And it's something in the mind, or the will, so small it is hardly noticeable at first. You do the same work, write your columns, do inter-views, cover the city hall, whatever. But you check your facts more carefully. You care about accuracy – you care. Because accuracy means justice to the people you write about. Inaccuracy is injustice.

'Also, people notice that your columns, instead of being always about funny things, sometimes ask questions that start people thinking – and perhaps caring. Care is catching, you see, Conor.'

'Go on.'

'That is it, Conor. That is all there is. Except that when you do see some obvious injustice, like this Mexican injustice, you do not cross the street and pass by. We are a caring people here in the Northwest, mostly, but we need journalists like you to tell us where our care must be focused. By revealing the injustices. If you do not do so, who will?'

'Paz will.' Con gave a chuckle.

'*Quatsch!* She is no journalist – have you not realised that by now? She is a failure as a reporter. Why do you think her research on the illegals is taking so long? Why do you think she has this mountain of evidence, yet nothing gets published? She has not the skill, Conor. Why do you think she keeps turning to you?'

'Jesus. Are you serious, Max?'

'My friend, if you were not so wrapped in your guilt and in the past, I would not need to tell you this. Everyone in the newsroom knows it. For a year already, the Citizen has been saying she will have to go, but Momma keeps saying we must giver her a chance. But the Citizen is right – Anna Paz belongs in social work. And Momma knows it in her heart, but her heart is kind. She cares about Paz. Care, Conor – sometimes even care can lead us astray.' Max smiled wryly. 'There is an irony to life, Conor. Anna Paz cares, but she cannot write. Conor Emmet can write – but he does not care.'

Con reached over and slapped Max's knee. 'Let's go play chess, old man,' he said.

16

The God who separated the waters above the earth from the waters under the earth did a botched sort of job around the Pacific Northwest. During the rainy season of autumn and winter the waters simply run together again, and people long for webbed feet.

But in spring and summer, when God manages to get the waters temporarily back where they belong, that land is a paradise.

With Paz in the paradise, Con experienced something approaching happiness.

They hiked together in the forests of the Olympic Peninsula; they swam in the rivers and lakes; they walked for miles through the driftwood that lay tangled along the Pacific beaches.

Once old Chuck Watkins took them by helicopter down the coast to Ilwaco. That was when Chuck's eagle eye spotted a couple making whoopee on a lonely beach far below, and took the helicopter down in a tight spiral right over the couple. The two men roared with laughter as the naked couple scrambled for cover, but Paz told them it wasn't fair and it wasn't funny.

'How would you guys like to be caught at it? Just tell me that.' Paz had to shout to be heard above the turbine.

'Wouldn't mind a bit,' Chuck yelled back. 'Would show 'em I c'n still make it!'

Paz had to laugh.

Max must have advised Paz to stop bothering Con about her Mexicans. She let it be, and beavered away on her own.

Most Fridays after work, Con and Paz would throw rucksacks in the back of Con's old Buick, and head for the start of some hiking trail in the Olympics. By nightfall the pair would be far into the mountains, and they would often sleep under the stars in a remote alpine meadow.

Paz was an ideal hiking companion. A quintessential Californian, she thrived on fresh air and sunshine. Although barely up to Con's shoulder, she was lithe, and could hold her own against Con's strides.

Paz had that outdoor look. Her graceful limbs might have stepped off a surfboard. Sometimes on the trail she would unloose her ponytail and the raven hair would tumble around her rucksack.

That hair must have come from her Latin father, as must those eyes so dark you could hardly see the pupils. And from her Connecticut Yankee mother would have come that apricot skin that tanned like a dream.

Once they were lying in knee-deep meadow grass in a forest clearing, amid the live murmur of a summer's day. The grass smelled sweet and the sunshine was like a caress. Paz was almost invisible save for her bent knees which peeped above the grass. She was wearing her hiking shorts: blue denim cut-offs of daunting brevity.

Con was thinking of Paz's skin, tanning there beside him like a waffle instead of blistering and boiling as his own lobstery skin did. Extraordinary damn woman. Wears no lipstick; rubs no cream in her face. Not even perfume: a lathering with soap and water every morning is Paz's notion of perfume. She smells so good, like . . .

'Hey Paz. Know what you smell like?'

'Huh?' Paz sat up, blinking.

'You smell like fresh bread.'

Paz thought. 'I'm not sure that's a compliment,' she said, looking sideways at him.

'It is, Paz. I remember as a child, the bread from McCann's bakery van, still steaming. Aroma was like heaven. It would make your head swim.'

'Do I make your head swim?'

'You're doin' it right now.'

There was silence.

'Paz,' Con said. 'Why don't you ever want to make love to me?'

'But I do. I'm longing to make love right now. Can't you feel that from me? It's just, I have this old-fashioned notion – please don't laugh – that the loving should come after some sort of commitment. Should be a kind of sign of commitment we already made.'

She reached through the grass and touched his arm. 'Does that make me some sort of fanatic? Sure hope not. But I've learnt from experience that when you do it just for the heck – it's a sort of a dead end. Never seems to lead to much worthwhile. Y'understand what I'm trying to say?'

'Experience?'

'What you expect, Con? I'm a big girl now.'

'Were you ever a nun, Paz?'

'No. Never. But I lived with a bunch of nuns for a while. Tell you round the fire tonight. Hey, guess we better get moving. We've a ways to go.'

'Gimme a kiss before we go.'

The kiss was long and lovely. Then they had shouldered their rucksacks and were back among the trees, walking single file along the narrow mountain track.

Everything about Paz was neat, Con was thinking, as he

walked the track behind her. That splendid little ass, neat as a boy's, tucked into those neat blue denim cut-offs. Neat breasts, pushing against their tartan shirt. Neat legs. They looked good even inside jeans: but in the cut-offs, hey! The cut-offs were for the mountains; blue jeans were for the rest of life. She never wore anything else.

Con wondered sometimes if Paz had been born in jeans. They seemed a part of her, like that apricot skin. Paz's notion of a splurge on new clothes was another pair of blue jeans.

But Paz could tuck a man's tartan shirt inside a pair of jeans and still look splendidly feminine. She could wear a frilly top above her jeans and look like a million dollars. She could throw an orange stole over her head and shoulders and look like the Sistine Madonna – at least from the navel up.

What's going on up there? Paz had stopped at a bend in the path. She was standing quite still.

'Paz. What is it?'

She made no reply. She did not turn around. Con ran up the path to her. As he came behind her, he could see over her shoulder, around the turn in the track.

In the narrow path, ten feet away, was a large black bear. It filled the pathway. It was on all fours, great snout raised, tawny eyes on Paz. It did not stir.

Con took Paz's arm and gently pulled her back behind him. 'Don't move,' he said softly. 'Until I say.'

The three figures remained motionless, as if in a tableau. The forest was silent. A bird began to trill in a tree overhead.

Con spoke softly, without moving his head. 'When I tell you, start moving back down the track. Slowly, mind – don't run. And quietly.'

'What about you?'

'Just do as I say.'

The bear reared up on its hind legs. It was all of seven feet high.

'Oh Jesus,' whispered Paz.

The bear stood there, eyes peering short-sightedly. Con noticed a white stripe on the chest that towered above him. The claws looked cruel.

'Start moving.'

Con sensed that Paz was moving back, although he could not hear her footfalls.

He could see the bear's breast rise and fall as the animal breathed. Its fetid smell reached his nostrils.

Suddenly the bear dropped on all fours and, with astonishing agility, lurched into the undergrowth that sloped down from the path. Con listened to it crashing through the foliage until the noise faded down the mountainside.

He ran back to look for Paz. She fell into his arms: she was shaking like an aspen.

'It's all right, little one. It's all right,' Con whispered, as he hugged her and felt the shudders move in waves across her body. 'It's all right. It's over now.'

He held her until she was easy in his arms. He helped her off with the rucksack, and they sat on the ivy-covered verge of the path. The apricot skin was pale.

Con took out a Thermos of coffee and filled their mugs. They sipped in silence.

'Maybe we should go back,' Con said.

'Huh uh.' Paz shook her head.

'Are you sure? I don't mind going back. Really.'

'We're more than halfway. It's only three hours to the meadows. Con, if I don't face it now, I'll never come again – I'll lose my nerve. Let's keep on. OK?'

'I'm for it. Shall we get moving then?'

'Will you stay real close to me? All the time? Please?'

'I'll be your shadow,' Con said.

The surrounding peaks were rosy in the evening sun when Con and Paz set up camp beside a stream in the broad alpine meadow. They were alone.

'Let's put the tent up, Con,' Paz said. 'I can't face sleeping in the open tonight. All those bears.'

'Good idea,' Con agreed, privately doubting if lightweight nylon would keep out any bear that had notions of sharing their tent. 'Tell you what, too. We hang the rucksacks, with all the food, from that tree there. I remember hearing that's what you're supposed to do when there's bears around.'

'What's it supposed to do?'

'Maybe it lures the bear away from the tent, so he spends the night trying to get at the food. Sort of occupational therapy for the bear.' He chuckled. 'Keeps him off our backs, so to speak!'

'Don't laugh, Con. It's not so funny when you've nearly had one on your back.'

'No, indeed. But bears only get dangerous when people start feeding them: there was a piece in the *Oregonian* about it only last week, warning people not to. It seems the bears start wandering into campsites looking for food, and then get vicious if they feel cornered. Like any animal.'

'Guess you're right. I'm glad our bear had somewhere to run. God, was I scared.' Paz shivered as though the evening had grown cold.

'Come on: let's get this fire going. Steak and baked potatoes, hey! The hunger's killing me.'

They sat closer to the campfire that evening. The leaping flames created a sinister outer darkness, full of rustlings and strange small sounds.

'I guess the cavemen must have felt like this,' Paz whispered. 'Sitting by their fire, listening to the wolves howling outside the cave.'

'Tell me about this nun thing,' Con said, partly to take Paz's mind off the bears. 'You actually lived with nuns once?'

'Twice. I was at a boarding school run by nuns after my parents split up. Then I lived in a hostel run by nuns in Seattle before I graduated. Stayed on after, too, for a while.'

'You graduated in journalism?' Con tapped his pipe on his boot.

'Nope. Social work, with a minor in counselling. Didn't know the first thing about journalism.'

'So how did you get to be a reporter?'

'Simple enough story, really. I learned about Mother Teresa from one of the sisters in the hostel. She gave me a book of her sayings, and one grabbed me. It went something like, Do not search for God in far lands – he is not there. He is here in the bodies of your own poor people, and in your lonely people, and even in the rich, choked with their own riches. Something like that.

'That clicked with me. I'd thought of being a missionary in Latin America, but instead I started spending my spare time with the down-and-outs around Pioneer Square. Some of them were Mexican – I had my own Latin America right there in Seattle. Hey, d'ya know the phrase skid row came from Seattle? It's where they used to slide the logs down to the water – the down-and-outs hung out there. It was skid road then. Got changed to row later. Before my time, of course.'

'The journalism, Paz. Where did that come in?'

'I'm getting to that. Anyway, I stayed on in the hostel after I graduated, and worked with the down-and-outs. Kept myself by waitressing. I see now it was crazy – I got too emotionally involved, and after a couple of years I was coming close to a breakdown.

'Well, I had done a couple of stories for the *Capitol Hill Express*, mostly about the down-and-outs, and the nuns suggested I try it full-time. Editor took me on, and I did OK.

'Then Jean Simms gave me a reporting job in Eatonville – the *Tribune* – and I spent a couple of good years there. Then I came here to the *Record* – and look at me weaseling back into social work. It's like a drug – I can't stay off it. I only hope I'm more mature this time. Con, I'm talking too much, I know. I'm so scared right now.'

'Scared?'

'All those bears.'

'Oh, those? Forget them, Paz: if there's any out there,

they're more scared than we are. Come on, I'll damp down the fire, and let's go to sleep.'

They stood. 'I'm so scared, Con,' Paz whispered.

He took her in his arms. 'Don't be. Look, I'm here with you. I'll be with you the whole night.' He kissed her gently.

She clung to him. 'Love me, Con. Love me now,' she whispered fiercely.

'But –'

'Don't mind what I said. Just love me. Please love me, Con.' Her voice was shaking.

On the grass, in the flickering firelight, he loved her. She was like a wild thing.

They never saw another bear that summer. Nor did Paz fear them any more: the night by the firelight seemed to have exorcised her terrors. And Con gradually got over his own fright, a fright he had carefully concealed from Paz.

That summer was an idyll. As the weeks went by, they explored more and more of the Olympic Peninsula, doling out precious hoarded vacation days, hiking and camping in the remote valleys of America's last wilderness. It was a time of blue skies, of sunlight filtering through forest leaves so they glowed like stained glass in a green cathedral. It was a time of falling asleep under stars like chandeliers, and of waking to see a blue canopy infinitely far above. It was a time of the water and the wood: the water dancing to sunlight; the wood vibrating to birdsong.

There had been a few rare happy times in Con's life, but in the end Con himself had always pulled the curtain down on them. Con wondered if happiness frightened him too much to bear it for long.

The new needles had not yet darkened on the Douglas firs, but, as the summer waned, so too Con's joy seemed to wane. For a while he could not tell what shadow was creeping into his soul. Paz noticed it, and was troubled. At length she asked Con about it.

'I don't understand it myself,' he told her. 'I think maybe it's this place, this Northwest. It's beginning to get to me. I never thought any place outside Ireland could be so lovely . . .' A wave of his hand took in all of Falls Lake, salmon-pink under the evening sky. They were sitting on the wooden jetty, feet dangling above the water.

'So it's lovely,' Paz said. 'So enjoy. How d'you mean, it gets to you?'

Con pondered. There are times when trying to explain a thing helps you see it clearly yourself.

'Do you remember that old song, "The Scottish Soldier", Paz? It was popular years ago. The soldier wandered far away – can you remember how it goes? Yes –

> For these hills
> Are not highland hills,
> Are not my land's hills . . .
> They are not the hills of home.

Aye, that's it, I think. That's what I'm feeling: these hills are lovely, Paz, but they're not mine.'

'You could make them yours.'

'I could. I think I'm beginning to. And maybe that's what's scaring me. Paz, I've got to see what I'm leaving behind. Or maybe what I left behind years ago, but never let go of. I've drifted for years, you know.'

He turned and looked into her troubled face. 'I need to see Ireland, Paz. Just for a few days. Just to – to get my feelings clear. I could wangle a week off. Make up the days later. That should be enough.

'Besides, I want to visit my father's grave. He died without anyone, you know . . .'

1 7

The farms of Shannon slid below the Boeing, with their stone walls and their quilts of fields in so many shades of green. As the plane banked, Conor Emmet had the momentary illusion that the silver wingtip would scrape the fields far below. Then the white lines of the runway were racing beneath the plane, and there was subdued applause as the wheels bumped gently, then gripped.

Con reached for his tweed fisherman's hat: the hat and the etching of all those years on his face should make him hard to recognise. Hadn't Lincoln said something about a man being responsible for his face after forty? Well, Con could answer for every one of those lines in that horse face of his. He smiled as he reached for his hand luggage and stood to join the people in the aisle.

Funny how people are hushed when they line up to leave a plane. Is it relief at landing? Tension released? People were even whispering. Like in church. Maybe busy with their thoughts – who would meet them, or what would happen during the visit.

Con had a thought or two along those lines. Am I daft to come back? They warned me never to. What if someone does recognise me? Sure, who'd know me now, and me gone all those years?

Maeve would.

But I'm not going near Maeve – even if she's still around. What'd be the point? Specially not now, with Paz back home. Home? Besides, Maeve might bring it all back. All the bad stuff. Maybe even the horrors. No way I'm risking that.

At Immigration a man with an astonishingly pink face gave Con a searching look as he took his US passport. He scrutinised the photo and then took another keen look at Con's face. Con's long body seemed to stoop a bit more. The man leafed through the passport. Then he stamped it, closed it and returned it smartly.

As Con waited for his bag to come up on the carousel, he felt conscious of two things: that people were looking at him, and that everyone had extraordinarily pink faces.

They can't all be looking at me – it's imagination. Stop being paranoid. Never realised the Irish look so pink. Me too? Face browner after the years, maybe. Must check, next time at mirror. As Con's hand reached out to grasp his passing bag, he noticed the hand was pink.

He took the green door at customs and a couple of chatting officials waved him through. Twenty minutes later Con's rented Ford Escort was humming north on the Galway road. 'LINKS FAHREN/CONDUIRE À GAUCHE/DRIVE ON LEFT', the sign had said before he swung the little car onto the main road, and the next half-hour was a confusion of dry lips and damp armpits and cars coming at him on the wrong side. Then it sort of clicked and Con relaxed, almost immediately causing a near accident at a crossroads.

After that he proceeded with less relaxation and considerable caution.

Whatever changes had come to Galway, the pubs had endured.

The Kelpie even smelt like the old days, but the taste was

different when you sat with a glass of Club Orange instead of a pint of thick, rich, black, cream-topped Guinness.

The old longing came back. Well, why not? First evening in Ireland. First chance in years to feel that texture on the tongue. And the tang at the back of the throat after you swallow. A pint, tonight. Just one. Then the wagon tomorrow. Close my eyes: imagine the taste. And the feel of it, the way it goes down.

Get outa here. Now. Con stood abruptly with his glass of orange and went through the door to where he remembered the Kelpie's restaurant. A girl with pink cheeks brought him a menu.

'Just tell me,' Con said, 'd'you still have steak and chips and sautéed onions?'

'We do, to be sure, sir.'

'Bring me lots and lots of everything,' Con said. 'I can see things haven't changed.'

But things had changed, fearsomely, as Con found when the bill came. It was the first hint that the green and lovely island, of easy-going folk with time for fun and enough to live on – the island he remembered – was hurting.

But morning was nostalgic.

Con slept late in the bed-and-breakfast on Newcastle Road, and caught up on jet lag. Even the breakfast was nostalgic, with rasher and eggs and black pudding and Hertrich's sausages, and the tea so rich and sugared and dark and strong you could trot a mouse across it. A meal to do you for the day, which was the idea. And with the mellow burden of that in his belly, Con strolled down the street to the university.

It was strange to walk again by the Gothic cut-stone façade towards the clocktower. He half expected to see Frank Flaherty or Ciaran O'Boyle come out from under the Archway and glance around looking for him. Or Maeve, with the red-gold hair tumbling down her back, resplendent in the corduroy breeches and the high, brown boots, striding smiling towards him.

But nearly twenty years had slid by. The last time he had set eyes on that Gothic archway, with its throng of students, was the morning he had climbed into a car to drive to Dundalk and prepare the raid from which he had never returned.

There was no one around the Archway at all. Of course: it was still the summer recess. But it seemed so lonely. He stood looking at the notices that meant nothing to him, about women's consciousness raising, and Goethe Institut sojourns in Westphalia. Things people had said on that spot came back to him. As when some girl had told him, after a debate speech, 'Y'know, you're the most admired man in the college.' He could almost hear the words vibrating in the air. Or Maeve's words: 'Come riding tomorrow, big fellow?' He could hear them again, there where she had said them.

Two Japanese students, young women – or maybe they were Chinese or Korean – came out from the Archway, gave him a passing glance and strolled toward the college gates. How come these oriental women manage to look so fragile, like porcelain figures? Bet they're far from fragile.

He wandered through the Archway into the quadrangle. Unchanged – the limestone arches of the cloisters, and the grass rectangles still looking slightly hungry, as grass looks when it's imprisoned by buildings.

Con turned towards the cut-stone entrance that led to the Greek Hall, where he had taken part in those debates and delivered his finest speeches. Inside the entrance there was just a row of doors. A young man came out of one of them.

'How do I get into the Greek Hall?' Con asked him.

'The what?'

'The Greek Hall – the big auditorium, right here.'

'It's all offices in there.' The young man paused for a moment. 'You know, I believe it used to be a lecture hall, but that was years ago. It's been offices since before my time. This whole building's all admin.'

'So where do they hold lectures?'

'Up by the river. All those glass buildings.'

'You mean there's a new extension?'

'I wouldn't call it new. Look, why don't you wander over and take a look? Go past the old cafeteria and through the trees. I take it you were here yourself?'

'I was. A while back, though.'

Con strolled through the trees. There, where cows had grazed by the river Corrib, stretched what looked like airport buildings, all modern glass and steel, topped at intervals with multistorey office blocks. A whiff of institutional cooking wafted from somewhere. In a concrete plaza rose an abstract sculpture in steel plate, twice the height of a man. Painted yellow, it made Con think of a company logo.

Con looked, then turned and went back to the street. He felt strangely empty. Thomas Wolfe had been right: you can't go home again.

The next few days Con spent pottering around Galway. Little had changed, except for that domed monstrosity of a new cathedral, which they told him in a pub was nicknamed the Taj Mícheál, after Bishop Mícheál Browne who had built it.

He wandered past Nora Croobs', and saw the high old house bricked up and waiting for demolition. He went down along the Claddagh and looked across the water to the line of little houses beyond the Spanish Arch. They had been grey then: now their rainbow colours danced on the river. A pair of swans moved over the water.

On the morning of his last day in Galway, Con checked out of the guesthouse and drove into Connemara. The day was warm but cloudy, with a hint of autumn. On the way to Inveran, he thought of the bridle path where he and Maeve had trekked with the horses for the last time. He parked the car, took off across the fields, and met the path almost at the spot where they had taken off their clothes to swim.

The sky was grey this time: it had been blue then. No

gorse bloomed. The tide was out, revealing brown, undulating seaweed and viciously sharp rocks. We could've killed ourselves on those rocks, was all Con could think. He turned to walk back to the car.

He drove to Clifden, returning through Kylemore and Leenane. The sun came out as he drove along the Maam Valley. At Maam Bridge he stopped. The heather was in bloom, and the hills were as purple as ever Paul Henry had painted them. Con leaned on the stone parapet, gazing down at the dark water like polished Kilkenny black marble. Flecks of foam moved across the smoothness.

Why does this loveliness hurt me so? Con found himself wondering. Perhaps if Paz were with me . . . ? No, she'd be lost here. This – this is something in my own soul. 'For these hills are not my land's hills.' But they are. I'm Irish and they belong to me.

No they don't. I'm an exile: I haven't even the right to stand on this bridge. They could shoot me for it. Oh dear God, I don't belong here any more. And I don't belong over there . . .

'Where in the name of Christ do I belong?'

He spoke the last words aloud. As if in answer, a trout broke the water, flashed silver and arced back into the dark surface. The flecks of foam wavered as the ripples widened across the stream.

Con turned away, climbed into the car, and drove non-stop the 158 miles to Newry. It was dark when he reached the border checkpoint, and no one bothered to halt him. It was after 10 p.m. when he rang the bell of the Iona guesthouse in Newry's Bridge Street.

Next morning, as he walked the few hundred yards to Chapel Street cemetery, the bleakness of Newry shocked him. His home town come to this. Gaping holes where he remembered busy shops. The gutted pub on the corner of Kilmurray Street. The six-wheeled armoured cars moaning through the streets.

The arrogance of the helmeted young soldiers who frisked him at a barricade. Maybe nervousness, not arrogance. They did not look that different from the young men at the street corners with hatred in their eyes, who spat when an army patrol passed.

God's curse on those who had set them apart. But who had? British politicians? Ulster unionists? Catholic bishops? Religious leaders?

Or men long dead?

Con pushed open the wrought-iron gate in the cemetery wall. He stood contemplating the rows of graves, with their tottering Celtic crosses and statues green with damp.

Men long dead.

Are we prisoners of the dead, of those who long ago established things so they still control our lives? Those who sowed the hatreds that still poison us? Those who created this pernicious system, with its built-in guarantee that people go on hating and killing? Are we their marionettes, dancing on strings from hell?

Con realised he was wandering aimlessly among the graves. This way he'd never find his father. He walked back and tapped on the sacristy door. An elderly verger checked a leather-bound volume, and gave him directions to his father's grave.

The Emmet plot was in an overgrown spot halfway down the hill that slopes to the Warrenpoint Road. A weatherworn, granite Celtic cross tilted above the pebble-covered plot. The once-white pebbles were greenish. Names of grandparents and of forebears were partly decipherable. Below them was the name of Margaret Emmet, and the date of her death. It was the same date as that of Con's birth.

More recently cut, but already weatherworn, were the words: ROBERT HUGH EMMET, MD. Dates of birth and death. Nothing else.

A wonder there was enough money to carve the name. The old man had left almost nothing. Whatever fees he got from the health service seem to have been spent on his poorer patients.

Con stayed a while. Memories of a kindly, shy old man, but little emotion. He tried a brief prayer, and hoped it was heard somewhere. Again Joyce's words seemed to console: 'O father forsaken, forgive your son.'

There lay all his kin. In Con's own land, no living relative. But then it wasn't his land any more.

Con turned and walked through the gate to Chapel Street. Ten minutes later he was sitting in his car, his bags on the seat beside him. One more errand: one short route to retrace. How's this you get to Edward Street and Corry Square? Ah yes, up to Dominick Street, over by Monaghan Street and turn right.

And there it was again, the red-brick façade of the police barracks, rising above the sandbags and barbed wire that now surrounded it.

Cruise slowly past, careful now over that ramp – up, and over; back wheels up, and over – hadn't been there that night, and just as well.

The little car passed the barracks and went down Edward Street. It turned right along the canal, right again up Bridge Street, and purred up the long hill towards Dundalk. At the top of the hill, where Cloughogue Church rears its blunt Romanesque tower and the road turns right under the railway bridge, Con swung the car left onto a side road, lined with stone walls like those in Connemara.

Well, at least it's ashphalted now, Con thought. Maybe it was then? No, sure don't I remember the van bumping all over the place that night? And me worried sick about Ciaran lying in the back – not that it mattered to poor Ciaran. Strange how I'm thinking about it without trying to block it.

And I'm actually driving the road again.

It was a grey day, not cold. The fields with their stone walls fell gradually away to the left of the road, yielding a panorama of river and canal and road far below, running through a spacious valley. Down there a couple of tiny cars moved silently along. Going to Warrenpoint. Not a car up here but my own.

Now the fir trees were on either side of the road, getting thicker and taller and blotting out the view. Glimpses of ferns beyond the little stony walls, and darkness under the trees.

Never realised how like the Pacific Northwest parts of Ireland can be. Except, the trees are taller over there, and there'd be no stone walls.

These little walls – so much a part of Ireland. I hid behind one that night, didn't I? There. I'm actually thinking about it. Thinking about the details, and not dying inside. No horrors: none at all. Was that why I came back? To exorcise the demon?

But I haven't reached the spot yet. See how I feel then.

Isn't there something about murderers coming back to the scene of the crime? What in the name of Jesus am I doing here?

Abruptly the forest fell away to the left of the road, and a vista of Carlingford Lough opened out, as though curtains had slid back from a Cinemascope screen. A thousand feet below was the gorge of Narrow Water, guarded by its Norman keep. From there the waters widened into the gunmetal expanse of the lough, which merged into sky at the horizon. Here and there a white wave glinted and was gone. Two mountains stood sentinel, one on either side of the lough. On the left, Killowen Mountain, most southerly of the Mournes, swept gracefully to the sea. On the right was volcano-shaped Carlingford Mountain, called Cooley on the maps. At the left of the panorama, the distant spires of Warrenpoint were like two needles, and you could see a gleam of buildings along the seafront. They'd be the old Victorian guesthouses. On the horizon a faint pencil line ran out from the Carlingford side. That would be Greenore: must be a good ten miles away.

And just ten feet away, the wall where Conor Emmet had machinegunned three young people to death.

He sat in the car, looking. He uncoiled himself from the seat and walked across to the wall. It was made of loose rounded stones, piled one upon the other. It seemed smaller, lower, than Con remembered. How had he managed to crouch behind it? Probably hadn't hidden him very well, but then it had been night. But wasn't there a moon? Or was there?

The wall had hidden him and that was that. They just weren't expecting him to come up from behind it.

There, I'm facing it. I'm actually reliving it. His eyes moved across the road. The car would have been – where? Just beyond where mine is parked.

He tried to think of the girl. He could not. Yet he was not blocking anything. He felt no grief, no anguish. Just emptiness. He thought of the two young men he had destroyed, and it was the same. The memories and the emotions were as dead as the three young people who lay in their graves somewhere near here.

Max had been right: the only meaning in it now was to leave them to God. A mist had come down on the lough, blotting out the mountains and merging sea and sky in an eternity of grey. '*Agnus Dei*,' Con found himself murmuring, '*qui tollis peccata mundi, dona eis requiem*. Lamb of God, who takest away the sins of the world, grant them rest. And grant me peace.'

He sat on the wall where he had sat that night so many years ago. Empty pipe in mouth, he gazed out over the empty lough, with a mind empty of thought, and hearing only the cry of a seagull and the distant sound of a vehicle ascending the road from the direction of the border.

The sound of the approaching vehicle grew slowly louder, and Con could hear the gears grind as it rounded a corner on the upward road. He sat on the wall, listening.

The vehicle came into view – a military-type Land Rover. It came slowly up the hill towards him, and Con could see dark uniforms in the front seats. The vehicle passed him by, then stopped.

A policeman stepped down from either side, each with a sub-machine-gun. He suddenly had a sickening sense of *déjà vu*.

Motioning with their guns, the policemen moved Con across to his car, spreadeagled him against it, and searched him. For an idiotic instant he thought they were going to charge him with what he had done on this spot all those years ago.

'Awright, Misther. Just turn around now.'

Con turned, letting his hands down to his sides, but carefully. The guns were pointed at his navel.

'Thon's a Free State kyarr. From Limerick. Whaddya doin' up here?' It was the clipped, northern sound.

'I rented it at Shannon Airport,' Con said.

'You're a Yank, be the sound of it?'

'I'm a US citizen, yes.'

'Show us your passport. And the hire papers for the kyarr.'

Con gestured questioningly towards the glove box, and the taller policeman nodded. 'Get them,' he said.

The taller one thumbed through the passport. Blond hair peeped from under the dark, peaked cap with the silver harp and crown on it. Both looked terribly young, almost as young as the two that – that I murdered here, Con thought.

'You were born in Ireland.' A statement. 'Where?'

'Newry. Emigrated years ago. Came back to visit my father's grave.'

A pause. 'Emmet's a Papish name.'

Another pause. The tall one was about Con's height. His young blue eyes held Con's. Gloved fingers tapped the passport. Then: 'Y'naver told us what y'came up here for.'

'The view. I've been around the world, and I've never seen its like. It's one of the things I came back to see. Look at it, lads – look at it there with the mist coming up off the lough. Did y'ever see the like?'

The three men stood together and gazed over Carlingford Lough, where the tops of the sentinel mountains were just now emerging from the mist. Their flanks were so clear and so textured you could almost reach out and run your hand over them. A shaft of sunlight broke through to caress Killowen Mountain. They gazed in silence.

We're looking at our birthright, thought Con. We're simply Irishmen looking at our birthright. His throat tightened.

The tall policeman turned to Con and handed him his passport, with the car rental paper folded into it. 'We'll be off now, sir,' he said, almost gently. 'Have a right nice holiday.' The men climbed into the Land Rover and drove off slowly. A minute later it had disappeared around the tree-lined curve.

A breeze had come up and Con shivered. All of a sudden he knew what he wanted to do.

I must see her. Said I wouldn't, but I've got to. It's my last night. Bugger the Movement. I'm not leaving without seeing her. But I don't even have her address. Or number.

Wait. I can make Dublin in two hours. Get hold of the phone book and ring all the Flahertys. All the Franks anyway. Can't be that many. But wasn't it unlisted years ago? Unless she'd be under Halloran. Can try.

The car bounced down the road towards the border, the vista dwindling as the road dropped. Con swung right where a sign said 'DUNDALK 12 MILES', and soon rejoined the main road. Nobody bothered to stop him at either customs post. A garda waved him on when he slowed at the Irish side.

Con drove fast towards Dublin.

'Doctor Halloran speaking.' The voice was quiet, assured.

'Maeve. This is Con. Conor Emmet.'

'Who?'

'Conor Emmet. You – do remember?'

'He's dead. Con's dead. Jesus Christ Almighty, he's dead.'

'Maeve. It's me. Really it is.'

'You're dead. You're – you're supposed to be dead. They said you were dead.' A silence. 'Oh Con, is it – you?'

''Tis, Maeve. The selfsame. Somebody musta been exaggerating – about my death, I mean.'

'Just – give me a minute, Con. I need – to get used to this.' Con could hear Maeve breathe. Then what sounded like weeping. He waited.

'Con. Where are you?'

'I'm here in Dublin. North Circular Road. Park Hotel, beside the Phoenix Park Gate.'

'Stay right there, and give me five, ten minutes. I'm only a couple of streets away. Just – don't disappear again. Promise?'

'I promise. Just you hurry.' The phone clicked off.

Among the sixty or so Flahertys in the telephone book, only one had the initial F. The man who answered had never heard of any Maeve. Finally Con had checked the *Golden Pages* under 'Doctors, Medical' and found Halloran, M.K., MB.

She evidently believed he was dead. How in God's name did that story get around? Where's my pipe? Did I leave it in the car? Ah no, here it is. He pulled the pipe apart and blew through the stem.

Maeve was standing in front of him, a vision in cream and gold. 'Oh Maeve,' Con said, and they were in each other's arms. She even smelt of the same violety perfume. He could feel her heart beat. Or maybe both their hearts.

After a while Con gently pushed her from him and stepped back, holding her by the fingertips, to look at her. She stood there smiling, but the eyes showed she had wept. Yet he could see how lightly the years had touched her.

The hair was short now, and curled in around her face. It gleamed in the light of the foyer, sort of burnished. Nary a grey hair. Tiny gold earrings glinted. The breasts were high under a tight cream rollneck sweater. She wore deep beige corduroy jodhpurs, loose at the thighs and tapering at the knees to slide inside soft brown boots.

'Still riding the horses?' Con asked.

'Very little. I hardly have time. Oh, you mean the pants? No, we call these fashion jodhpurs. Nothing to do with horses.'

His eyes came back to Maeve's face. A couple of crinkles at the edge of the eyes were the only changes, and he could see they came from smiling. She must smile a lot. She was smiling now.

'So how's Frank?' Con said.

Sadness chased the smile, as cloud shadows chase across a meadow. 'Frank's dead. You never heard? No, of course, how could you? Frank's dead these three years.'

Con sat down. He motioned for Maeve to sit. 'What in God's name was it?'

'The Brits got him. Frank stayed with the Movement, as

you might guess. Well, he went up to Belfast to brief a local group, and the Brits raided the house. They put Frank in Long Kesh – that's their concentration camp. Of course they call it an internment camp, but it's the same thing.

'They took him off to some interrogation centre. Hooded him for days on end. Kept him in total silence. Then deafened him with noise. Put him in a cell so tiny he couldn't stand up or lie down. Kept him awake for days with lights and noise. Threw him out of a helicopter blindfolded – only a few feet from the ground. It's one of the cases gone to the European Court. In the end it was his heart. Just gave out.'

'Maeve, I never knew.'

'Och, I'm over it now.' The voice was matter-of-fact. 'Not over it – living with it. Took me a while, I can tell you. We never had children. Did you know that? Sometimes now I wish we did.'

Con saw the eyes filling up with tears. He reached over to touch her arm, but she shook her head. Then suddenly her chest was heaving and she was sobbing uncontrollably.

Con moved over beside her, and put his arm around her shoulders. He said nothing, but let her weep her fill.

At length Maeve grew quiet. She seemed to take control of herself again, and turned to look at Con. 'I'm used to Frank being dead, Con,' she said. 'But by Christ I'm not used to Conor Emmet being alive. Wait – tell you what. You're checked in here? I'll get you out of that – they won't mind. You'll stay at my place: it's only a few streets away.'

Maeve's brass plate was set into an old-fashioned door with polished brass letter box and knocker. It was a red-brick two-storey artisan's dwelling. Late Victorian.

'Frank and I bought the house just before they got fashionable,' Maeve said. 'Now they cost a bomb. But there's lots of the real old Dubs still around, and they won't sell at any price. A lot are my patients: they're a breed unto themselves. That's the surgery, left of the door. Used to be the parlour. It's gin-and-tonic or nothing, I'm afraid, or a cuppa tea. Tea? OK. Come in the kitchen and talk to me while I'm making it. I want to hear your story, right from the start.'

Con told his story, with its highs and lows, sparing her nothing.

They carried in the tea, and a gin and tonic for Maeve, to the tiny living room. Maeve sat on the sofa, legs curled under her, hands cupped around her glass, leaning forward, nodding occasionally.

Yes, she said, they had seen some of Con's columns – people in the States used occasionally send clippings. But not for years now. She had heard about Con's marriage and the death of his bride.

Con told about hitting skid row. 'I suppose I sort of went off the radar screen for everybody,' he observed. It must have been around that time, they agreed, that people got the notion that Con was dead. He had been, in a way.

Con told about Momma and her dogs and the job at the paper, and Max and the fishing and the chess.

'So what's next?' Maeve asked.

'Nothing's next. It's Rainhaven for me, for the foreseeable future.'

'But what are you doing with your life, Con?'

'What am I doing? Y'know, you remind me of somebody I work with. What I'm doing is achieving tranquillity, as far as a newspaperman can. Staying sober. Licking my wounds, maybe. Not caring too much about anything.'

'Don't you want to achieve something more than tranquillity?'

'Dammit you do remind me of someone back at the office.' Con's voice rose. 'Why do people always want me to achieve? I've achieved enough, aye, and unachieved it again, if there's such a word. As for doing something for the underdog, there's lots of them right where I live, with Mexican names, slaving away in the forests, selling their souls to the company store just like the bad old days.'

And he told Maeve about the migrants, about the dirt wages and the hovels and the cheating and the chain saws, and the slavery of debt and the disappearances.

'And you're doing something about it?'

'Well, yes. We're, uh, preparing a couple of articles that will expose some of this.'

'You've changed, Conor Emmet. Well, I don't know – maybe that's the right way for there. But you know what we say here? The Armalite and the ballot box. Persuade and communicate, but everybody knows the guns are there. It's the only way with the Brits. God, I wish the Movement had you back. Someone that could communicate like you can – God, what we couldn't do with you.'

'Maeve, am I in danger here? I'm banned from Ireland, you know. Meeting you put it out of my mind. Will there be trouble that I called to see you? Could anyone know? I've even been wearing this hat to look different.'

Maeve leaned back with her hands behind her head, stretched out her booted legs and laughed until the tears ran. 'Oh, that's powerful, that's too good entirely,' she said, and started to laugh again.

'What's so goddam funny?'

'Sorry for laughing, Con. Don't know why. Maybe it's just relief at finding you alive. I'm laughing at the thought of you peeping over your shoulder and wearing your hat over your eyes.' She got another fit of laughing.

'Fact is, they've forgotten you years ago. Sure didn't they think you were dead? Nobody would even remember what you did. Anyhow it's a new scene here – that sort of thing happens every day now, whether we like it or not. The lads would welcome you with open arms. You'd be the long-lost brother. Really.'

'Well, I declare to God. That sure is good news. You know, I nearly didn't contact you. You can't imagine what a relief this is.'

He stood up in the tiny room. 'Y'know, I really have been

wearing this hat over my eyes, just as you said. And my dark glasses too, sometimes. Hey, how does this look?'

Con grabbed his tweed hat and pulled it down. He took sunglasses from a pocket and placed them on his nose, and turned his collar up around his ears. He hunched his shoulders. 'Would yih say I'm furtive enough for the good of me health, doctor?' he said in a hoarse stage whisper.

'I'd say you'd just about do, my good man,' Maeve said, grinning. 'Only couldn't you do something about that awfully long nose?'

They laughed, and Con threw himself on the sofa with a sigh. 'Well it's good to find I'm not on the run, I can tell you that,' he said.

Maeve turned her gaze on him. 'It's a good job you aren't, Con. There's no way you could ever make that old hatchet face into anything else.'

She leaned over and kissed his cheek.

He put a hand on her knee. 'That'll do about me,' he said. 'How about the story of Doctor Halloran?'

'There isn't much to tell, really. I'm still with the Movement, of course. I've always been on the political side – they can't touch us here in Dublin, though everybody knows we're just the front for the lads with the guns.

'I never stopped working with the Movement, even after they got you out of the country. You know, of course, Frank was the only one to survive the raid, besides yourself? They say now the raid was totally inept. It was that girl who got shot at the Flagstaff that nearly finished the Movement. Oh Con, I didn't mean to –'

'No, it's time somebody filled me in.' Con was pushing tobacco into his pipe. 'Maybe I know most of it, but tell me just in case. I think I can face it – though for years I couldn't.'

'Well, after you ... after that girl got shot – she was a Newry girl, name of Prunty, did you know? and she'd left home after a row, and was staying with friends – anyway, after she got shot, the Dublin government really cracked down. The Taoiseach went on the wireless and said all the usual rubbish about a Christian nation not tolerating such carry on – you can imagine. I remember he ended with Good Night, and we all called it the Good Night Speech.

'It was pretty well goodnight for us. We didn't have much support at the time, but we had bloody well none after that. The Movement hibernated for years. Almost no support, north or south.'

The doorbell rang, a pleasant chime. Maeve went to answer it. Con could hear a woman's worried tones, then a child's piping voice. The surgery door closed and there was only a murmur. It opened again after a few minutes, and he could hear the woman's 'Thanks awfully, doctor. Goodnight now, doctor.'

He heard Maeve say, 'Bring him back in the morning if he's not all right. Goodnight now.'

Maeve came back in, then went to the kitchen to pour another drink. 'Nothing for me,' Con said. She came back to the sofa.

'You know of course how it started again, in the late sixties? Did you know it was Martin Luther King and that Selma thing that started civil rights in the North of Ireland?

'Imagine, Con, an American Baptist preacher as hero for Irish Catholics! We even sang "We Shall Overcome" on the marches. We were marching against all the old things, like discrimination in jobs and housing, and the way the elections were gerrymandered. One of the chants was 'one man, one vote'.

'And, as you might expect, those thick police, with their Brit cousins, started moving in on the marches. They beat some of the marchers to pulp – there's TV footage that went round the world. Then they started killing: on one occasion soldiers killed thirteen unarmed marchers. And again it was the TV let the cat out of the bag.

'Dublin of course huffed and puffed, and the Taoiseach here said he wouldn't stand idly by, but sure what could he do against the might of England? So when the people found nobody would stand up for them, they turned to us, to the Movement. And we had been waiting our time.

'That's about it, Con. We grew stronger and stronger, mostly due to the Brits' stupidity. And now our aim is Brits out. That simple. Their soldiers out; their pinstripe ponces out. Get rid of the Brits, then we'll see what comes next.'

'But the killing, Maeve. There has to be another way.'

'There isn't, Con. Not with Britain. Wherever they were kicked out from around the world – Aden, Cyprus, Malaya, you name it – they stayed and stayed until the killing got intolerable. Only then did they quit. That's their rules for the game. Try any other way – talking, negotiating – and they laugh. They force us into force.'

'Maeve, you're talking to someone did the killing. I'm not your ordinary listener. And I'm telling you there has to be another way. The agony's too much. It only starts the day of a killing. But it lasts a lifetime: long after the reasons for killing are forgotten. Not just for the families left behind: it's worst of all for the men that do the killing. Theirs is the real hell: it starts instantly, and it's forever. I know.

'Maeve, you say you want the Brits out. But at least they're preventing some of that killing. If they left, both sides would slaughter each other. At least the soldiers keep them apart.'

'Why not UN troops? It's one option, if not a likely one. But you're right – it could be civil war. And you could have the South sending up troops to protect the nationalists, and the whole island could go up.' She leaned forward. 'But Con, that mightn't be such a bad thing. The fight has to come, so get it over with. Clear the air. Clear out that pathetic Southern government while we're at it, and make a whole new start with some sort of people's republic.'

Con put his head in his hands. 'Maeve, I don't think you have an inkling of what civil war is. It is quite literally the most horrific conceivable thing that can happen to any human group. It is the world's worst evil; brotherhood turned inside out. Everything human reversed. So it's not a couple of thousand dead like in Northern Ireland in nine years – it's fifty thousand a month until the population's halved. It's towns razed and every male massacred and every woman raped and then bayoneted – by Irishmen. It is loathing grown to satanic levels. Read Hemingway, about Spain. Ronda. It means machinegunning twelve-year-olds like in Lebanon. Disembowelling young girls for a photo, like in Algeria. It means the country never recovering, I mean never – not in five hundred years. It means dictators, terror –'

'Con. Con. Will you stop it, for Christ's sake. Do you think I don't worry about such things? Do you think I like killing? Do you think I don't wake up at night crying over what happened to Frank? Do you think it's easy? Listen, don't you forget what this is all about . . .' Maeve gave a sigh. Her voice softened. 'Look, forget what I said. I was just – wondering out loud, anyway. Sure, who knows what will be next? Nuclear war's a lot more likely anyway, and then we'll have no problems at all.'

There was a pause. 'I'll tell you one thing,' Maeve said. 'If you were here you could be working to head off a catastrophe like that. There'd be a place for you on the Movement's political side. You could be a journalist on the *Press* or the *Times*, with a lot of influence. And no one need ever know you were with us.

'Tell you what, Con. Tomorrow evening there's a couple of people I'd like you to meet. No, not from the Movement – just a couple of media types.'

'Maeve. I'm leaving tomorrow. I'm on the midday flight out of Dublin. To New York. Didn't I tell you?'

She stared at him. 'But sure – but – Conor Emmet, don't do this to me. You come back from the dead; you walk into my life, just like that. And not twelve hours later you're going to walk right out again? No way. What in hell are you playing at?' Her eyes filled up with tears.

She stood up. 'Con. Don't do this to me,' she pleaded. 'Can't you get another flight?'

He stood to face her, and put gentle hands on her shoulders. 'It's APEX: they won't change it. But that's not the point. The point is I stand to lose my job if I don't get back on time. I've a boss would fire me at the drop of a hat, and there's no union to back me up. And I won't get another job. Not like the one I have now.'

Maeve was silent for some moments. 'Will you be back?'

'Of course I'll be back. Now I know I don't have to hide. Sure I can come and go as I please, now.' He laughed. 'All I need is money.' His hands gripped her shoulders. 'Maeve. Darling Maeve. This isn't goodbye. In fact it's only hello. Don't you understand that?'

Maeve smiled and wiped away a tear. Con saw now how those crinkles functioned – those little smile crinkles at the edge of the eyes.

They stood there, literally at arms' length, gazing at one another. Then Con drew her shoulders towards him and they were in each other's arms. Maeve's arms went around his waist and the burnished head nestled in against his chest. They rocked from side to side. Maeve looked up and her mouth opened slightly to receive Con's.

He could feel her heart thumping. Then her tongue came probing.

1 9

On Saturday Paz and Max were at Seatac Airport to meet Con. It did not go splendidly.

Con was tired when he came off the DC-10 – there had been a long wait to change planes at New York, and he had had little sleep and a lot of cramp, jackknifed in the narrow seat. Even before they reached the car, Paz said, 'Did anything happen over there, Con?'

'How d'you mean?'

'Something's not the same. What happened?'

'Willya lay off, Paz,' Con said irritably, 'Nothing happened over there. I've got a dose of jet lag. And a cold as well. Now willya lay off?'

There was little talk during the drive down Highway Five. Paz drove in mournful silence and Max, never one for small talk, sat up front with her. Con stretched himself as best he could in the back seat of the old Falcon and fell asleep.

The car scrunching across the gravel wakened him. He unravelled his cramped limbs, rummaged for his keys, then remembered he had left them with Paz. She handed him his bags and opened the apartment door.

'I put the heating on, Con, and there's stuff in the fridge

for tomorrow. I'll take Max home. I know you're tired and you'll want to sleep now.'

'You don't mind? I really am flattened. Look, tomorrow's Sunday – we've all day.'

'I can't, Con. I have to go to Seattle on a story. You sleep all you can tomorrow. Best way to beat jet leg.'

'See you Monday, so.' He kissed her on the cheek, noticing the pained look in her eyes, but was too tired to think about it. 'Bye Max. Thanks for coming. See you both Monday.'

But Paz wasn't there on the Monday. Shinn said there was some lead in Seattle she needed to follow, and she had weaseled a week's leave out of Kane so she could stay on there. Con felt momentarily hurt that she hadn't rung to tell him. But it was a snap decision, he told himself, and she wouldn't have wanted to disturb him when he was sleeping off the jet lag. She'd ring later.

She did ring that afternoon, and was concerned about his cold and his jet lag. She was sorry to be away so soon after he got back, but she was on to a good lead. 'See you next Monday, then,' she promised.

With Paz away, Con found his mind turning to Ireland. For years he had erased it from his thoughts. Now it existed again: he could go there when he wanted.

Images floated into his imagination: a green laneway with cart tracks in the grass, and the yellow gorse tumbling over the stone walls; a cottage above Lough Corrib, with those hundreds of islands fading into the blue distance; Carlingford Mountain rearing out of the mist. Sometimes Maeve's face floated among the images, but the face was more symbol than person, just as those scenes were tokens of Ireland rather than real places where people walked and sun shone and rain fell.

Con thought he understood what was happening: an exile realising his native land was no longer barred to him, and the exquisite relief that brought. One made up for the lost years by the intensity and abandon of one's vision. It was good to know that life in Ireland was again an option. Not indeed that I'd want to, he told himself, with all I've got here. Especially Paz. But it's good to know Ireland is back where it used to be. There, if I want it.

So it was understandable that when Con sat down to his column for Saturday's paper, he should write about Ireland. Or rather, about Northern Ireland, as he had just read a half-assed editorial in the Seattle *Times* which referred to 'the religious war in Northern Ireland'.

So Con headed his column, 'DO CATHOLICS FIGHT PROTESTANTS IN IRELAND?' He led by saying the vast majority of the Irish were not fighting about anything:

> The Republic, which is four-fifths of the island, has been Europe's most peaceful country in the past half-century. It was not even *in* World War Two. So peaceful, indeed, that Germans and French flock there to get away from it all.

He explained that in the other one-fifth of the island, called Northern Ireland, less than one per cent of people were even remotely connected with any fighting.

> And the fighting is not between Protestants and Catholics, but between descendants of colonists and natives, like the fight that goes on wherever Britain has tried to plant its flag.

Con explained to his US readers how, three hundred years before, in an effort to subdue the rebellious northern part of the island, the colonising English government threw the natives off their land and homesteaded thousands of English and Scots settlers on the confiscated farms.

> In previous 'plantations' of this kind, the colonists had always ended by marrying the natives, thus frustrating

the divide-and-conquer policy. But not this time: the Reformation meant colonists and natives would no longer intermarry, because their religions were different.

It was a godsend in keeping the two sides apart.

And whenever the sides started to come together, the English government fomented religious bigotry to set one side against the other, on the principle of divide and conquer.

Finally the English government succeeded so well that the two groups were identified as Protestant and Catholic, instead of colonist and native. To this day the children of each group learn at separate schools, and, quite incredibly, the clergy of both groups want it kept that way.

But, said Con, each group desperately needs the other. An island people can grow inbred. In previous centuries, it was the recurrent invasions – Dé Danaann, Formorians, Firbolgs, Celts, Vikings, Normans, English, Scots – that kept Ireland healthy. However uncomfortable they were, those invasions brought desperately needed new blood, once the marrying started, which was usually sooner than later.

But this time, the invaders have remained an undigested lump. Yet we native Irish need them. We need their blood, we need their genes, to renew the Irish people.

And by God they need us: they've been marrying their own kind now for 300 years.

We need each other's cultures too: the settlers could do with the native Irish creativity in word and song, and we natives could benefit from their hard-working Protestant ethic.

Can you imagine, Con asked his readers, what a brilliant Irish nation would evolve from two such splendid peoples?

But they are kept apart, through killings by extremists

on both sides, but worse still, by churchmen of both sides, who will not even let children of different faiths share a school. The churchmen fear the children would grow to trust each other, and would then intermarry.

Which is precisely what would happen. And is precisely what Ireland needs. But churchmen of both sides prevent it, because it would weaken their churches and they would lose power and control. And especially money.

So it's still divide and conquer, but now it's our own people doing it to us – our churchmen.

Meanwhile, back at the barricades, the fighting goes on. It used to be one side wanting to unite with the southern Republic, and the other side wanting to return to the good old days of colonial rule, backed by Britain. But now it's just killing for killing's sake.

Indeed only one thing is still clear – that whatever the extremists are fighting about, it isn't religion.

There was more, but it was the colonist–native concept that clicked with readers. From the phone calls it seemed it was the first time many Americans had seen Northern Ireland in terms they could understand.

Although it contained nothing new, the column created a mini-sensation in the *Record*'s circulation area.

It was fishing and chess with Max that weekend. 'Like the old days,' Max said with a smile. 'Like the days before Anna. But do not languish, Conor. Your Anna will soon be back.'

Paz was not at her desk on Monday morning, and somebody said she was not back from Seattle. Con felt bothered that he had heard so little from her in the last few days.

While he was scrolling through a list of Associated Press stories on his computer screen, he noticed the catchline IRISH WAR. He called it up on screen: it was his Northern Ireland piece from Saturday's paper, with his byline. AP had evidently decided to run it nationwide, maybe even worldwide. Why not? Con thought. Maybe it'll clear up some of that confusion I find everywhere.

Con felt lonely all day. That evening, cooking supper alone, he willed Paz to call him, since he had no number for her in Seattle. Finally she did, but neither of them had much to say. And Paz's voice seemed sort of – small. I'll be back tomorrow, she said.

Next day, just before deadline, she was at her desk. When Con saw her tidying up around midday he sauntered across, hands in pockets. 'How about a bite of lunch?' he asked.

Paz shrugged. 'Why not?' she replied in the small voice. Jeez, she even looks small, Con thought. Sort of mousey.

He sat on the desk, watching her put her papers in various drawers and locking them. 'What's wrong, Paz?' he asked.

'What happened over there, Con?'

'Over where?'

'In Ireland. You know what I mean.'

'Whaddya mean, what happened?'

'Was there – is there a woman over there?'

'No.'

There was silence for a few moments. Then Paz gave a decisive nod. 'Let's go,' she said.

There was silence in the car on the way to Rosita's. Not tense, just people occupied with their thoughts.

They ordered *huevos rancheros* from Rosita, who gave them a searching look. While they were waiting, Con broke the silence.

'Can I take something back, Paz?'

She nodded.

'I said there was no woman. Well, there is one.'

Paz nodded, studying the tablecloth.

'This woman, she's called Cathleen Ni Houlihan. Sometimes we call her Róisín Dubh – Dark Rosaleen, in English. There's even poems about her, but you mightn't much want to hear one. And I've been in love with her for a long time. Still am, I suppose.'

Paz looked up. 'So this Cathleen Ni – whatever. When did she pop up? You never as much as hinted at her before.'

'She's always been there. She was around before I was born. And she'll be around when I'm dead and gone. There'll be thousands like me in love with her then, as there are thousands now. She's forever.'

Paz gazed at him, eyes dark and wide. There was silence for a moment.

'This Cathleen Ni What's-her-name,' Paz said. 'I think I understand. She's your country, OK? It's Ireland that's got a hold on you. That's what you're trying to tell me. OK?'

'It is surely what I'm trying to tell you. Look, bear with me a while. I'm one of those who were sent to walk hard streets in far countries. For years and years Ireland was out – didn't exist for me. Now it does. That takes getting used to. I've just been there, and I keep thinking about it.'

'You wanna go back there?'

'This is where I belong. Here, with all this.' Con gestured vaguely at the evergreens beyond the window. 'But I need time.'

'Just don't take forever, Con Emmet.'

Con reached across the table and took her hand. The food came and they started to eat. Paz looked up at Con. 'Can I ask you one more thing, Con?'

'To be sure.'

'Y'won't get mad?'

'Try me.'

'So, OK about this, uh, Cathleen What's-her-name. But, well, was there any other woman, y'know, a real flesh'n'blood one, while you were over there?'

Con looked into the dark eyes. 'Promise you'll believe what I'm going to tell you. Promise? Right. Yes, there was another woman. A woman I once loved, many, many years ago. So long ago, she thought I was dead. Well, I saw her again – and

I can tell you for certain I do not love her. Love doesn't survive nearly twenty years and my presumed death, and then just revive like that. And that's what I meant when I said there was no woman. Please don't ask me more. Just take my word: I do not love her. Right?'

'Honest Injun?'

'Honest Injun. Or better still, as they say in Ireland, cross me heart and cut me throat and hope to die.'

Paz smiled gently. 'I believe you, even if thousands wouldn't. Isn't that an Irish saying, too?'

'Indeed it is, Anna dear. By the way, just to get some balance into this, do you know what James Joyce called Ireland?'

'What?'

'Well, he didn't call her Cathleen Ni Houlihan, that's for sure. He called her The Old Sow that Eats her Young!'

20

As usual, Friday had been a heavy day at the paper, with everyone scrambling to get the weekend sections finished. Afterwards Max went with Con to unwind by the seashore. Paz was away in Tahola, digging out some salmon fishing story.

The day-long rain had ceased, and a watery sunset was trying to arrange itself in the western sky. The two figures were imprinting the only footprints on the rain-textured sands beyond the airfield.

A flock of tiny birds whirred past and disappeared towards the breakers that curled in the fading light.

The boots splashed across flowing water where a stream had etched its meandering into the sand.

Between men and dunes lay the driftwood, acres of ivory-pale, sea-bleached, writhing tree limbs, beseeching humanoid shapes in the twilight, forest skeletons washed down the rivers of Oregon and Washington, picked clean by the claws and teeth of the waves, then tossed back to whiten under the sun and the rain. The water and the wood: blood and sinew of the Northwest.

'It is like a graveyard of the gods,' Max said. 'No, not so.

I know what it is. It is that battlefield in the Bible, which Isaiah saw in a dream. You remember? The bones lay scattered over the valley, dry bones. Then the Lord spoke and the bones came together, each with the other. He spoke again and flesh grew upon the bones. And he spoke once more and they came to life and stood up, a mighty army. Look around you, Conor. Cannot you see these great bones even now moving in the twilight? Soon an army to challenge you, or perhaps to follow where you command.'

'Except that I've done with armies, Max. Know what, though? I got a letter this morning from an old comrade – from the old fighting days in Ireland.'

'It is this report you wrote? I have been hearing of the letters that are reaching your desk from all over the world.'

'Incredible, isn't it? A piece with nothing original: AP puts it on the wire, and it takes off. Herb Paterson called me from AP in Seattle: listed me some of the papers round the world that ran the piece, or ran a translation. Like *Asahi Shimbun* in Tokyo, *Frankfurter Allgemeine*, even the *Scotsman*.

'Goes to show – the thirst for real understanding of Northern Ireland. Nobody has a clue.'

A helicopter clattered down along the shore and swung inland. dropping sharply as it came. It passed in front of the two men. In the gloom they could just see a helmeted figure at the controls. Then they felt the wash of the blades.

'Looks like old Chuck, coming home to roost for the night,' Con observed. 'Probably lifting out cedar for somebody.'

'This old comrade who wrote to you, Conor. What did he say about your article?'

'She, actually. In fact, an old flame of mine. She says the *Irish Press* – one of the national dailies – ran the piece, and the old crowd, that thought I was dead, suddenly realised I wasn't. That I was very much alive. She says some of them are saying why wouldn't I come back and work with them again. It seems they need writers to state their case.'

'It would certainly appear that Ireland's case needs stating, if one is to judge by how your article has been received,' Max said. 'And you, Conor. Do you wish to go back?'

'My place is here, Max. You know that. This is where I belong.'

'That was not what I asked, *lieber Freund.*'

'I dare say it wasn't. Max, I think a lot about Ireland. You remember before I went on that visit, it was eating at me. I think I hoped the visit would get it out of my system, but instead I have images of Ireland flitting through my mind like ghosts. Doesn't make sense, does it?'

'This – old comrade. Does she have anything to do with it?'

'I don't think she does, Max. Truly I don't.'

'Conor, may I ask you something? Is she still *Mitglied* – still belonging to those revolutionaries, you know what I mean?'

'The Movement? She is, Max. She was always in the Movement's political front, and I suppose always will be. Although she's a doctor by profession: seems to have a fairly good practice too. The Movement's her love, now, Max. She doesn't need me. And I don't need her. I have Anna Paz now.'

Max was silent, and there was no sound but the crunch of boots on the rain-dappled sand. Con was momentarily dazzled by the flare of Max's lighter as he lit a cheroot. He noticed how dark the sky had become, except for the line of light along the western horizon.

'It's not that woman, Max,' Con said. 'Believe me. And I'm not fooling myself. But Ireland's another matter: I don't seem to get it out of my system. I love Ireland so much, Max. You can't imagine how much.'

'And why cannot I so imagine?' Max sounded almost angry. 'Will someone explain to me, *Du lieber Gott* will someone tell me, why the Irish think they are the only ones who love their country?'

'Do you think, Conor, I did not love my country – that I did not weep tears when I had to leave it? Oh yes, I loved my country, but in the end I had to let it go. This whole continent is built by people who loved their countries but had to let them go. And now they love this country – and look what that love has built here.' Max pulled on his cheroot, and the tip glowed like a harbour light in the darkness. 'Tell me something, Conor,' he said. 'In Germany they speak of the Fatherland – the country is the Fatherland. Is it so with the Irish?'

'How d'you mean?'

'Is Ireland the Fatherland?'

'Oh, I see what you mean. No, we speak of Mother Ireland.'

'Yes, I thought you would.'

'And then I was telling Paz how the poets speak of Ireland as a girl –'

'Mother Ireland will do nicely for my point, *danke*. Conor, can you remember your Christian Bible? Can you remember what the Christus said: a man shall leave his father and mother and shall – *sich anhängen* – shall cleave to a wife? You know the words?'

'I think I'm beginning to understand –'

'There is your problem. You are a *Muttersohn* – a mother's boy, Conor. Or, as they say here, you are tied to your mother's apron string. Only your mother is Ireland. Cut this last string, Conor.'

The cheroot swung in the darkness as Max stopped and faced Con. 'There is only this tiny string left, my friend. You left your Mother Ireland many, many years ago. And you have told me enough so that I know how you were then. You were a frightened, unwanted, and very dirty child – no matter your real age. Dirty with what you had done.

'But you have had many years to grow. This land has nourished you, and you have come slowly to manhood. Here, among the waters and the woods. The waters have washed you clean, and the woods have given you a haven of peace. It is part of the *Wunder* of this place, a gift from God. I too have found peace here.' Max turned, and the two men started walking back they way they had come.

'I may be wrong, Conor, but I think I am not. I think it is time at last to let go of your mother and also to cleave to a wife. She has been waiting, Conor, waiting some time. You are both ready now.'

They trudged through the darkness, guided only by the faint whiteness where the breakers curled, and by the sky glow from the little town that nestled beyond the dunes.

'One last thing I wish to say, Conor. But perhaps – perhaps I have already said too much?'

'Go ahead.'

'This one thing. Well, two. If you were to go to live in Ireland, I think Anna Paz would not go. Ireland would not be right for her, and I think you would not want her there. But what I really wish to say is this. If you went back to Ireland I think you would also return to childhood. A man who goes back to his mother's house, often reverts to the ways of his youth. And your youthful ways were the ways of violence.

'Conor, my intuition is that this other woman would involve you once more in violence. Perhaps not directly, but you would be involved. Let me ask you something, Conor. What does Anna's family name mean? *Paz*, in Spanish – what does it mean?'

'Peace?'

'Exactly. Peace is what it means.'

The men clambered up the sandy track to where Con's old Buick Wildcat was parked. Max paused at the car door and turned to him. 'And do you know something? It is Anna Paz who has given you that measure of peace that you now have. When you came to us you were like this twisted driftwood that lies around us here. She took you to herself, as the river receives the driftwood and carries it to the peace of the sea.'

'My cold mad feary father.'

'Please?'

'Nothing, really. Something Joyce wrote, about reaching the sea. By the way, will you be at Manuel's party tonight?'

190

'They asked me, Conor, but I said I am no party man.'

'It's a sort of thankyou to Paz – only she doesn't know it yet. Would you not come?'

'I shall leave it to the young, Conor. Like Anna and you, who have things still to work out between them.'

It seemed to Con the entire Mexican community was crammed into that frame house, which even on ordinary days was crowded with its three families.

Infants crawled the floor in peril of extinction by trampling, toddlers wandered in a forest of well-pressed pants legs. Mexican men do not go for denim jeans at a party: mostly it was grey or fawn dress pants, ironed by the wives to razor-sharp creases, topped by an open white shirt that made those moustachioed faces seem like copper.

Con marvelled, as always, at the quietness of it. Mexican parties do not begin boisterously. Aye, but wait till the music starts. Then they'll let go. Yet even now in the quietness there were smiles and sparkling eyes, and a can of Schlitz beer in nearly every hand.

An ice-cold can was pressed into Con's hand. '*Mi casa es tu casa, amigo.*' Manuel was smiling at him, looking like a trim young attorney rather than a man who had slaved in sun and rain for half nothing.

'This stuff's bad for me, Manuel,' Con said. 'Would you have a Pepsi in the house?'

'Sure thing, Con. I get you a Pepsi.'

Little hands tugged at Con's fingers: he looked down to see Lucy and Loopy smiling up at him. Like dolls, he thought. He let them tug him across to the corner of the room and sat on the floor with them.

'Do I get a kiss from Lucy? And one from Loopy? Wow, it was worth coming just for that. Made my day, them kisses did. Nobody else gets kisses but me – right?'

The three-year-old whispered something to the four-year-old. 'Lupita says crack y'fingers, Unca Con!' Lucita announced.

'She has to ask me herself. Come on, Loopy. You're a big girl. You ask.'

'Quack fingers.'

'Certainly, modom. Would the big knuckle on the first finger be suitable, modom?' Splat. 'There you are, modom. Perhaps modom would prefer a thumb? Very special crack from thumbs, y'know, modom.' Splat. 'Top knuckle on the little finger? Very delicate, refeened sound, modom . . .'

No, these are not oriental eyes, Con thought. The little ones were sitting on his outstretched legs, watching him silently, the same shy smile puckering each face. Not oriental – nowhere are there eyes like Mexican Indian eyes. The eyes of Benito Juarez, which gaze from the Mexican peso note. Slanted, tawny eyes – the eyes of an Aztec idol, glaring down from a pyramid since before Cortés. Eyes that watched an eagle slay a serpent. Quetzalcoatl eyes.

Watchful eyes.

And here comes the original, thought Con, standing to greet Consuelo. That's where the eyes came from. And that elfin delicacy. Consuelo was wearing a poncho over her ripening belly. Shy, as always.

'*Buenas tardes, Señor Con. Quiere algo de tomar?*'

'Manuel's bringing me a Pepsi, Consuelo. And here he comes. Thanks, Manuel.'

Manuel caught his wife's eye, cleared his throat, hesitated. '*Con, amigo,*' he said. '*Quiero pedirte un gran favor?*'

'A favour, Manuel? You know, if there's anything I can do –'

There was a burst of applause and Con saw that Paz had come in. She looked tired. By God, when she's tired her eyes slant like the rest of them. But of course – she'd have some of that blood too. Standing there with the eyes slanting and the hair drawn back, she was indeed lovely.

Paz came across and Con got an all-American hug and kiss. Nothing restrained or Aztec about that. She was in her designer jeans: a special concession.

People were forming a circle around her. Silence fell. Manuel coughed, and began to speak. Con just about got the gist of what was being said: ' . . . *y queremos darle las gracias a la Señorita Paz*', thanking her '*por todo lo que ha hecho por nosotros*' – for all she had done for them. And then '*con mucho cariño y estimación*' they were asking her to accept '*este pequeño presente*' – this little gift.

Someone stepped forward with a large package, which was placed in Paz's arms. It hid her face completely. She stood for a moment then lowered the box to the floor. Her face showed surprise and delight. She had not been expecting anything.

'*Abrelo! Abrelo!*' everyone shouted.

Finally there stood exposed a top-of-the-line kitchen blender with enough accessories for a gourmet restaurant. Paz looked as if she might protest, but caught Con's eye.

'It's fabulous. *Absolutamente fabuloso. No sé ni que decir . . .*' And she clapped her hands with delight.

Everyone started clapping and it went on and on. Someone put on a record of *cumbias* and in no time everyone was dancing. Con helped Paz with the box, carrying it to the front porch.

On the way back he felt a tug at his hand. It was Lucy. 'Lupita wants you crack her fingers for her,' she whispered.

'He'll do nothing of the sort,' Paz snorted. 'Conor Emmet, you, at the kids' knuckles now? Look at me. That is corrupting the young. I'm ashamed of you.'

'I swear – I never cracked their knuckles.' He reached down and lifted the two in his arms. 'Tell her, kids. Tell her I never. Tell her or she'll eat me without salt.'

'I will, too,' Paz said, and tickled them all three. The kids cackled with delight.

Con looked around at the throng of dancing people. 'You know, Paz,' he said. 'I keep asking myself, how can folks like this ever be called aliens? It sounds so wrong. Do they look alien to you?'

'That, *amigo*, is what I have been wanting you to ask yourself for quite a while. It's been bothering me a lot longer.'

Manuel came across, leading Consuelo by the hand. 'The favour, Con. I ask it now?'

'Try me, Manuel.'

'Consuelo and me – we want – we want to – *este* – *queremos que tu y Anna sean nuestros compadres.*'

Con looked at Paz enquiringly.

'They're asking if we'd be godparents for the new one, the one that's coming. It's OK by me.'

'I'm not religious, Paz. Wouldn't I have to oversee that the wee critter's learning his catechism, and so forth?'

'Don't worry: with them it's just an honour they're doing you. And you'd honour them.'

'Tell them we'd love to.'

Paz turned to the couple. '*Claro que sí,*' she said. '*Nos daría muchísimo gusto.*'

Manuel gravely shook hands with them both.

2 1

Afterwards they called it the Day of the Raids. Newspaper work is a bit like the military: a lot of the time it can bore you all to hell and then suddenly everything happens at once.

Immigration struck first. They made their first raid – or rather, raids – that Monday long before dawn. They hit almost every forest work camp in western Washington while the men were sleeping, picking up the rest of the illegals by the vanload as they arrived at the camps for work. They hit the houses in the towns, where the wives and kids were holed up. That's what the Immigration Service calls a 'drive'.

And their information was plumb up to date.

Then there was the other raid. Two men walked into the Rainwater County Hospital and up to the pharmacy counter. Meg Zimmer, the 28-year-old pharmacist, found herself gazing down the blue barrel of a .38 pistol.

'Give us all your class-A drugs,' said a man with a beard.

'Somebody get the police,' screeched Meg, right into the muzzle of the gun. The man's jaw dropped, and he turned to run, along with his companion.

A security guard heard Meg's screeches, drew his gun and chased the raiders as they fled to the parking lot. The bearded man killed him with a shot through the chest, and both raiders jumped in their car and roared away.

But all that was later. The Immigration raid came first.

Con learned of it around 6 a.m. while driving to work along Evergreen Boulevard, wet under a dreary dawn sky, deserted except for a Dodge van cruising ahead of him. There seemed to be a roadblock at the corner of Pike and Evergreen, and all of a sudden the Dodge van slammed on its brakes, the back doors flew open, and bodies galore stumbled out and started running, scattering down Pike Street and through the yards of the houses. Whistles shrilled as men in uniform raced after them.

The roadblock consisted of a couple of big Ford Fairlanes sideways across the street, leaving a narrow gap in the centre. Each car had US BORDER PATROL stencilled on the door.

Con pulled in, turned his collar up against the drizzle, and strolled across to the roadblock, where men in uniform capes were hunching under the rain.

'Morning, all. Name is Emmet, from the local paper.' He passed his ID card to one of the Border Patrol officers. 'You men are a long ways down from the Canada border. Can I ask what's going on?'

'Hi, I'm Will Stein – Blaine detachment. INS called us in to help round up the illegals. Biggest drive in years: they're moving on all fronts, right across the Northwest. And it looks like for once there's been real surprise. Catchin' 'em like flies.'

Con's heart was starting to thump, as the significance for Manuel and Consuelo dawned on him. He forced himself to appear unconcerned, and pulled out notebook and pen. 'Where d'you take 'em?'

'Compound back of the sheriff's office is assembly point for Rainwater County. Then Seattle for processing. Then they bus 'em down Highway Five and dump 'em off deep in Mexico. Of course if any of them's carrying false papers, INS can refer them for prosecution. That means a prison camp. Like Safford. Routine. But for most it's just the bus ride to Mexico.'

'Don't a lot of them come right back?'

'That's the trouble, Mr Emmet. It's a losing battle. We're only putting out fires. Picked up seven thousand in Washington State alone last year, and we know damn well far more than that came back up Interstate Five. No way we can keep on top of it.'

Con jotted a few notes, but his newsman's instinct for a story was taking second place to his concern for Manuel and the family. 'Well, good hunting, men. I'll be off and file my story.'

'Call Lar Drewsky at our Bellingham office. He's chief there, and he'll give you the big picture.'

After inching through the barricade, Con raced across town towards the south side where Manuel lived. He was crossing the railway tracks when Paz's old red Falcon slithered through the rain, flashed its lights and honked. Con stopped and ran across. A weeping Consuelo sat beside Paz, and the children sat solemn-eyed in the back. Con said 'I see you already . . .'

'Yep. I was covering my police beat and I heard it right there. Look, Con, I'm taking them to your apartment for right now – that OK with you? Mine's too cramped, and we've no time. OK?'

'Uh, Ye–es. Yes, that seems like a good idea. Sure, no problem. But where's Manuel?'

'We're not sure. Didn't come home last night. Either they picked him up early, or he got a tip-off. Consuelo's climbing walls – she says if they send her back they might dump her hundreds of miles from Manuel. Could take months to meet up.'

Con reached in and put a hand on Consuelo's shoulder. '*Todo estará OK*,' he said gently. '*Estará bien*.' Consuelo nodded and smiled through her tears.

'Unca Con,' a piping voice said from the back of the car. 'Lupita says you c'n kiss her new doggie.' A whitish blur with a pink tongue and no apparent eyes was hoisted up for inspection.

'Aw, goddammit Paz, whaddya have to bring that mongrel for? The bloody thing's not house-trained. And I promised Momma I'd take her dog tomorrow. Goddammit Paz, there's limits . . .'

'Take it easy, will you, Con. Look, it's no big deal. Anyway Consuelo'll see to it. We'd better get going.'

'Yeah, OK. Sorry. Look, I'm a bit uptight, that's all. Listen kids, I'll kiss the doggie tonight an' that's a promise. OK? Paz, there's a roadblock further up. Show your ID, tell them Consuelo's your sister and she's due any minute – God knows, she looks it – and you gotta get her to the hospital right away. That should do it. Hey, you sure she's not going to . . .?'

'Could be, after what she's been through. But we'll deal with that if it comes.'

'Get back to the paper quick as you can. It's going to be busy. And Paz, good luck!'

The sweet–sour tang of adrenalin and sweat hung in the newsroom. Or maybe just sweat: Con wasn't sure if you could smell adrenalin. But it was surely flowing. People were clustered around the radio scanner, which squawked intermittently with garbled police utterances.

'Mornin', Con.' Marty, the city editor, was speaking. 'Look, would you and Paz take on this thing? You two are closer to the illegals than any of us. Handle it any way you want – but this is big. Every county west of the Cascades, AP says. Biggest drive in years. Hey, where's Paz, anyway?'

'She's on her way. Sure, we'll do it, Marty. But who'll dummy my Northwest pages?'

'Kane'll do them if I ask him. He's pretty good at times like this. Oh, and skip the page one meeting. Take it Kane'll want this for page one, by the way. So that gives you a bit longer – ten-twenty at the latest.'

'Can I have Earl?'

'Good idea. Here he comes now. Earl, you're photographing this aliens round-up, OK? Con'll brief you.

There's Kane, too. OK, let's go.'

The page one meeting started immediately behind the glass of Kane's office, interrupted momentarily to admit one overlooked doberman, which was scratching and whining at the door. As soon as Paz got in, Con held his council of war with her and Earl.

'Paz, can you get down to the sheriff's office? Find out how many they've picked up so far. And how many more due in. Any other details you can. Earl, see if you can get a picture of the men in the compound, or being taken out of the cars. If there's chains or leg-irons, get them. Paz, call in whatever you get. Then drop across to the police and the highway patrol and see if there's anything doing there. And after that, Rosita's – she's open for breakfast, and the legal Mexicans'll be there. Some of the illegals too, I bet.

'You'll hear things there you'll get nowhere else. And bring me some good quotes. Then hightail it back here.'

Con paused for breath. 'By the way, I take it everything's OK – uh – back at the ranch?'

'A-OK,' said Paz.

'Oh, and Earl? Y'know Gómez's work camp on Cedar Mountain? That's the nearest to here. If you still got time take a run up there. Sure to be raided, and you might get some good shots. But send your first films back with Paz before you go up the mountain. Good luck, both.'

Con had to yell the last bit, as the two were nearly out the door.

He huddled at the desk and drafted a quick list of phone calls to make.

Check out the other neighbouring counties: sherriff's office, Pacific County; sheriff's office, Gray's Harbor. How many raids there? How many picked up?

Then Lar Drewsky, Border Patrol HQ. Immigration and Naturalization Service, Seattle, for the big picture. Seattle attorney Stein: specialises immigration law. Vic Harris, Parco

Legal Services: really cares, good for comment. Joe Telford of Mexican-American Affairs Commission.

Subcontractors themselves: Madden and Hal Schwartz down in Busy Bay; the Stokes sisters over at Rockham; Andy Hafner in Tacoma; Gómez, right here in Rainhaven. Which of them employ illegals? Aware of employing illegals?

Then the big guns: Smith Pulp Corporation; Westhoff; Dave Rasmussen of Poltek Paper. Did he know who the subcontractors hired? Any comments on the raids?

Con pulled the phone towards him and started spinning the dial, and the raw material of the story poured in, transformed into apparently meaningless squiggles on his spiral notebook.

Bert Mason saying Immigration *told* him to hire illegals to stay competitive. Rasmussen saying Poltek can't get locals to do the work, so has to get out-of-town contractors. Knows nothing of the men those contractors hire.

Border Patrol's Drewsky unavailable, but Ken Giddings of the Bellingham office talking of wretched resources and total lack of policy on aliens.

And the count coming in: 134 in Pacific County; 123 so far in Gray's Harbor; a massive 261 here in Rainwater County. No comment from Smith Pulp. No comment from Westhoff. No comment from . . .

Someone put a cable on the desk. Tear it open quickly. ARRIVING FRIDAY TWO DAY VISIT STOP CAN YOU MEET BA87 SEATAC 14:20? STOP MAEVE. What the fuck . . .? No time to think. Later. Shove it in the jacket pocket. Yes sir, we know you only hire the contractors. But do you – phone dead. Well, fuck you too. Try Stein. You mean you can be deported even after twenty-five years here? If you came illegally at first, you mean? Now that's something. Thank you. Thank you indeed. Jeesus here's Paz back. Soaking wet – must be pouring outside. Paz, go change soon as we get done. So what you got? Sit here, read me the main points, and I'll tell you what I need. Great. Can use that. And that. Any good quotes from Rosita's? What? Wait a minute, did I hear you right – they told you

Gómez paid nobody for four months and they're certain he blew the whistle? You mean, called Immigration to get out of paying? They're saying that? Gawd almighty, that creep'll be found dead. I better get on to him and see what he says. Tell you what. Whyn't you do a sidebar on the scene at the sheriff's office, where they're bringing 'em in? We need colour: Kane'll find space for it. Ten inches, no eight – has to be short. Hey, did you drop in Earl's film? Good. Let's get going. Get outa those clothes soon as you're done here. Mr Gómez please. This is the *Record*. Oh. Well, is there anyone I can talk to? Look, ask him to call me as soon as he gets in, tell him it's most urgent . . .

Marty was beside him. 'Citizen says you got twenty-five inches, not counting the head. He'll jump the last 'graphs to the back page. And he'll run a five-by-seven pic on A-one, if Earl comes up with the goods. Nothing written yet? Hey, get moving, man. Look at that clock.'

Con felt the iron bands lock across his chest in the old familiar panic. Then it was gone, and there was the exhilaration, the heady certainty he'd make it, the dampness at the armpits and a brief whiff of one's own gorgeous unconquerable sweat.

He ripped the pages from their spiral, spread them on the desk, and for a few moments moved them around like cards in solitaire. When he had them in the order he wanted, he pulled up close to his computer terminal, touched a switch, and the green cyphers came up on the screen.

WHAT NAME? the screen asked. His fingers traced EMMET on the keyboard.

PASSWORD? He typed his initials: HCE – Hugh Conor Emmet. The screen cleared for the story.

Under SLUGLINE at the top he entered the word SWOOP, paused an instant, and then his fingers started their silent dance around the keyboard:

GOVERNMENT agents today (Monday) apprehended more than 1,200 illegal aliens as part of a massive drive against undocumented forest workers.

In simultaneous pre-dawn swoops throughout Western Washington and Oregon, officers of the Immigration and Naturalization Service, backed by members of the US Border Patrol . . .

Total concentration. Story building itself on the screen in front of you, bits moving off the paper and slotting into exactly the right place on the screen. As if the story already existed like a jigsaw puzzle and these were the interlocking parts going to their preordained spot to make the complete picture. Total concentration, yet a tiny part of the mind still free to enjoy the sensation of building, making, creating – free to wish this kind of pressure could come more often, for the lift it gives you; free to ask, whoever said reporting wasn't creative?

But total concentration. Clock hands slithering around to deadline. A bubble around you, screening out the noise and havoc – screening out whatever was going on over there at the radio scanner right now, people jostling around it with occasional squawks from the scanner coming through the bubble, something about late-model Ford Fairlane, hospital pharmacy, dead on admission, Burnt Gulch Road. What in hell . . .? Concentrate. Find out soon enough. Keep hitting that SEND key, so as not to lose the story. Screen says fifteen column inches gone in – just a couple more now and leave the rest for Paz's sidebar. Head could take ten more inches, but that's Kane's baby. Momma in red – scarlet galleon sailing up the newsroom, Plato at the helm; nose for the high moments, Momma has. Never misses' em. Total concentration: tighten that bubble around you . . . Clock hand just touching deadline.

That's it. Done. Hit SEND key and wipe story off the screen. Stretch your limbs – God, pains in the back like after running a marathon. Stick head into Kane's cage and tell him SWOOP story's filed, ready for editing.

Stretch again and yawn. *Post coitus tristitia*. No, fulfilled, actually. Feeling great. Now what the hell is going on over at that scanner?

Marty filled him in. 'Two guys tried to rob the hospital pharmacy and killed a guard. All we know so far. Made a getaway north, up Burnt Gulch Road – means they gotta be from outa town. No locals would be that dumb: that road goes nowhere. They'll end up in the forest with no way out.'

'Who's covering it?'

'I sent Paz up to the hospital to see what she can get. She's to call down here right away – there'll not be time for more than a few 'graphs. Wish those assholes had timed it better. I'll get Kane to hold page one as long as he dare. The rest we'll run tomorrow. Barrett's headed after the police up Burnt Gulch, and Earl just came back and he's gone after him. Should be big in tomorrow's paper.'

The scanner's red dots stopped running and a voice was squawking: ' . . . prolonged shootout . . . now ended . . . Burnt Gulch Road . . . Caucasian male, bearded . . . dead at the scene . . . officers had no option . . .' The dots started running again. Then: ' . . . companion escaped . . . forest north of Burnt Gulch . . . search under way . . . canine units . . .'

The phone shrilled. 'Paz on the line, Marty,' someone said. Marty went across to take the call. Con stayed by the scanner.

Suddenly over the scanner came the unmistakable pulsing whine from inside a helicopter cabin, and Con recognised the clipped tones of Frank Lindstrom, sheriff's deputy: ' . . . fled northwards from point of entry . . . fugitive . . . as of now, no sighting from the air . . .'

Con waited for Marty to put down the phone. 'Marty,' he said. 'One second. There's a chopper up there. Could only be one of Chuck's: he's probably at the controls. If I'm out at the airfield when they come in to refuel, maybe I could bag the centre seat and cover the chase from the air. Whaddya think?'

'Do it,' said Marty. 'And one more thing. On your way home could you stop off at this address' – he handed Con a scrap of paper – 'and try to interview a girl called Meg Zimmer. Pharmacist from the hospital. Paz says she was quite a hero today. Well, heroine. She's at her parents' now – pretty shook up. Get what you can.'

'Nearly forgot,' Con said. 'Could someone finish tomorrow's op-ed page? It's all done bar a couple of heads, and the Oliphant cartoon's there in my tray.'

'Leave it to me,' Marty said.

22

By midday the rain, which had begun as a spiteful drizzle, was roaring in from the ocean in curtains of water. It was as if the ocean itself had moved over the town and hung suspended between sky and earth.

At the airfield down beyond the harbour, a helicopter sat on the drenched asphalt, rotor blades lashing like a whip. It was a Hiller J-3 Soloy, utterly functional – little more than a perspex bubble and a scorpion-like tail. There were three men in it: old Chuck Watkins in the left-hand pilot's seat, Conor Emmet jackknifed in the centre, and Frank Lindstrom on his right. Lindstrom had a waterproof cape over his sheriff deputy's uniform. He held a 12-bore Remington 8-70 police shotgun on his knees, pointing through the space where the door had been removed. Little rain came in, most being whisked away by the rotors.

Glancing back, Con could see the sting-like tail shimmering in the gases from the howling turbine behind their heads. He looked up through the bubble's roof at that wilderness of rods and spindles, from which in a moment their lives must hang. The rotors whirled with an oiled smoothness and yet with a sort of violence.

The instrument console was shaking as the rotor blades beat upon nerves and brains with a merciless thump-thump-thump. The cabin flickered slightly with their passing.

The vibrations grew smooth and the rotor faded to a ghostly parasol above their heads. Chuck eased the left-hand lever slightly upwards, feeling the skids just teetering on the asphalt. Up came the lever a few more degrees, and Con saw the skids come away from the ground about a foot. The helicopter hung there.

Abruptly but smoothly the right-hand lever moved forward, the right-foot pedal moved forward with it, and the left-hand lever arced up and back. The helicopter gave one splendid leap outwards and upwards; the watery world fell away and the tops of the evergreens were points piercing the murk far below.

The machine banked and swung across the town towards the nearly invisible hills, beyond which was a manhunt.

'To keep him pinned down is all we can hope for,' old Chuck had told the sheriff. 'Weather's too filthy.'

'Hafta do, then,' the sheriff had said. 'I just hope they get him quick. If it goes too long, dunno how I'm gonna pay you.'

'I'll give you today for the cost of the gas,' Chuck had said. 'We all gotta do something.'

As the helicopter trundled above the town, Conor looked down, seeking the squat old red-brick building that housed the *Daily Record* offices. It was hidden in the murk. They'd be getting their breath down there now. How remote it all seemed from here. And insignificant. Like the astronauts looking back at Earth. Hard to imagine the Citizen yakking away down there. Helluva morning it had been.

Con tried to stretch his muscles in the tight space. He leaned his head back against the bulkhead, letting himself relax.

Ahead rose the hills. The rain reduced everything to monochrome, making each sawtoothed ridge a flat plane, painting successive ridges in diminishing tones of grey. Like a Chinese silk painting.

The cable. God, he'd forgotten the cable. Con clapped a

hand to his shirt pocket, so that Lindstrom looked across concernedly, as if Con were having a heart attack.

He tugged it out and unfolded it. It said no more than the first time. ARRIVING FRIDAY. Maeve was coming: that was all.

Could she be on her way somewhere else, to LA maybe, to address some Republican meeting? And dropping off here for old time's sake? Helluva way round for a social visit. Could Maeve be that lonely? Or wanting to water a friendship that had budded again in one brief evening in Dublin? God only knew.

Or could it be something to do with that article? Con cursed it sometimes. It reminded a lot of people of Con's existence, and he wasn't sure he wanted that.

A nudge in the ribs. What was Lindstrom saying?

'Can't – hear – you,' Con yelled over the howl from the turbine behind their heads.

'I said – not a hope – a seein' anythin' – down there right now.'

'That so? So what are we – doing – up here?'

'Pinnin' him down. Keeps him from runnin' – till the dogs can git him.'

'That so? Poor – bloody – bugger.'

Con's mind came back to the cable. Well, he'd have a few days till Friday. And then Maeve – nearly two decades older, yet still with style. He felt a twinge of excitement. Then a twinge of apprehension: what about Paz? It would be awkward. Awkward indeed.

Why the hell was Maeve coming?

'Ya want – some – orange hard candy?' Lindstrom was hollering again.

'Please.'

'Helps – the ears. Makes ya swallow.'

Jesus, willya pipe down, Lindstrom, Con thought. Leave me to my brooding.

The helicopter had settled into a sort of grid pattern of flight, clattering along close to the treetops. Chuck had taped one of the Westhoff Corp's logging maps to the console, and from time to time he reached forward to mark the map with a pencil.

With the rain roaring into the trees, and a ground fog on the clear-cut sections, none of the men was keyed up for dramatic developments. But the hunted man down there would not know how much or how little they could see. Pin him down: keep him from running. Till the dogs get him. That was it.

The airman, the lawman and the newsman settled into their private thoughts. A howling Hiller is no place for conversation.

The deputy adjusted his earphones and thumbed a knob on the radio. He leaned across to tap Chuck's shoulder. 'They located him,' he yelled. 'He's back near Burnt Gulch again. Want us to sit on top of him. Let's go.'

Chuck tapped a dial on the console. 'Can't,' he yelled. 'Gotta refuel.'

'Son of a bitch!' the deputy yelled. 'Why now? Why's it always happen to me?' And he slapped his hand on the butt of the shotgun in frustration.

The helicopter swung around, put its nose down, and soon the airfield appeared beyond the harbour mudflats where the trees ended. A flock of sandpipers wheeled far below, like a shoal of tiny fish. The airfield rushed upwards and suddenly toy buildings were full-size hangars, beside which the Hiller touched one skid and then the other, squatting like a seagull on a piling. The banshee whine died and the slowing rotor blades were snapping whips above the men's heads as they ducked away.

'I'll not go back up,' Con told the men. 'I've a heap to do at the paper. But I'll join you tomorrow – if you're still searching. OK?'

Con slept with difficulty that night. He was tired and edgy: the euphoria of working under pressure had worn off, and he was hankering after his more lazy, laid-back features-and-column routine. But more than anything he was troubled by Maeve's cable.

Interviewing Meg Zimmer had been easy enough. He had called to her parents' home, where she was cocooned by family and friends. There was a glass in every hand. It was a kind of post-trauma party, and Meg kept going back over the security guard's death, and asking Con if she hadn't done 'a dumb thing' by calling out for help.

'I was taught in pharmacy school there are two things you should do when they try a drug heist. Give them what they want, and the last thing you should lose is any kind of human life. You can act very dumb, and lose what you can't get back – somebody's life. And that's what I did.' She took a sip from the bourbon and soda someone had shoved into her hand, and her hand trembled a little. 'But it was already a kind of a hard morning and I was tired, and it just kind of happened.'

She held Con's hand as if for reassurance. 'I'm sick at heart thinking how somebody got killed,' Meg said. 'If I had just gone along, maybe Bill Hagen'd be alive now. An' I dread tomorrow, when people will be asking me what happened.'

'Have you met problems like this before?' Con asked.

'Well, I've met drug people before, and I don't like them. You get them trying all kinds of stuff at the pharmacy counter. God how I hate them. We're trying to provide a compassionate, quality care service at the hospital and it's just hard that people keep gumming up the works. Like, perverting it to their own ends. People like that just take up the time you could be using for something else.

'There's amateur drug abusers, and there's thieves,' Meg said. 'And there's these. It's just a pain.' And the tears came at last in torrents, and before she realised it, Meg had buried her head somewhere in Con's chest. Con held her shoulders until she had cried her fill.

On the way home, Con had stopped off at Rosita's, hoping Paz would be there. She was.

'Any word of Manuel?' Con asked.

'Not a thing.'

'Consuelo OK?'

'No problem. I gave them your spare room. One of the kids cried a bit, but I looked in a while ago and they seemed fine. Except that Consuelo's worried stiff about Manuel. He wasn't in the sheriff's compound, and there's no sign of him anywhere.

'Hey, but you and me, we still gotta eat. How about *enchiladas?* I waited to eat with you.'

'*Enchiladas*'ll do nicely. Did you bring the paper?'

Paz handed him the *Record*. Earl had done a splendid picture of men in single file entering an old, corrugated Greyhound-type bus with US BORDER PATROL across the top of the windshield. The faces showed utter defeat. There were no leg-irons or chains. Kane had run the picture five columns wide above the fold. Below it was the five-column headline

ILLEGAL ALIENS LIFTED
IN SHOCK DAWN SWOOP

and then the story, with Con's byline. Kane handles front pages well, thought Con grudgingly.

Enchiladas came, with mugs of Rosita's rich, delicious coffee. Without a word, Con took the cable from his pocket, opened it and handed it across to Paz. She read it silently, then read it again. Still holding it, she put her hands in her lap and the dark eyes searched Con's.

'Well?' Con asked.

'Well what?'

'What – what do you think of it?'

There was a pause. 'That's the woman you told me about, right?'

Con nodded. Another pause.

'I think she's coming to take you back to Ireland,' Paz said quietly.

'Good God, woman, don't be ridiculous. What's in that bit of paper to give you such a notion?'

The conversation left Con strangely disturbed as he let himself into his apartment that night.

There was no sign of Consuelo or the kids or their con-founded puppy – they would be asleep in the spare room long since. The apartment had been picked up and polished, and was quite bereft of its cosy bachelor grubbiness.

The table was laid for one, and Con found a foil-wrapped tuna sandwich in the fridge. Well, the sandwich would keep, but Consuelo had been kind to think of it.

As he stood by the fridge, Con felt a longing for a golden glass of beer, beaded bubbles winking. None there, mercifully. He undressed, climbed into bed, read the rest of the *Record* and turned out the light.

Sleep eluded him. He lay there stony-eyed, Paz's words going round and round at the back of his skull: ' . . . take you back to Ireland . . . coming to take you back to Ireland . . . back to Ireland . . . to Ireland . . .' The old, familiar images floated into his mind: the green laneway with the cart tracks; the gorse licking the hillsides like yellow flames. Maeve's face. No, is it Paz's face? Paz walking that Irish laneway? Can't be sure any more. No, Paz belongs on a logging trail in the rainforest. I think.

And then the Irish lane floats into view again and Maeve is striding towards me in the high boots and the corduroy breeches and never seeming to get any nearer. No, she's on that Galway pony and she cantering silently down the lane to me, cantering ever so slowly, ever so slowly, and she's Cathleen Ni Houlihan and her red-gold hair is streeling behind her like a flame . . . No, it's that logging trail beyond Burnt Gulch and it's Paz running towards me away from those raiders and she's wearing the denim cut-offs that hug her neat little ass, and the big hiking boots and the thick socks that set off the slender thighs, and those pointy breasts pushing at the red check shirt and the sun is glowing on the apricot bare arms and she's smiling and she's opening her arms and now she's reaching me and I'm clutching her and something inside me is pumping away and... am I awake or am I sleeping?

23

By Thursday the fugitive had been four days in the forest. Everyone engaged in the manhunt was praying he be caught, if only to let them home out of the rain that was a wall of water and made cataracts of forest trails. Even the men in the helicopter were wet. Water had seeped past Con's shirt collar, making him cold and irritable.

The Hiller was flying its grid pattern, Chuck's hands caressing the two control sticks, eyes making their own grid pattern along the ground. This was Con's third time up, and the novelty was wearing thin. But at least there was time to think. His mind kept coming back to Maeve's impending visit, as a moth flits around a flame.

His thoughts came back to the business in hand. Down there lurked the symbol of what threatened the peace of Rainhaven – a man from 'a car ride away' (as the paper had put it) who could bring big-city violence right to the rainforests. It was a poison that spread. Marty had mentioned how people were oiling their guns and talking of doing something about it all.

The helicopter put its nose down and turned for home to refuel. Soon the men were drinking coffee and drying out in the shed that served as terminal.

'I'll be editing this afternoon, you guys,' Con said. 'And I won't be with you Friday. I've to meet a friend at Seatac that's flying in from Europe.'

'We could hold the action till you get back,' Chuck suggested with a grin.

'Wouldn't wish it on you, Chuck. Anyhow the bugger'll drown if you don't catch him soon. You might even drown up in the chopper.'

Afterwards, chugging around the timberyards to the *Record* office, Con wondered if there was any fugitive at all by now. Sheriff and police seemed to think there was, and had pulled in reinforcements and tracker dogs from several counties. They should know.

With a start Con realised he had given little thought to the other fugitives – those Mexicans who had evaded Immigration. And what of the ones dumped back in Mexico? Had Immigration lifted Manuel, and was he frantically searching for wife and kids all over northern Mexico? Hardly likely: he only had to telephone Paz to find out they were still in Rainhaven. But he hadn't telephoned.

Consuelo had to be sick with worry. Con resolved that this evening he would try harder to reassure her: the scramble of the past days had left so little time. But Paz had been in regular touch with Consuelo and the kids. And Con'd do better tonight.

Momma's pick-up stood in the *Record* parking lot. Wasn't she supposed to be off in DC? There was no doberman in the back. Through force of habit Con put his nose to the cab to get a screech out of the dachshunds. But the cab was empty. Of course – Plato's over with me. The other'd be at Barrett's.

Con nodded to the folks in advertising, and pushed open the door to the newsroom. Inside, he sensed that electricity you get among journalists when something highly newsworthy has just been ferreted out. The *Citizen's* cage door was shut, and behind the glass Kane was huddled with Marty, Barrett and Momma.

Kane beckoned to Con. Curiosity kindling, Con entered the glass cage. There was silence. Kane's bleary old eyes looked up at Con; he tugged at his moustache. 'You're a buddy of ole Max Stern, right?'

'We're friends. You know that.'

'He's on a week's, uh, vacation,' Kane said. 'I guess he'd be at home, would he?'

'Probably,' Con said. 'But why ask me? Why don't you just call him?'

'I'm, uh, getting to that. Now listen. Pete here has been working on some, uh, Nazi story for a while, an' now it seems he's got something solid. Real solid. An' it's about your buddy Stern.'

Con looked around for a chair, but there was none.

'Maybe you'd like to ask him a couple of questions, huh?' Kane went on inexorably. 'Seeing as you're an ole buddy an' that. It seems our ole Hebrew friend sold his soul to the Krauts. His name was Jacob then, by the way. Seems he did know Treblinka OK, knew it, uh, very well indeed. He was a guard there.'

Barrett's nose was wrinkling, and Momma was looking down at her dogless lap.

'We've volunteered you to ask him about it,' Kane said.

The afternoon was a nightmare. As features editor, Con spent Thursday and Friday afternoons on layouts for Saturday's picture page and features, as well as editing the tabloid section, grandly named *Pictorial Record*, which would be folded inside Saturday's paper. There were photographs to be cropped, and scaled to the required size. There were cutlines – photo captions – to be written and measured. There was the picture page to build – the pictures were about the Quinault Indians' new fish hatcheries down at Taholah, and the tab section was mostly about one of those bores who make ornaments from driftwood.

Con stood by the angled layout counter, his mind a maelstrom. Maeve was forgotten. He stared at the blank grid sheets and the waiting pictures. The unthinkable: Max, kindly, decent Max – his friend, who had piloted Con through seas of guilt and never once asked a direct question – Max had played a part in the Holocaust. Had been a guard in an exter-mination camp. First a prisoner in Treblinka. Then put to work in the camp's printing press. Then they had given him a gun and a uniform.

Con found himself thinking about whiskey.

Paz was beside him. 'Move over,' she said. 'I'll do the cutlines: you scale the pix. OK?'

Somehow between them they got the layouts done. The work seemed to come from Con's fingers, not his brain.

Afterwards they took the road past the airfield. They sat together in Paz's Ford, facing the ocean where the road ends, while the rain drummed on the dunes and lashed the drift-wood around them. The faint line of breakers seemed almost unmoving in the murk, and far away.

'It's a watertight case, Justice Department boys told Barrett.' Con shivered, and rubbed his hands for warmth. 'Barrett wouldn't dare play with this one, Paz. And he's been staying close to Justice office in Olympia. But it's still – completely – unbelievable. There's no way the man I know could have helped run a death camp. Much less have turned against his own people. That's the most unthinkable part of all. That, I simply – that I cannot accept.'

Paz put a hand on his knee, but said nothing.

'Barrett says Justice have a task force for sniffing out people involved in war crimes from World War Two. Says they're in-vestigating over 360 cases across the States, and they don't mess about. Says if they leaked him this about Max, then they're ready to move.'

'They're going to arrest Max?'

'No. Barrett told us they'll start a public process to denaturalise him. He'll be charged with concealing his past when he immigrated here and when he filed for citizenship. And when they have him denaturalised, they'll move to deport him. Barrett says it could take ages: Justice's in no hurry, and they're quite happy to drag it out.'

A squall lashed the side of the car, and rain cascaded down the window.

'So what's to happen right now?'

'Well, the *Record*'s goin' to let him go, that's for sure. Kane and Momma are in a dilemma whether to run it as a news story before it hits the *PI* or the *Times* up in Seattle, or just fire him and hope he'll be gone before the story breaks.'

'But does he get a chance to speak for himself? Does he not get to answer the charges before they fire him?' Paz was shocked.

'They've asked me to talk to him. And I'm going to – but not because they want it. I got to: he's my friend, and there has to be something – something in this we don't know. Something – that would explain things.'

'What is there to explain?' Paz asked. 'What's Max supposed to have done? I mean, lots of people were guards in the war. It's not the end of the world.'

'A guard in a death camp is different, Paz. It means you were part of a machine expressly designed to exterminate. It means you helped make the Holocaust happen. Besides, as a guard Max would have known the things they did there. He'd have known about the Lazaret.'

'The Lazaret?'

'A nine-foot-deep pit, where a fire always burned. They called it the Eternal Fire. Old people were taken there, to be shot in the neck and tumbled in. And people who were so sick they couldn't be rushed to the gas chamber. And children of unknown parents.'

'And Max is supposed to have shot them?'

'Nobody's saying he did. Nobody knows what he did

in Treblinka. Just that he worked there, helped run a death camp.'

Paz thought for a moment. 'So, for all we know, he could have been secretly helping the victims? Or keeping his head down so's not to get shot himself?'

'Nobody's saying that either. No one's come forward to say he helped them. Or that he hurt them. No one seems to know anything. But it's enough for Justice that he was a guard there, and that he concealed the fact.'

There was silence in the car, except for the sound of rain drumming on the roof. The two sat staring through the water-blurred windshield at the line of distant surf.

'I can't believe it,' Con said. 'I'll never believe it. I know Max, and he's simply not a wicked man.'

Paz turned to him. 'I want to ask you something, Con. Is a man who once did wickedness a wicked man? I think you're already asking yourself that – only it's yourself you're thinking about, as much as Max.'

She heard Con's intake of breath. He kept staring through the windshield.

'I've known for ages, Con,' she said gently. 'You didn't have to tell me. But we're close enough for me to have guessed at a couple of things by now.'

'Did Max say something?'

'Never. But I just know there was – something. An' I don't ever need to know what. But don't ever forget there's a thing called repentance. And if there was anything in Max's past – I'd say the man we know is one who found repentance.'

'Con, this visitor who is coming – would you like to invite her to Falls Lake on Saturday? That way you could come yourself, and do some fishing.' Max had been tying a trout fly when Con walked in. Con sat in an armchair, watching him in silence. Darkness had fallen, and beyond the yellow-lit window the black sky seemed blue.

'Max. There's something I've got to ask you.'

'Yes, my friend?'

'Max. They've got something down at the paper about you. About – about you're supposed to be – about you being a guard at Treblinka.'

Max's fingers stopped moving around the fly he was tying. He did not turn from the table where he was working. Con could not see his face.

'Do you believe it, Conor?' Max asked quietly. He turned and looked directly at Con. 'No, I can see that you do not wish to believe it, and I am glad. I know what this is about, and I will tell you. But first I need some time – I need to be alone.'

He stood: '*Geh*, my friend. Please go now. I must be alone. I will tell you on Saturday what you must know. That I solemnly promise. Leave me until then. Please, my friend.'

Paz's car was outside Con's apartment when he pulled into the parking lot. She was just leaving: been visiting Consuelo, no doubt. Con parked and went across to her.

'Max'll tell me Saturday. Right now he wants to be alone. And Paz, I need to be alone too. Would you mind terribly? Please.'

'Sure, Con. Phone if you need me. Is – is Max OK?'

'He says he knows what they're on about. That's all he would say.'

They kissed, and Con walked up the steps to his apartment. As he let himself in, Consuelo opened the door of her room, eyes questioning. She was holding the wriggling puppy. Con shook his head. 'No news of Manuel,' he whispered. '*Todavía nada. A la mejor, mañana.* Maybe tomorrow.'

Tears welled in the dark eyes, and Con put and arm around her shoulder.

The children stirred in the bedroom behind her. 'Unca Con,' Lucita called. Con went in and sat on the bed. The little lynx-eyed girl reached up and hugged him. She smelt warmly of sleep. They both looked at Loopy, still sleeping, one tight little fist on the pillow, the edge of the duvet in her mouth. Consuelo stood by the door, watching.

Con suddenly felt an overwhelming tenderness for this little family, and his heart hurt him as he gazed at the children. Maybe that's how a father feels when he sits by his children's bed.

'Unca Con,' the child whispered. 'Lupita says, when's our dad coming home?'

24

Maeve was already waiting when Con arrived at Seatac Airport, midway between Seattle and Tacoma.

Con was tired after a sleepless night focused on Max, followed by the hectic Friday morning schedule at the paper. He had told Kane there'd be nothing from Max until Saturday, and old Kane hadn't liked it. Con had rung Max's number a couple of times, but Max seemed to have gone to earth.

Heads turned as Maeve stood to greet Con. She was wearing an exquisitely cut suit in palest mauve. Glint of gold at ears, neck and wrist. Flecks of gold in the grey-green eyes. A hug, redolent of fine tweed and that perfume of violets. Then Con took her bag and they headed for the parking lot.

At first they were shy.

'You'll stay with me, of course,' Con said, as the car began the ride down Interstate Five.

'Graciously accepted. I'll be only two nights, then San Francisco to meet a group there.' Maeve smiled. 'You don't object to a young widow under your roof, I hope?'

'You'll be only the fourth woman in the house,' Con said dryly. He told her about Consuelo and the children.

Con endeavoured to put Max to the side of his mind, to

concentrate on the driving and on his guest. He found himself chattering like a tour guide, pointing out Mount Ranier's snowy summit suspended in the sky to the east, then the military complex of Fort Lewis that stretched for miles on either side of the freeway. The hillside city of Tacoma rose up to the right, and was gone. Then Olympia, with the state capitol dome on its bluff above Puget Sound.

Below the bluff the car swung west off Interstate Five, onto the fifty miles of highway that leads to the Pacific Ocean. Far ahead a bank of clouds cut across the clear evening sky, extending from horizon to horizon like a roof.

'Looks like rain up ahead,' Maeve observed.

'That's just the coast for you. Once we slide under that lid of clouds it's a different world, almost like Ireland. Except quadruple the rain. In the rainforests they measure the rain in feet, not inches. No kidding. But an Irishman can hack it – we grow webbed feet!'

The trees grew taller on either side.

'When I was a boy,' Con said, 'I could never quite understand those Grimm's fairytales about Hänsel and Gretel getting lost in the forest. I suppose because we didn't have much forest in Ireland, compared with Germany where the tales came from. But here I can understand being lost. Those trees go all the way to Canada – well, to the straits of Juan de Fuca, then Canada. Planes can crash there and not get found for ten years. People say there's ape men in there –'

'You're joking me.'

'Not at all. They call them Sasquatch, or Bigfoot. Sort of our local Loch Ness monster. There's even photos of the footprints.

'But the place is so vast they could be there for years without being seen. Right now there's a man in there on the run, and in five days they haven't seen hide nor hair of him. Even with tracker dogs and helicopters.'

'One of those illegal Mexicans?'

'No, it's a murder hunt. Hold-up men shot a hospital guard. Police killed one and the other's on the run.

'Speaking of Mexicans: reminds me, did you ever try Mexican food? I could take you to Rosita's. Rosita's a sort of mother to all the young fellows from Mexico. The newsroom people often eat there. Want to try it?'

'Certainly. I'd love to eat Mexican. I think. Beans and things, isn't it?'

'Over there is something people aren't too happy about.' Con pointed to the southern horizon. Lights like a city crowned a ridge against the fading sky. 'Nuclear plant. Up there's a couple of reactors half built – costing twenty times what they reckoned. People are worried about wastes that'll have to be guarded for half a million years.'

'I often think,' Maeve said, 'if America has trouble placing nuclear dumps, even with the Rockies and all those deserts, how can islands like Ireland and England manage? I mean, every spot you choose is beside someone's house.

'You know, of course, Britain's pumping all its waste into the Irish Sea? Already they've made it the most radioactive stretch of water on the globe.'

Montesano slid by on the right. The car glided through Aberdeen and Hoquiam and swung northwards through Amanda Park. For mile after mile, not a human habitation. The car lights bored through seemingly endless tracts of forest, dark and deep as the day the first settler came.

'And miles to go before I sleep,' Maeve quoted, drowsily.

As if in answer, a few houses flashed by. Then a drive-in cinema, advertising *Naked Fiend*. A roadside lot full of hideous garden gnomes, each like a tumour.

The real trees fell away and the manmade ones appeared – grotesque growths, one topped with a yellow McDonald's M, others with Exxon and Mobil logos, and one with a monstrous barrel of Fried Chicken. Lights danced on water; the car strummed across a metal lifting bridge and entered downtown Rainhaven.

'Faith, I've seen prettier places,' Maeve murmured.

'Wait'll you see the hillsides in daytime. If tomorrow's sunny, you won't believe how lovely it is. And you'll not meet better people.'

'Seems to me they've just improved on the log cabin,' Maeve sniffed.

Girders reared ahead and the car strummed across another bridge, swung right and pulled into the lot of a small, low block of apartments, at the edge of which water glinted.

'I'll leave in your bag,' Con said. 'Then we'll go eat. I'm in number five. It's no chateau, but the view of the river's really something. You'll see in the morning.

'By the way, you get my room. I take the couch: it opens into a bed. The Mexicans have the spare room. Oh, and there's a couple of dogs – a vicious dachshund I'm babysitting, and a sort of a pup belonging to the Mexicans.'

'And here was I feeling sorry for you, you poor solitary man! How wrong can a girl be?'

'Mind if I make a phone call before we go? Won't take a minute.' Con went in, put down the bag, and dialled. 'Dammit, Max, where are you hiding?' He came back out. 'Let's go to Rosita's,' he said.

Rosita herself welcomed them, giving Maeve a keen scrutiny.

'I'm on my diet again,' she told them. 'Can't even eat my own chilli. And they're watching to see I don't cheat.' A sigh. 'Kata!' she yelled. 'How many calories in a taco?' To Con: 'Hey, your buddies from the paper are in the bar. Your friend Paz, too.'

Con and Maeve sat down. Spanish-speaking voices sounded quietly all around. A group sauntered in from the bar, Paz among them, and sat down at a table. Paz saw Con and came across. 'So this is your visitor from Ireland? Hi. I'm Anna Paz. I work with this creep.'

'Anna, this is Maeve – Maeve Halloran. Won't you sit down – join us for a bit?'

224

Paz sat down.

'Looks like the rain has backed off, doesn't it?' Con said, hopelessly.

There was a cheer down near the cash register. Four young men had come in, dark, with Indian eyes, and people were crowding around them. Handshakes.

'Hey, Rosita.' Con called to her as she passed by. 'What's going on down there?'

Rosita grinned. 'It's some of that bunch the Immigration picked up Monday. Shipped to Mexico. These kids came back up I-Five from Tijuana. Just got in. There's more coming later tonight.'

'They've been there and back already?'

'You bet.'

Paz was eyeing Maeve. 'You gonna take this guy from us?' she asked.

'Sure what would I want to do that for? I'm just an old friend.'

'Bet you are,' Paz said. 'Just remember, he's happy here. And he's sober here. And he's doing good work here. And he's where he should be.'

'If you say so.'

'I'm off to eat,' Paz announced.

'Wouldn't you – care to have a bite with us?' Con asked.

'Thanks all the same. Got some of the gang over there. Catch you later.' Paz trotted off.

Maeve leaned over to Con. 'One of the friendly folk you were telling me about?'

'Paz's all right. You'll see.'

25

Consuelo must have decided to leave Con in peace with his visitor. Neither she nor the children were to be seen when Con and Maeve got back.

Con tapped gently on the bedroom door, and Consuelo opened it a few inches. She was in a nightgown.

'Some of the men are back from Mexico,' he whispered. He tried again with his halting Spanish: '*Algunos muchachos – ya regresaron. Tal vez más, esta noche.* Maybe more tonight. Maybe – *tal vez Manuel.* Maybe Manuel's on his way.'

She took his hand and pressed it silently. She smiled briefly at Maeve, shook hands silently, and closed the door.

'I got in gin and some tonic,' Con said. 'Still your poison? Ah, good.'

Plato glared from the sofa, perfecting his quiet snarl.

'Don't mind that little bugger,' Con said. 'Not that he isn't wicked, mind you. He'd bite you only his mouth's too small. Like a coral snake – just as vicious, but mercifully just as tiny.

'Afraid this is a bachelor's quarters,' Con added. 'And I know it's got a bachelor smell. Paz told me.'

'She comes here?'

'Occasionally.'

He mixed a gin and tonic for Maeve and put the gin, a six-pack of Schweppes, and some sliced lemon on the coffee table. 'You'll not be wanting ice, I expect?' He smiled. 'Daft American custom.'

'No ice. Just lemon.'

They sat looking at each other in silence, then both smiled with embarrassment.

'So tell me the latest from Ireland,' Con said, for something to say. 'All we ever hear is when a bomb goes off in Belfast, and AP doles us out a hundred words over the wire.'

Maeve raised her glass to say cheers, then took a sip. 'Well, you saw yourself what it's like. Down south, the Republic has this crazy inflation and unemployment, and nobody gives a damn about the people in the North. Nobody except the Movement, that is.'

'And does the Movement give a damn?' Con asked quietly.

Maeve stared at him. 'How could you even ask that, Con? Of course the Movement cares. It's the only thing left to care: everyone else has sold out. Even the Irish government is wagging its tail and trying to suck up to the British. And of course the Brits are laughing at them – they laugh at everything except force. It's their nature.'

'But this violence, Maeve. Will that bring the northerners together?'

'I don't suppose it will, Con. That may have to wait. Listen, the priority is, get the Brits out. We don't like violence any more than – than George Washington did, over here. But the Americans had to use force to get rid of the Brits, and so do we. Remember we're dealing with the most violent nation the world has ever known.'

'Maeve. Come off it. You're exaggerating.'

'Am I, Con? Listen. How did the British grab one third of the globe? Here's how – because they were more violent and more cunning than the nations they enslaved.

'And the Brits held their empire by the most savage violence the world has seen. To be sure, they called it Colonial

Administration, and they dressed up their violent men in the red robes of judges and the white suits of district commissioners and the khaki of officers and gentlemen. But those fancy-dressed savages lugged along their gallows and hanged and hanged and hanged their way around the world – do you know, they even had a mobile gallows on a truck in Kenya in the Mau Mau days? Sure, they called it Colonial Administration and –'

'But Maeve, look at the Germans –'

'The Germans went berserk for twelve years under Hitler. But the Brits have been at it four hundred years. Con, who invented the concentration camp? The Brits, in the Boer War. Who ran the slave trade? The Brits – it made Liverpool rich. D'you know they fought a war to sell opium in China – and made fifteen million addicts? Even today's drug barons don't go to war to win addicts. The Brits did.

'Con, who used to cut out your bowels for standing up to them? The Brits, Con. It was part of being hanged, drawn and quartered. That's how they dealt with "traitors".

'And they went on executing and torturing until, one after the other, the colonies met violence with violence and sent the Brits packing back to the miserable little island they came from.

'And Con, the Brits never let go of any people until their fingers were prised from their necks – here in America, China, India, Pakistan, Africa, Palestine, Egypt, Malaya, Cyprus, Aden – you name it.'

'They're gone home now,' Con said quietly.

'Ah, but they're not, y'see. They still have one bit of empire, Con. Six teeny-weeny counties in the north of Ireland. And they're playing all the old imperialist games there. They can't hang like they used to, since the world's watching. But they've subtler methods, like shooting unarmed marchers in Derry. And they can still torture.

'In fact they torture more than ever, Con, only now they call it deep interrogation – it's how they killed my husband.

'Con, their own Graham Greene wrote that British torture in Northern Ireland is – wait'll I get the words – is on a different level of immorality than hysterical sadism or guerrilla bombs. Those are his words. He called it – something organised with imagination and knowledge of psychology, calculated and coldblooded.

'That's one of their own saying it.'

Con had never heard Maeve like this. Same energy; same power of words – but now, all to do with hating. It used to be sacrifice, love, ideals. Now, hatred.

'And you know what, Con? they're not only the world's most bloodthirsty people, but the world's most brilliant propagandists.

'What's the best cover for the massacre at Glencoe, or the massacres at Amritsar or Derry, or all the other colonial savagery? It's this notion of the English gentleman – the pukka sahib, kindly, suave, stiff upper lip, that wouldn't hurt a fly because it would be jolly bad form, old chap.

'They've conned the world, Con. Just as they conned it that they're the honest brokers in Northern Ireland, keeping two wild tribes apart, when it's they themselves are the one and only aggressor tribe, holding this last pathetic bit of empire because it's all they've got left.

'They spread their lies and their lies and their half-truths like Beelzebub the Father of Lies. They can make rape seem like rescue.

'Now, can you tell me how to get people like that out of your country? Any other way, short of violence?'

'But, Maeve, it's not just getting the British out. Northern Ireland's more complicated than –'

'It isn't, Con. It's absolutely simple. And it's precisely Brit propaganda's aim to make it seem complicated. It's as simple as this, Con. The Brits are in Northern Ireland. One group wants them out, and the other wants them to stay. The group that wants them out are the Irish. The group that wants them to stay are the Brit settlers that the Brits put there – the so-called loyalists. It's that simple.'

'They're there three hundred years – that's hardly settlers, any more than we are. And we're descended from settlers, too. Just earlier ones. Anyway, after you use violence to get the Brits out, will you then use violence on the loyalists to make them accept you?'

'If we have to –'

'And let's say you do, and you whack them into line. Do you keep them in line by violence for the next hundred years? That won't leave you too different from what you say the Brits are –'

'Hold a minute –'

'It's my turn, Maeve. I listened to you. Now you listen. What kind of violence will you use to keep them in line, Maeve?'

'It might never happen. We can face it when –'

'Face it now, Maeve. What violence will you use? Bombs are no good, once you're in power. Too inaccurate. It has to be hangings and torture, Maeve. Perhaps you could hire the Brits to teach you deep interrogation –'

'Con –'

'Or a few more executions? Maybe they'll sell you their mobile gallows: they've nowhere left to use it.'

'You're being grossly unfair, Con. And let me tell you –'

'I'm being more than fair, Maeve. Oh Christ Jesus it's not about fairness anyway. It's about killing.'

'What?'

'I killed people. I know what killing is. I killed and I killed, and all that's left in the end is bodies. Bodies and blood. No new Ireland – just dead boys and girls. I thought I only killed three – it was four, because I died too. When you kill, you die. You die inside, and forever: that's the price you pay to kill. Look at me, just look: the walking dead, here facing you. The world ends for you once you kill: that's why thou shalt not kill. Oh Jesus, Maeve, don't ever pull a trigger.'

Con put his head in his hands. He spoke more softly. 'It's

the end of the world for the people at both ends of the gun.'

'What are you talking about, Con?'

'I'm talking about evil. Something happens when you kill. You pull that first trigger, and you take a step back into the evil that's out there waiting. And the second time you pull the trigger you move further back into evil, until finally your soul is fixed in evil. Like the Nazis and the godfathers. And those imperialists you were talking about.'

'So you're evil, you're telling me? I'll take your word for it. So how the hell do you dare lecture me on avoiding evil? How goddam dare you? Unless maybe you had some bloody marvellous conversion.'

'As a matter of fact, I had.'

'I don't doubt it. Something had to make you go soft. Wouldn't want to dirty our hands with any of this rough stuff, would we? Who got your balls, Conor Emmet? That little lady I met?'

'Rough stuff, is that what we call it now? Don't be a hypocrite, Maeve. Use the real name: call it what it really is. Killing. Heads hanging off necks. Guts hanging off lampposts. No, I don't want to dirty my hands: they're dirty enough as it is. Blood's very dirty, Maeve – and it sticks. It doesn't wash off. Not ever. Not ever. I should know.' Con started to weep.

Maeve waited in silence. She waited until Con was done weeping.

Then she said quietly: 'A few minutes ago you called me a hypocrite. Don't ever call me that again. It's you're the hypocrite. You're just about as big a hypocrite as those Irish government types that condemn our violence and then head off to negotiate with the Brits . . .'

Con raised his head. 'What's hypocritical about that?'

'Aw, stop fuckin' pretending. The Irish government knows, and you know, and everybody knows, it's only because of our violence the Brits bother to listen to them.

'Say we laid down our arms. The Brits would go right back

to that stinking colonial regime, and, when the Irish government would go cap in hand to urge a solution to the problems, the Brits'd laugh and say, what problems? look it's all nice and peaceful.

'Because the Irish government'd have no teeth. We're their teeth, Con. Though no one admits it. And without us the Brits would laugh in their faces. And I'd laugh in your face, Con. Jesus, would I laugh.'

Con was angry now. 'Well, I'm laughing in your face right now – if I didn't, I might spit in it. I'm laughing because you haven't changed that much since the Galway days, God help you.

'When I saw you that last time in Ireland, you know what, I could hardly believe how little you'd changed. I thought it was the most fantastic thing. You hadn't even acquired a wrinkle. But Christ now I know why you didn't change. You never bloody well grew up. You look the same as you did twenty years ago – same corduroy breeches, same perfume, same gin. And you're still mouthing the same old slogans, hating the same old England. You're the same old bellows full of angry wind, and you've never even thought there might be another way –'

'How goddam dare you, Conor Emmet.'

'At least I've changed. I was a killer once: I'm not now. I was a drunk: now I'm dry. I loved nobody, not for a long time, and I love somebody now. Yes I do, and I don't give a goddam who knows it, you or anybody else. And I'm learning to care, which I never did before –'

'Con –'

'But you? You never learned a new thing in twenty years, like the monkey in a cage that goes on pulling the lever – you never learned a new trick. Christ, I wish you had a few wrinkles – it might signify a few new ideas. In twenty years you learned nothing – and forgot nothing. Like the Bourbons.'

It was Maeve's turn to weep.

But Con wasn't done. 'Yes, I thought time had stood still

for you. It had. And it has. You're still chasing an Ireland that stopped existing years ago and that can never be again. And you're hating people for what their grandfathers did. And you're using methods that stopped working fifty years ago, if they ever worked. Which I doubt. You haven't changed, the way a mummy doesn't change.

'You're like the bloody country you come from, and that I come from, more's the pity. With its woe and its weariness and its one-track minds and its wounds that never heal. And its cruelty that goes on and on, because no one can think of an alternative.

'You say the Brits are tyrants? You're a tyrant yourself, Maeve – only you're not on top yet.

'I said you hadn't changed? I was wrong. You've changed all right – you're eaten up with hate. It's got into your soul. I don't think I've ever heard as much hatred in – in a lifetime, as you've uttered in the last hour. You're not the Maeve I knew. You're in darkness. In a black cave, and you're scared to turn round to the light seeping in. For fear of seeing your hands. Your hands, Maeve. Instead you make more darkness, to keep from seeing what's on your hands. You've given your soul to darkness.

'You're evil, Maeve. As evil as the imperialists.'

'Oh God, Con, you're so unfair. So desperately unfair.' Maeve had her head in her hands, and tears were coming through her fingers. 'Con, what do you think my profession is? I spend my days, and my nights too, relieving suffering. Be fair to me. Please, Con.'

The anger had spent itself. They sat there, avoiding one another's eyes. Con had his arms around his bent knees, and Maeve sat with her head in her hands. The clock went tock tock tock tock on the wall.

Con gestured to the gin: help yourself, the gesture said. Then, instead, he leaned over, poured a generous measure of gin into Maeve's glass and took the cap off a fresh bottle of tonic.

'How much?'

'That'll do. Thanks – Con.'

There was silence.

'Oh Maeve, Oh Maeve,' Con murmured to himself. 'Too long a sacrifice . . .'

Silence again.

Maeve turned to look at Con.

'Con,' she said quietly. 'I've thought and thought and anguished and searched and even prayed for some other way. I found none.' She wiped a tear from her cheek. 'Con, tell me, for God's sake. Is there something you found, that I don't know? Another way?'

'This I have found: killing is no way at all. I've done it, and there's only bodies and blood at the end of it. No solution – just bleeding bits of boys and girls. Cut in pieces to feed this Moloch we call Mother Ireland. Which isn't Ireland, but a monster we've created and feed with human sacrifice.

'Another way? There has to be, since this isn't one. I find myself thinking, did Gandhi or Mother Teresa have some kind of secret? I mean, Gandhi got the British out of India without violence.'

'So what's their secret?'

'If there is one, it's something awfully simple. With Mother Teresa there's some sort of – respect for people, as individuals, just as they are. I dunno – love, maybe.'

Maeve smiled ruefully. 'So it's love the Brits, is it?'

'Take that word Brits, Maeve. It's easy to hate them and kill them when they're a faceless swarm behind that word. But see them as folks like us, that maybe pronounce a few vowels differently. They sweat like us; they have babies; they die of cancer like us. And they're just as frightened. Then you realise most have done none of the things we blame the Brits for. Here, wait till I show you . . .' He rummaged among papers on the coffee table and came up with a scrap of photocopy. 'Let me read you this. It's from the *Northern Star*, one of those English radical papers from the last century. This is from 1838:

We have no colonies: our aristocracy and merchants possess colonies all over the world, but the people of England do not possess a foot of ground in their own country, much less colonies in any other. What are call-ed our colonies belong, not to us, the people of England, who derive nothing from them but the loss of blood and treasure: they belong to our enemies, to our oppressors and to our enslavers.

I'm using that in my column next week. Makes the point, doesn't it?'

'And the point is, I suppose, that we see people as individuals, and then care about them? Then it gets hard to kill them, right?'

'More or less.'

'Won't work, Con. Too many people. You can't get to know a whole nation as individuals. Much less the whole bloody world.'

'But Mother Teresa found something. Look, I never met her or Gandhi, but I met a couple of folks here on the same wavelength. There was a little nun helped me when I was drinking. And there's someone here who works with those Mexicans . . .'

'That woman I met?'

'Huh? Yes, as a matter of fact.' Con grinned. 'Though I must admit she was pretty shitty to you this evening. Of course, she's not in the same league as Mother Teresa. But she's searching.'

'So what have these people got?'

'I honestly don't know. Maybe it's – the rest of us seem locked in a three-dimensional world where the only workable logic is violence. But Gandhi and Martin Luther King found a fourth dimension that lifts them out of the box where you need violence. They found solutions without it.'

'And this, this fourth dimension – what is it, Con?'

'I really do think it's some sort of love, Maeve. Maybe it's love for Allah or God or whatever's out there. Or in here – right inside us. Maybe if you love enough, it spills over the whole world. Maybe it's God's love works through you. I dunno. I'm not exactly close to God, to put it mildly.'

'Same problem – you can't love everybody in the world. There's too many. You can't even know them.'

'Well then, maybe it's grace.'

'What?'

'Remember "Amazing Grace" – I once was blind but now I see? Supposing, in a blinding flash, I saw the goodness in the Brits or those Protestant loyalists. The sheer downright goodness and decency that's in ordinary people, in spite of the fears they're stuck with. In spite of their prejudices, spawned by those fears. And then supposing I could say to them, So I love you, and I ask your forgiveness. It would take a helluva lot of grace to say that – but then, they say grace can do anything. Like the song says. And then supposing grace enabled them to say, We're sorry too. Will you forgive us for all we did down the years?

'Y'know, sometimes I think all we lack is imagination. We go on confronting and hating because we can't imagine any other way. Well, maybe grace could cut right through the hate, and make us see what Gandhi saw. That it's not all about winning or losing, but that you can love people into changing so that nobody needs to win or lose.'

'And where's this grace to come from?'

'Maybe you just ask. Ask and you shall receive. We could try. Or maybe it grabs you if you leave yourself open. If you take your eye off the evil for a moment.'

'You said you had some sort of conversion, Con?'

'Did I? Oh yes, that was in the heat of the argument. No I haven't changed much, but I suppose I sort of sniffed a whiff of goodness here and there. A bit like sniffing smoke – you can't mistake it: there's gotta be fire somewhere. And maybe it's lit a tiny spark inside me, and maybe if I breathe on it it won't go out. But a conversion? Hardly.'

They sat in silence. Con topped up Maeve's glass.

Maeve sipped and put the glass down. 'Con, there's something I have to tell you.' She was looking at her hands, linked on her lap. 'It may not be welcome. Only thing I ask: please don't hate the bearer of bad news. If it's bad. Please don't hate me. Please, Con?'

'What is it?'

'Con. I didn't come just on a social visit.'

'I know. Nothing could be clearer.'

'I came because the Movement sent me – to bring you an official message. You're under orders to return to Ireland, immediately. And permanently.'

'If I say no?'

'Con, don't. Your oath still holds, as you well know. You never leave the Movement. You know that. And you know what happens to deserters.'

'Do you really mean that?'

'Con, I wish I didn't. But it's God's truth. Anyone classed a deserter or informer is shot, and that's it. No matter where they are in the world. It's one of the absolutes. You'd have a couple of months at most.'

'Great God,' Con whispered. 'The fuckers. The goddam lousy motherfuckers!'

Con sat for a long time, then got up and went to the lavatory. When he came out, he sat staring in front of him. Maeve watched him sadly.

Con looked longingly at the gin bottle. He stood up. 'I'm going to make coffee. You want some?'

She shook her head.

'Please yourself.' Part of Con's mind marvelled at the civilities between a man who had just heard his death sentence and the person who had pronounced it. He busied himself with coffee grounds and filters, and noticed his hand tremble as he poured the coffee. He carried it in and sat down. Maeve looked tired.

'That fucking column,' he muttered. 'Why the hell did I write it?'

Maeve reached over and touched his knee. 'Can I say something, Con?' She spoke gently. 'Con, they're not asking you to have anything to do with violence. Ever. You paid your dues long ago.

'Listen to me, Con, just listen. That's all I ask. It's the political side needs you, to help them run their PR – to state their case internationally. You know it's just a matter of getting their case across to a world that hasn't heard it. You could take a job with the *Times*, or the *Press* or the *Indo* – they needn't know you're working for us.'

The dog gave a commanding yelp.

'Excuse me a moment, Maeve. He's gotta go out.'

Con closed the front door behind him, breathing the comforting, slightly gamey smell of the river and the scent of cedar wafting from the nearby shakemill.

He watched the weasel-like creature sniff around the grass, lifting a leg in salute and sharpening claws with arrogant little backward kicks. The tinkle from the bell on its collar wandered out of the cone of light towards the base of the willow tree.

Lucky brute, Con thought. Eats and sleeps and pisses, and no one to say come back or we kill you.

After a leisurely session of leg-lifting, the tinkle drew near again, and the needle nose passed Con without a glance of appreciation.

'Get in, ya little Brit,' Con murmured absentmindedly. The dog emitted a quiet snarl and led the way into the apartment.

Maeve was asleep.

Con gently lifted the booted legs onto the sofa, and Maeve sighed in her sleep. He went to the bedroom, brought out the duvet from his bed, and tucked it around her.

He stood looking at her. Sleep gave the features a childlike look, and Maeve seemed nineteen again. The face was pure Botticelli.

He turned down the light and tiptoed to his bedroom.

26

Young Robbie Kekkonen and his father were not quite the first to reach Falls Lake that Saturday. It was shortly after dawn, but a couple of boats were already silhouetted far out on the still water, like grey mirrored islands, and the muffled splash of an oar and the brief purring of a marine outboard carried across the hushed lake water.

The day held the promise of brightness and even warmth, once the light mist had burnt away. But for now the world was a lustrous grey – water like mother-of-pearl, sky luminescent, and trees like ghosts.

The twelve-year-old helped his father unload the boat from the pick-up and carry it to the ramp. They clamped the outboard in place, loaded their gear, tugged the rip cord, and set off.

The trout were greedy and the fishing was good.

After a while the boy said: 'Hey, Dad. There's something about that boat over there. There's not been a move out of the guy for ages. Maybe it's just the fog. Wanna have a look-see?'

They started the motor and puttered across to the outline of boat and man.

'It's old Stern from the *Record*. I'd know the old sonofa – I'd know the old guy anywhere. Wonder if he's ill or – Christ Robbie don't look. Do as I say. It's real bad. I'll see to him.'

The body, wedged in the V of the boat's prow, sat precariously upright. A shotgun leaned with its muzzle still on the ruined chest. Eyes and mouth were open; blood had soaked the clothing and mixed with the water slurping around in the boat. A trout rod lay across the seats, and below it a freshly caught two-pound trout, as though old Max Stern had wanted to savour, one last time, the most joyous experience he knew.

Projecting from the jacket pocket they found an envelope addressed to Conor Emmet. One end of it was blood-soaked.

Around the same time a telephone shrilled at the bedside of Conor Emmet. It was Paz.

'Con. Sorry to call you so early. Listen. They've located that guy in the woods. All hell's broke loose – I'm getting it on the scanner here. Chuck's been up with the helicopter for over an hour, and the dogs are in full cry. Loggers near Burnt Gulch caught him trying to sneak food from a truck, and he ran away when they challenged him. Another thing: one of the logging camps reports a rifle missing. But the loggers who chased the man say he was carrying nothing. So he's probably not armed.'

'OK Paz. Did you brief Marty? Good. Earl? Well, then call him. Tell him to get up there fast. I'll hitch a ride with Chuck when he comes in to refuel. Hey, would you mind coming here for Maeve? Take her up to Burnt Gulch to see the action. Do you mind? I don't know what else to do with her. Thanks, Paz.'

Con went out to the living room and shook Maeve. 'C'mon, Maeve. Wake up: things are happening. You can shower later.'

Only war or a manhunt could require a helicopter to do the things Chuck Watkins's helicopter was doing. This was a manhunt.

Anyone who has ever hunted, with gun or line or trap, knows the exhilaration of pitting skill, perseverance and cunning against a quarry that is part enemy, part victim.

But a manhunt is different. There is the same brutally male drive every hunter feels: the drive to take the quarry, whether the taking be capture or death. But in a manhunt every now and then comes the lurching reminder that down there is a human being, running for his life, heart pounding as the baying of the hounds grows nearer, bowels loosening and lungs screeching and skin crawling for fear of the searching eyes in the helicopter sitting there above the treetops.

And one pair of those eyes belonged to Conor Emmet.

He sat pinned in the centre seat of the Hiller, between a sheriff's deputy whose skilled hands held a 12-bore Remington 8-70 police shotgun, and a pilot whose skilled hands held their lives. Con reflected on the legendary skills of Chuck Watkins: right now old Chuck was using every last bit of those skills.

Trees clawed at the helicopter as it growled and shrieked and thudded and manoeuvred along narrow forest paths and in and out of clearings that seemed surely too small to contain the disc of the thrashing rotor. The fog had long since lifted, and the late-morning sun glinted on high-tension transmission lines that were spider webs beneath the Hiller's skids, and the helicopter began thudding along above them, as though the lines were rails.

The cyclic-pitch control stick touched Con's knee as the machine banked and slithered down beside a transmission pylon, and for one awful moment it seemed as if Chuck were going to squeeze his helicopter underneath the power lines. Down there a police car stood on the rough dirt track, where a uniformed figure was talking into a microphone beside the open car door. On Con's right, deputy Lindstrom was leaning out of the doorless cockpit, polished shoe resting on the top of the skid, talking into the microphone in his left hand. Con glanced apprehensively to see if Lindstrom's seat belt was secured.

The man on the ground pointed westward. At a signal from Lindstrom, Chuck hurled his machine up and over power lines and trees.

A logged-out canyon gaped between steep rock walls, and the men in their helicopter clattered down into it, a monstrous sheriff's posse riding the wind. The rock walls rose higher on either side, and last autumn's leaves and pine needles swirled up in the rotor wash as the helicopter moved along, swaying slightly only a couple of feet above the brushwood in which a terrified man might be hiding. The canyon curved in an arc, and ended abruptly in sheer cliff, like a dam across the canyon. Without pause or effort the pilot's left hand moved up and back, the Hiller lifted vertically like a soaring bird, and the rocks and treetops slithered away beneath.

The helicopter paused, swaying slightly, as if hanging from a thread. It swivelled around, still hovering, and the sun dazzled the men in the perspex bubble, the rotor blade shadows flickering like a strobe light.

The pilot rotated his machine to take the sun out of the men's eyes. In the pause that followed, Con faced the thought he had been blocking all morning. I'm the hunter now: soon I'll be the hunted. They're going to kill me. If I don't go back, that is. *Can't deal with it now.* Max – think of Max instead. To-day is Saturday. Keep thinking of that.

The deputy leaned across to Chuck, pointed with his left hand, and the helicopter gave a leap, turning in the air as it did so, and spiralled down toward something on the ground. Not the hunted but the hunters: two men with a dog that sniffed his way along as leisurely as if he were sniffing lampposts. Con could see the tail wag.

The dog handlers gestured urgently westwards. Somewhere ahead was the quarry. A line of dogs and their handlers, in the manner of beaters, was forcing that quarry westward to where others would be waiting. Including the men in the helicopter.

'Pin him down,' Lindstrom had said. 'Keep him from run-ning. Till the dogs get him.' Lindstrom had explained it during the refuelling stop. 'It's having the helicopter up there that makes the difference. When he hears us he'll freeze right there. Even with the dogs hot on his trail. And if it gets real hot and he starts running, we can hop right after him.'

Lindstrom had paused. 'It's not a good feeling, hunting a human being with this.' He tapped the shotgun breech.

'What happens if we get to him first?' Con had asked.

'Depends. If Chuck here can get me in close, I may be able to jump out and apprehend him. If it's a position that we can't land, I can keep him at bay with the shotgun till the dogs get here. This mother's a high security risk, so we're taking no chances.'

The helicopter was weaving slowly westward, almost touching the tops of some tightly packed hemlocks. A logged-out area appeared below. Once again Con felt excitement clutch at his gut – the hunter's cruel longing to see the quarry break and run. He glanced at the figures beside him, whom he knew as humane and decent men, and it struck him that circumstances had made them – and him – enemies to the running man on the ground. Enemies with no personal hate, but enemies none the less, who were using a fearful machine to deprive him of his freedom, and perhaps of his life.

Hadn't Yeats a line or two on that, about the World War One airman? 'Those that I fight, I do not hate... in this tumult of the skies.' More or less. We're just three cogs in the grim, grinding engine that starts to turn once a crime has been done.

But will I live much longer than the running man on the ground? Being up here won't save me. Can't stay up. Must come down and face – what I have to face.

Lindstrom adjusted his earphones, then leaned across to signal to Chuck. The helicopter swung around as though on a spindle, and plunged into another logged-out, rock-strewn canyon, heading back to where the dogs and the man would be coming from. Suddenly there was a flurried movement almost under the skids. A terrified young doe scampered down the canyon, then raced up the sloped sides until it was high above the helicopter. It paused against the sky, head cocked, then vanished over the ridge.

The canyon broadened into a treeless, stump-littered shallow V, the wide end of which was blocked by a curtain of Douglas firs where the logging had stopped. It was a natural amphitheatre. Where the forest started again, the front line of trees resembled the curtains of a gigantic stage. They were almost bare of lower branches, so the men in the helicopter could see between them into the forest darkness beyond.

It was from there he must come. Con found himself listening for the baying of approaching hounds, but could hear only the howl of the turbine and the thump-thump-thump of the rotor blades.

They waited. Holding the Hiller's nose to the forest, the pilot slowly patrolled the hundred-yards-wide curtain of trees, jockeying his machine sideways from one end of the trees to the other. From beside Con came the terrible, unmistakable clack-*clack* of a Remington police shotgun being cocked, louder even than turbine or rotor.

They waited. In moments now the quarry would stumble out from between those curtains onto that awful stage. Con's heart was pounding with the rotor: it was the joy of the hunter at the kill.

Something slammed into the helicopter and it bucked like a wounded animal. 'Christ, he's behind us,' yelled Chuck, fighting to hold his machine. 'Sum-bitch is shooting.' Chuck's right foot kicked and the Hiller swivelled clockwise ninety degrees on its axis. A hole appeared in the perspex above Con's nose and there was a clang over his head. Crouched only feet from the helicopter was a man stripped to the waist, a rifle to his shoulder. The police shotgun spoke once: the naked torso leaped in the air and the rifle arced away into the brushwood.

For the briefest of eternities the three men sat in their perspex womb like unmoving foetuses. The rotor blades seemed silent and slow-moving. The Hiller swayed gently.

Things moved. The helicopter dropped a foot or two towards the tangled ferns, the deputy snapped open his seat belt, poised on the skid and jumped off, running to where the man had fallen. Con clambered out to the skid and jumped after him. The lightened helicopter gave a groan of relief and clawed its way back into the sky above the trees. It paused, put its head down, and trotted across the sky to the ridge on the north of the amphitheatre, where it squatted and whined into silence.

Con stood with the deputy and watched Manuel die. He lay on his belly by a tree stump, as he raised his head to look at Con. In a grotesque orgasmic parody Manuel's body coiled and convulsed, and gouts of blood came out from the neck with each lurch.

And her dying eyes were fixed on Con as she tried to raise herself from the seat of the car. And great gouts of blood spurted from a cavern that once had been her throat.

And then Con was holding Manuel's shoulders, half whispering, half crying: 'But why, Manuel? In Jesus' name, why?'

Manuel tried to speak, but pink foam sprayed from where the vocal cords had been.

So Con just held his shoulders as he pumped out the last of his blood and died. And then the deputy held Con's shoulders as he vomited and vomited up everything but his soul, down there among the tree stumps.

By the time Con's last dry retchings were done, the thirsty ground had soaked up Manuel's blood. Maeve was kneeling beside Manuel, and Paz was beside her. Dogs were baying and yelping and the amphitheatre was filling with blue police uniforms and brown deputies' uniforms and white ambulance uniforms. On the north ridge, red and blue lights were flashing.

Medics carried in a stretcher. Maeve closed Manuel's eyes and stood. Paz was weeping.

Barrett was standing watching Con. The reporter's hard

nose twitched. 'You're gonna have to get used to this sort of thing, y'know,' he said.

Con looked at him blankly, wiping the vomit from mouth and nostrils.

'Gotta learn to take it. Happens all the time in our trade. I mean, look at ole Max – here today, gone tomorrow. Way the cookie crumbles.'

Con stared at him.

'Mean y'hadn't heard? Your ole Jewish buddy? Wasted himself with his shotgun this morning. Blew himself right outa Falls Lake. Y'didn't know? Jesus H. Christ, a newsie and he doesn't even have the news. Whaddya know!'

Con went on staring.

There was a crack like a pistol shot where the flat of Con's hand snaked out and collided with the side of Barrett's head with stunning force. Then Con's hands were on the throat, fingers tightening and thumbs digging into the windpipe, and Barrett's head was back and his tongue was out and his eyes were bulging. 'You motherfucker,' roared Con. 'You murdering lousy fucking motherfucker. You killed him. I'll kill *you*. I'll kill you. I'll kill –'

It took Lindstrom and another deputy to tear Con's hands from Barrett's throat and pull him away. They pinioned Con's arms while he struggled and cursed and swore and gasped for breath. Barrett sank slowly onto a tree stump, a look of horror on his empurpled face. His hands plucked shakily at his throat where cruel bruising was coming up. A noise like a death rattle squeezed out of him.

Paz and Maeve elbowed their way up to the men holding Con. 'It's OK, Con,' Paz said, almost in a whisper. 'It's OK. Take it easy. Just – take it easy.' She caught Lindstrom's eye and the men relaxed their grip. Paz's face was stained with tears.

Barrett looked up at Con. 'You're gonna – pay – for – this,' he croaked. 'You're done for this time. You know that? These guys saw what you did.'

'Saw what?' Lindstrom asked.

From his tree stump Barrett looked slowly from one face to another. 'So that's the way it is,' he said.

'C'mon, Con.' Paz took his arm. 'Right now. I'm taking you home.' The men stood aside, and Paz and Maeve led Con away. They climbed the ridge to the flashing lights. 'Sheriff or one of the deputies'll give us a ride,' Paz said.

'I can't go home, Paz,' Con said. 'I can't walk in on Consuelo and the kids and tell them we killed their father. Jesus, with his blood all over my shirt? I can't do it. Not yet. Not ever.' His voiced firmed. 'Rosita's – that's where I'm going. You two please yourselves.'

When Con walked into Rosita's with the two women, he had on Paz's anorak over his bloodstained shirt.

Eyes widened but no one commented, when he ordered double brandies for all three. Con's remained in front of him, untouched. They sat in silence, Con with his chin resting on his closed fists, staring in front of him.

Paz reached inside her shirt and pulled out an envelope. 'Max left it for you,' she told Con. 'It's only a photocopy – sheriff kept the original. One of the deputies brought it up to Burnt Gulch for you.'

Con opened the envelope and pulled out a solitary folded sheet of paper. He unfolded it. It was the photocopy of a printed page. He looked at it, examined the black stain that was photocopied blood, turned it over in his fingers. Then he started to read.

It was from *Europe* magazine. Part of an article about Max's heroine, Simone Veil. It referred to her girlhood spent in Auschwitz for the crime of being Jewish, and described how she had lost her father and brother there. Max had circled a quotation from Madame Veil:

> Even the nicest people become animals under concen-
> tration-camp conditions, stooping to anything in order
> to survive. That was the most appalling aspect of the

whole concentration-camp experience – that it degraded not only the jailers but the victims.

There was nothing else.

Con put the scrap of paper slowly down on the table and sat staring out the window. No one said anything. Life at Rosita's moved quietly, almost respectfully, around them.

Con seemed to rouse himself. He turned to Maeve. 'I'm not coming back with you,' he said.

Maeve did not reply.

'Tell them,' Con said, 'I'm not coming back. Tell them I don't judge them, but that I know what I have to do. Tell them that.'

Tears started in Maeve's eyes. Paz was looking uncomprehendingly from one to the other.

'And Maeve,' Con said. 'Tell them I won't go gentle. Tell them that, Maeve.' He was silent for a moment. 'Maeve,' he said then. 'Ask them will they give me three months. Tell them I need three months before – before ... Tell them there's things I have to finish. Do that for me, Maeve.'

Con noticed his untouched brandy. He picked it up and held it to the light from the window. He squinted through the amber liquid.

He poured half of it into Maeve's glass and half into Paz's. 'Pity to waste it,' he said.

He turned to Maeve. 'Go now, please. I can see a cab out there by the door. If you pick up your things at my place, you can still catch the bus for Olympia. Leave the key under the mat.'

Maeve stood up, wiping tears from her cheeks. She put a hand on Con's shoulder and squeezed. Then she walked to the door.

'Maeve!' Con's voice stopped her. 'Tell them I'd be no use any more. Tell them my work is here now. Try to tell them that. Will you, Maeve?'

Maeve nodded through her tears, and walked out to the cab.